WHAT PEOPLE A[...]
ABOUT SARAH [...]...

In *First Impressions* Sarah Price has crafted a lovely setting with memorable characters and a fascinating plot—all specialties for this talented author. The conflict is realistic, and the ending will leave you satisfied but wanting more. I can't wait for the next one!

—KATHI MACIAS
MULTI-AWARD–WINNING AUTHOR OF MORE THAN FORTY
BOOKS, INCLUDING *THE SINGING QUILT*
WWW.BOLDFICTION.COM

Sarah Price's *First Impressions* is a heart-warming story of faith, family, and renewal. It will delight fans of Amish fiction and those who love a tender romance.

—AMY CLIPSTON
BEST-SELLING AUTHOR OF
THE KAUFFMAN AMISH BAKERY SERIES

[*First Impressions* is] a sweet, engaging story that will satisfy Price's many fans.

—SUZANNE WOODS FISHER
BEST-SELLING, AWARD-WINNING AUTHOR OF
THE INN AT EAGLE HILL SERIES

Sarah writes so well in so many different genres, it's dazzling. There's never a dull moment reading Sarah's work. [*First Impressions*] is a real treat.

—MURRAY PURA
AUTHOR OF *AN AMISH FAMILY CHRISTMAS*

Sarah Price continues to explore new territory when it comes to writing Amish Christian fiction. Her ability to forge new paths is a true statement to her talent and skill, not just as writer, but also as a masterful storyteller. Her talents are a true gift to her readers.

—PAMELA JARRELL
WWW.WHOOPIEPIEPLACE.COM

Sarah Price writes with an authenticity that pulls at the heartstrings and triumphs over self in a way that gives you renewed faith in love and friendship, showing us all the hand God has in our lives.

—SUE LAITINEN
DESTINATION AMISH

Once again Sarah Price has woven a tapestry of beautiful imagery, timeless wisdom, and sigh-worthy romance into [The Matchmaker]. Endearingly sweet and positively delightful!

—NICOLE DEESE
AUTHOR OF THE LETTING GO SERIES
AND A CLICHÉ CHRISTMAS

Highly recommended to anyone who reads Amish romance!

—BETH SHRIVER
AUTHOR OF THE TOUCH OF GRACE SERIES AND
RUMSPRINGA'S HOPE

SECRET SISTER

An

Amish

CHRISTMAS TALE

3 1526 04774501 0

WITHDRAWN

SECRET SISTER

An

Amish

CHRISTMAS TALE

SARAH PRICE

REALMS

Most CHARISMA HOUSE BOOK GROUP products are available at special quantity discounts for bulk purchase for sales promotions, premiums, fund-raising, and educational needs. For details, write Charisma House Book Group, 600 Rinehart Road, Lake Mary, Florida 32746, or telephone (407) 333-0600.

SECRET SISTER by Sarah Price
Published by Realms
Charisma Media/Charisma House Book Group
600 Rinehart Road
Lake Mary, Florida 32746
www.charismahouse.com

This book or parts thereof may not be reproduced in any form, stored in a retrieval system, or transmitted in any form by any means—electronic, mechanical, photocopy, recording, or otherwise—without prior written permission of the publisher, except as provided by United States of America copyright law.

Unless otherwise noted, all Scripture quotations are from the King James Version of the Bible.

Scripture quotations marked MEV are taken from the Holy Bible, Modern English Version. Copyright © 2014 by Military Bible Association. Used by permission. All rights reserved.

Copyright © 2015 by Sarah Price
All rights reserved

Cover design by Studio Gearbox
Design Director: Justin Evans

Visit the author's website at www.sarahpriceauthor.com.

Library of Congress Cataloging-in-Publication Data:
An application to register this book for cataloging has been
submitted to the Library of Congress.
International Standard Book Number: 978-1-62998-219-9
E-book ISBN: 978-1-62998-220-5

Lyrics from Leroy Beachy and Edward Kline trans., *Songs of
the Ausbund: History and Translations of Ausbund Hymns*
vol. 1 (Millersburg, OH: Ohio Amish Library Inc., 1998).

First edition

15 16 17 18 19 — 987654321
Printed in the United States of America

Wives, be submissive to your own husbands as unto the Lord. For the husband is the head of the wife, just as Christ is the head and Savior of the church, which is His body. But as the church submits to Christ, so also let the wives be to their own husbands in everything. Husbands, love your wives, just as Christ also loved the church and gave Himself for it, that He might sanctify and cleanse it with the washing of water by the word, and that He might present to Himself a glorious church, not having spot, or wrinkle, or any such thing, but that it should be holy and without blemish.

—EPHESIANS 5:22–27, MEV

A NOTE ABOUT VOCABULARY

*T*HE AMISH SPEAK Pennsylvania Dutch (also called Amish German or Amish Dutch). This is a verbal language with variations in spelling among communities throughout the United States. In some regions, a grandfather is *grossdaadi*, while in other regions he is known as *grossdawdi*.

In addition, there are words such as *mayhaps* and the use of the word *then* at the end of sentences and, my favorite phrase, "for sure and certain," which are not necessarily from the Pennsylvania Dutch language/dialect but are unique to the Amish.

The use of these words comes from my own experience living among the Amish in Lancaster County, Pennsylvania.

A WORD FROM THE AUTHOR

*I*N THE TWENTY-FIRST century we have lost many things.

One of them is the art of letter writing. Beautiful handwritten notes in precise penmanship have been replaced with quickly typed statuses, often limited to 140 characters. Whenever I receive a letter from a reader, I sink into my reading chair, admiring the handwriting on the envelope long before opening it to pull out the letter.

Each letter is a gift. In many ways, the letter writer is my secret sister, since most of my readers I will meet only through my books. Some readers find me on social media and we communicate on my Facebook page or through e-mail. I do enjoy interacting with my readers, and I'm quite thankful the Internet affords me that opportunity.

But there is something else that I see on the decline that is akin to those letters I receive: giving for the sake of giving without any recognition at all. To me, that is the true definition of philanthropy.

The Amish are masters of philanthropy. They donate time, material, and labor to help anyone in need. But the most beautiful art they have mastered is that of being secret sisters. Unlike in our culture, where secret sisters are typically created through a church or women's group with structure and rules, the Amish truly embrace the term *secret*.

In many ways, secret sisters provide a form of ministry to each other, especially the elderly, who may be in need of a little extra support during hard times. One of the most common "gifts" sent from a secret sister is a neatly written Bible verse on a single sheet of paper. Of course, other small gifts are sent along the way, but scripture is usually the most impactful gift.

In most cases, the secret sister is never discovered. The identity of the secret sister is never discussed or speculated, not even among friends; to do so would be a form of pride. Typically, the giver's identity forever remains a mystery. The only reward for being a secret sister is the knowledge that someone else received encouragement through the actions of a completely anonymous person.

Yet the receiver will treasure these gifts, the token objects, and the many handwritten Bible verses that are sent to her.

Giving for the sake of giving. Not for the glory of being recognized as the giver, but solely for the sake of knowing that joy was received.

Just one more lesson we can learn from the Amish.

PROLOGUE

August 3, 2015

*G*RACE WALKED OUT of the kitchen, careful not to let the screen door slam shut behind her. The little metal spring at the top needed to be fixed; she just hadn't the time to repair it of late. In her hands, she carried a tray with two empty glasses and a green plastic pitcher. The humidity of the afternoon was slowly dissipating, but it still felt warm enough for a nice cold glass of mint tea.

He sat on the small front porch in the metal garden chair, the cushions faded with age but still plush enough to support his hunched back. As Grace set down the tray, he lifted his eyes, so tired and dull, and watched her. She tried not to notice the dark circles under his eyes or the gauntness of his cheeks. In her mind, she remembered a different vision of her husband, one of sparkling green eyes and a flashing smile. In his youth, he had never been one to sit around, not in those days. But the vigor of a twenty-two-year-old man is not something that can be bottled up, like a medication, and stored for use in later years. Now, just getting out of bed required Grace's assistance, and most of his days were spent sitting in a chair.

No. Grace Beiler much preferred the memory of those years when Menno used to come calling, not caring that people knew of his affection for her. He would drive his courting buggy down her father's lane, whistling a tune she hadn't heard before, then stop right in front of her house and jump down with a spring to his step.

"I came to take you for a buggy ride," he'd say. He never asked. He just told her the way it was going to be. And that was fine with her.

Her *maem* hadn't particularly cared for Menno's unconventional approach to courting. She'd purse her lips and look the other way, pretending to busy herself with some insignificant chore by the sink. As for her *daed*, he would scowl and leave the room, never having approved of this young man or his interest in his daughter. Grace felt torn between respecting her parents' feelings and following her own. While the former tugged at her conscience, the latter won over her heart.

"Aw, Grace," Menno said to her. "What's the point in being so secret about courting, *ja*?" He smiled out of the corner of his mouth. "I already know that I'm gonna marry you anyway."

She caught her breath at his proclamation. She was only eighteen at the time, and Menno was the first boy to call on her. But one look at those eyes, so bright and so alive, and Grace knew she would never say no to Menno Beiler.

They married just three months after their courtship began.

Now, fifty years later, the brightness had faded long ago, and even though neither spoke of it, they knew the unpreventable and inevitable limitations of their future time together. First came news of cancer, metastasized from his lungs to his liver, and then, more recently, a stroke.

"I have your meadow tea, Menno," Grace said as she began to pour the drink. Made from fresh mint leaves, meadow tea had long been Menno's favorite drink.

"What was that?"

His words weren't very clear; they hadn't been for weeks. Sometimes when he spoke, a white film formed in the corners of his mouth. She always made certain to have a handkerchief in her apron pocket to wipe it away.

"Your tea, I said." This time she spoke louder and slower, hoping he could hear her better. "It's warm outside, and I know how much you like your fresh meadow tea."

"You made it?" At his emphasis on the word *you*, she felt a warmth in her heart. He always said that no one else made a finer meadow tea than his *fraa*, Grace.

"*Ja*, Menno," she reassured him as she poured some of the tea into the glass. "I know just the way you like it."

Reaching over, she placed the glass of tea in his hand, making certain that his fingers wrapped around it before she released her hold. It was only half full; she knew better than to fill it much more than that because his hands often shook when he tried to take a sip.

"You always made the best meadow tea," he said after he swallowed a mouthful. He tried to smile, but only one side of his mouth lifted. "Reckon I'll miss that, Gracie."

Startled at his words, she looked at him. He hadn't told her he wanted to go visiting anyone. She needed to arrange transportation and hire a young man to help her. Such visits could no longer be spur of the moment. "You plannin' on going somewhere, then?"

His attempt at a smile tugged at her heartstrings.

When he didn't respond, she poured herself a glass of tea and sat down in the chair next to him. It took a few shuffles of the pillows to feel comfortable. At last, she could take a deep breath and enjoy the evening. Humidity or not, she loved the lazy warmth of late summer. She delighted in watching the birds that sat on the ugly *Englische* electrical wires or visited the bird feeder. At least no one complained when Menno hung up the bluebird boxes. Grace diligently chased away the pesky sparrows that tried so hard to steal the nesting boxes. With the help of Hannah Esh, one of her close neighbors, Grace learned that hanging a thread over the birdhouse opening often kept the sparrows away.

"God sure has given us many blessings this summer, *ja*?" Grace set her glass down on the table and looked at Menno. "The farmers surely cannot complain."

"Reckon not," he managed to say.

"And we have the autumn communion and baptisms coming up." For a moment, she felt twenty years younger as she smiled to herself, clasping her hands together in delight. Each year, she looked forward to those special occasions at worship service. Seeing young men and women join the church simply brought her joy. And the communion service with the foot-washing ceremony reminded her of the need for humility, as Jesus had showed His disciples.

Of course, following those two important services came the next wave of gatherings: weddings. Between young folk getting married from their own *g'may* and the children of their cousins, nieces, and nephews, they used to get invited to upwards of ten weddings a season. Ever since they had moved, however, and later when the *g'may* split, there seemed to be fewer weddings, so Grace knew they might be invited to attend just a few of the joyful celebrations this year. Still, Grace looked forward to each and every wedding, knowing there would be new *bopplis* within a year or so; and that meant she could knit pretty blankets to give in exchange for a few moments of holding the babies.

Grace loved babies and wished that she and Menno had a larger family. But God's will was His own doing, and she felt blessed enough with the four He had given her.

"I wonder who will be announcing their weddings this October." Unlike Menno's approach to courtship, most young men still honored the art of secrecy in their pursuit of a wife. The older women liked to speculate which of the families might be hosting a wedding feast in November. The first clue came at the kneeling vow service in October, since marriage was typically a catalyst for baptism. The second clue was hearing whispers of large orders of celery, a staple in the wedding feast. "Won't that be right *gut* fun, Menno?"

He grunted in acknowledgment, and she wasn't certain which way to take that. Clearly he was not in a talking mood. That was Grace's signal to keep talking and to expect no answers. Ever since his stroke, his impaired speech seemed to frustrate him. So she compensated by talking more and asking fewer questions.

"And then Christmas. Oh, I simply cannot wait to see those children in their pageant. They always glow, especially when they sing 'Silent Night.'" She couldn't help herself; she laughed in delight. "Remember last year when that little Rebecca Lapp forgot the words and started to cry? Bless her heart!"

Menno remained silent for a few minutes. Grace let the sounds of nature speak for them. Birds chirped as they flew back and forth to the bird feeder near their porch. In the distance, she could hear the familiar beat of horse's hooves rhythmically pounding the pavement, accompanied by the gentle whirring sound of a buggy's wheels. Grace looked up as the buggy passed their driveway and waved to the driver, a man with a long white beard whom, without her glasses, she couldn't quite identify.

"Grace," Menno said before clearing his throat. He repeated her name again. "Grace. It's time for me to go."

She frowned. "Are you sleepy already, then? It's a bit early, but let me help you change and get into bed." Immediately she stood up and began to assist him to his feet. She managed to give him his cane, but she still held his arm as they walked to the front door. She'd return later to clear away the tray of refreshments. It would take at least thirty minutes to prepare Menno for bed.

As the door shut behind them, a small brown sparrow landed on the birdhouse. After looking around as if making sure no one was watching, it pushed aside the white thread and dipped its small body into the hole, disappearing for the night into the safety of its new shelter. It would stay there to celebrate the arrival of a new day and a new sunrise.

A new day and a new sunrise that Menno would never see.

CHAPTER ONE

September 27, 2015

*G*RACE SAT ON a cushioned chair in the front of the women's section at worship service. Her wrinkled hands held the worn-out *Ausbund*, the Amish book of hymns, as she sang with the rest of the members in her *g'may*. She didn't need to open the small, chunky book to reference the words of the hymn, for she knew this particular song by heart. They were lovely words, words that she often sang to herself when she was home alone, sitting in her dark green recliner that rocked if she pushed with her feet against the well-polished hardwood floor. It was a soothing motion and a soothing sound.

Now as she sang, her gray eyes wandered to the men on the other side of the room. The older ones, more confident in their voices or simply not caring if they were off-key, sang louder than the younger men, a few of whom snuck a peek at the *Ausbund*, probably because they had not committed Song 100 to memory yet. But without question, everyone sang from their heart.

With joy we want to sing
As we have resolved
All we who want to bring
This offering unto the Lord
Joyfully we want to commence
In peace and unity
Therefore is our desire
That to the Lord with songs of praise
This offering be prepared.

When the hymn ended, the bishop stood and paced for a few long seconds before the *g'may*, his hands behind his back as he did so. David Yoder, just a few years older than Grace, had been the bishop only a few months. With his long white beard and balding head, he carried an appearance of deep scriptural knowledge and wisdom. Indeed, even in his youth, David had hung on to every word during worship services and often spent time after the service talking with the preachers. Not long after Menno and Grace moved to Akron, she had been pleased to discover David's familiar face at worship service, as well as his younger sister, Hannah, now her neighbor and married to James Esh. Through them, she had met David's wife, Lizzie, and Hannah's sister-in-law, Mary Esh, along with Mary's husband, Stephen. The old ties to Ephrata helped her feel at home in their new church district in Akron.

With his serious devotion to God and Scripture, David Yoder carried on the conservative stance of his predecessors, something that Grace appreciated during his sermons on Church Sunday. In fact, David ruled the *g'may* with strict abidance to the *Ordnung,* the unwritten rules that governed each church district. Although he often reminded his church members that times were changing and recognized that external pressures on the Amish made it difficult to shun worldliness, David preached that assimilation and conformity to the modern world were dangerous to their faith.

Grace appreciated his concern for the spiritual life of his *g'may.* Before his death, Menno also often expressed his appreciation for the wise and caring leadership of Preacher Yoder. During Menno's decline, Preacher Yoder and Lizzie had been frequent and diligent in their visits. Today, however, something clearly bothered the bishop. His pacing indicated that he was deep in thought and pondering exactly how to approach whatever issue weighed so heavily on his mind.

Grace knew she had only to sit quietly and wait. It wouldn't take long for David Yoder to form the ideas that would make for a forty-five minute sermon. She clutched the *Ausbund* tighter in her hands and shut her eyes, not from weariness at having to leave so early in the morning for worship service, but in prayer that God would lead the good bishop to find the words that he clearly and desperately sought.

"We have much to be thankful for," David began. His voice took on a higher pitch than normal, with a singsong quality that Grace liked about David's preaching. "God has blessed each and every one of us over the past year: bountiful crops for our farmers, a good economy

3

for our market workers, and few have had need of medical care. God has blessed each one of us indeed!"

Grace felt disappointed in the direction of the sermon. She wasn't one to argue with others, especially a bishop, but the past year had not been kind to Grace.

Each morning, before she changed out of her nightgown in preparation for the day, she knelt by her bedside and prayed, asking God to lift the burden from her shoulders. In past years, Menno had taught her to pray for larger shoulders, but Grace didn't think there were any shoulders big enough to help her through this trial of loss.

In the empty house the cold autumn air filled each room, as a deep sense of loneliness, an emotion Grace had never known existed, filled her heart. Without Menno, her days were filled with long hours of nothingness. The house was so clean from daily dusting and mopping that the furniture shone, the floors sparkled, and not one cobweb filled a ceiling corner. And often she would read the Bible, the worn pages torn in some places from years of repeated reference.

Her neighbors were kind to her, regularly stopping by to check on Grace and to sit for a short visit. But for the most part, Grace spent her days alone, and every evening, she struggled to find new ways to count her blessings.

Though she had grown up and raised her *kinner* on a farm in Ephrata Township, Grace now lived in a plain little house along one of the main roads that bordered Akron, Pennsylvania. Years ago, her son Ivan had taken over the family farm. For a while, Menno and Grace lived in the *grossdawdihaus* and Menno continued helping Ivan with the farmwork. It wasn't the largest farm in Ephrata, and with a teenage son able to take on more of the chores, Ivan didn't need his *daed's* help as much. At least that was what Menno told anyone who inquired about their move to Akron.

Years before, the farm had been much larger. When Menno's grandparents worked the land, it had been twice the size. In order to accommodate two of their sons, Menno's grandfather had split the land, giving one lot to each son. It was a common story throughout the area and one that Grace knew today was hurting the Amish style of life in Lancaster County.

Because the farm was small and Menno was growing older, Menno had convinced Grace that it was time to retire elsewhere. After all, when Ivan's oldest son, Levi, married, he would benefit from living in that small house as he started his life with his new bride. Like many other aging Amish couples, Menno and Grace moved to an *Englische*-style house. They removed the electricity and installed a hitching post to accommodate visitors. At first, Grace disliked the noise of the cars rumbling by, especially on warm evenings when she and Menno sat outside. But after a while, she found there were some benefits to living in a less rural area, one of them being that she could visit with her neighbors.

When they had lived on the farm, they seldom saw their neighbors in between worship services. There was always so much work on a farm: from milking cows to mucking stalls, from making bread and cheese to cleaning the house or washing clothes. From before sunrise to well after sunset, Grace and Menno worked. With just four *kinner* to help, there was enough work to pass around to everyone, but not enough help to ever complete it.

This time was meant to be their golden years. A time to visit distant relatives, reconnect with lost friends, and possibly even travel. Menno often talked about taking Grace on a cruise to Bermuda with a small group of Amish couples or on a bus to Canada to see Niagara Falls.

Neither of these trips had ever happened.

"Yet I continue to hear complaints." The bishop's words were now strong and fierce, breaking her free from her private thoughts. "Complaints about the government. Complaints about the cost of land. Complaints about the limitation of cell-phone use among our church members."

Unknowingly, Grace nodded her head. She had heard those complaints from several women in the *g'may* as well. The farming families couldn't afford land for their newly married sons. The changing laws forced the Amish to conform in ways they didn't want to, such as contributing to government programs and services they would never use or having to buy into health-care programs when they were quite satisfied with their Amish Aid program. And the cell phones…

Some of the women complained about the fact that the men were allowed to use cell phones for their businesses but they abused the privilege by receiving personal calls after work hours. Yet the women were not permitted to have cell phones for their own use when they went to market or worked outside the house at a store.

Grace never opened her mouth to contribute her opinion. She had learned long ago that opinions were best kept to oneself, especially when they were the opposite of the opinions of those speaking.

"But what are we doing about those complaints? What can we do about them?" The bishop paused, looking at the many pairs of eyes staring back at him. "We can pray. We must pray. Turn your complaints into prayers for the leaders of this country, for the leaders of your *g'may*, and for the leaders of your homes. Pray that they make proper decisions, decisions we can abide without sacrificing our commitment to the Plain way of life. Pray that we can accept, or at least adapt to, those decisions that do not. Prayers can solve all problems. Only prayers. You must turn your concerns and problems and complaints over to God." And then he quoted Psalm 5:

"'Give ear to my words, O LORD, consider my meditation. Hearken unto the voice of my cry, my King, and my God: for unto thee will I pray. My voice shalt thou hear in the morning, O LORD; in the morning will I direct my prayer unto thee, and will look up.

"'For thou art not a God that hath pleasure in wickedness: neither shall evil dwell with thee. The foolish shall not stand in thy sight: thou hatest all workers of iniquity. Thou shalt destroy them that speak leasing: the LORD will abhor the bloody and deceitful man.

"'But as for me, I will come into thy house in the multitude of thy mercy: and in thy fear will I worship toward thy holy temple. Lead me, O LORD, in thy righteousness because of mine enemies; make thy way straight before my face.

"'For there is no faithfulness in their mouth; their inward part is very wickedness; their throat is an open sepulchre; they flatter with their tongue. Destroy thou them, O God; let them fall by their own counsels; cast them out in the multitude of their transgressions; for they have rebelled against thee.

"'But let all those that put their trust in thee rejoice: let them ever shout for joy, because thou defendest them: let them also that love thy name be joyful in thee. For thou, LORD, wilt bless the righteous; with favour wilt thou compass him as with a shield.'"

Immediately following the worship service, the room transitioned into a flurry of activity with every man, woman, and child working feverishly to transform it into a dining area. The men lifted the wooden benches and placed the legs into the trestles that converted them into tables at which the membership would sit for dinner and fellowship. The women hurried into the kitchen to finish dishing the food into serving bowls. The young boys gathered the *Ausbund* books and placed them neatly into the crates that would house them until the next worship service in two weeks' time. Meanwhile, the young girls hurried to cover the newly formed tables with white cloths and set out the utensils and plates for each member of the church. The only ones who were excused from working were the elderly.

Fitting into that category, despite not feeling elderly, Grace stood with her friends near the back wall, watching the commotion with a smile on her lips. It felt like years since she had been one of those young maidens, hurrying to prepare the tables for the fellowship meal. After she had married Menno, she would often help with the food preparation until she had her first *boppli* and needed to tend to her needs. When her *kinner* were older, she was in charge of washing dishes and overseeing the other women. Now, however, she was considered "elderly," and that meant she didn't have to help as much with Sunday services.

"Now, Grace," a voice said from behind her. "You've been hiding in your *haus*!"

Turning, she smiled when she recognized her neighbor Hannah Esh.

"You know how I feel about the cold and rain, Hannah," Grace replied lightly, pausing as two other women joined them: Hannah's sisters-in-law Mary Esh and Lizzie Yoder, the bishop's wife. She greeted them with a warm smile too. "It's just been too miserable to go walking in the afternoons."

Stephen and Mary Esh lived just a few houses down from hers. Like many of the elderly farmers, they had also retired into smaller *Englische* homes, choosing a home close to Stephen's brother and Hannah's husband, James. With Mary, Hannah, and Lizzie being related to each other through marriage, holidays and birthdays tended to include all three of their families. Often they invited Grace to join them, but most of the time, Grace refused, for she was afraid of feeling like an outsider at their family gatherings.

"Has Linda or Ivan stopped in this past week, then?" Mary asked.

Grace shook her head. "*Nee.*" If she felt a moment of resentment that her two children did not visit, she quickly shoved it away into the dark recesses of her mind. They had lives of their own, and who was she to place one more burden on them by insisting they visit her?

An awkward moment of silence followed her response. No one ever asked about Susan, who had left the faith, and of course, no one ever mentioned Grace's son James. It was almost as if they had never existed. But Grace knew that the Amish grapevine, that powerful line of gossip connecting the different families, commented about the fact that her other two children didn't visit her more often, especially with Menno's recent passing. The silence became uncomfortable, as if no one knew how to respond.

Finally, Lizzie clucked her tongue and shook her head, breaking the silence. "Such a shame Linda lives so far away."

The other women nodded, mumbling about children being forced to move their families farther away and start new communities. Still, everyone knew that thirty miles was not that far; Linda could always hire a driver to visit her mother. And no one wanted to comment that Ivan lived only two towns away from Grace's home. It wasn't like the Amish to speculate about the reasons for a splintered family, at least not in the presence of the family. The grapevine was about facts and information, not judgment. In this particular case, Grace knew that most people guessed the reason anyway. She wasn't about to correct them. What was done was done, and there was no sense in rehashing the past.

"And all is *vell* with your family, then?" Grace asked, expertly changing the subject by steering it onto something more pleasant. After all, everyone knew that Lizzie Yoder loved to talk about her children and grandchildren. As the wife of the bishop, Lizzie had many opportunities to do so. Whenever a member of the *g'may* sought out the bishop for advice, Lizzie was always nearby to visit afterward. Even better, the bishop and his wife were often invited to visit at different houses in the district right after the worship service. The endless (and almost always one-way) discussion about the Yoders' family filled a lot of empty air at the supper table on those Sundays.

"Oh, my!" Lizzie laughed cheerfully, her cherubic cheeks glowing with maternal pride. "My *grossdochder*, Catharine, has been enjoying herself so much teaching this year!"

Grace smiled, not surprised that Lizzie mentioned her granddaughter. But in this particular case, she didn't mind, for Catharine was a fine young woman. "Oh *ja*! I heard that she was the new teacher."

The news of sixteen-year-old Catharine Yoder's appointment as the teacher of the small one-room schoolhouse on Peach Road, just two and a half miles from Grace's small home, had been announced long ago. However, with the upcoming autumn baptisms, communion, and then the wedding season, there had been much more news to discuss than a new schoolteacher's appointment. After all, Catharine was held in high regard in the community, her pleasant demeanor and her faith in God well known to all, so her appointment by the Amish school board hadn't been surprising.

"She's doing well, I presume?" Grace asked, truly interested.

Lizzie smiled, her rosy cheeks glowing. "The school board sure thinks so. And she has the students working on something extra special for the Christmas pageant this year."

Mary nodded. "I heard about this from my Jacob's youngest daughter. They're all being quite secretive about it."

Both Lizzie and Hannah appeared amused. "They sure do love that Christmas pageant. Wasn't it last year that the students gave homemade candies to all the families? And they sang that song in High German! Quite impressive!" Hannah said.

"Why, I'm sure that whatever Catharine has planned," Lizzie interjected, "will be just as impressive!" Her pride in her granddaughter did not go unnoticed, but the three other women were too polite to say such a thing. She was, after all, the bishop's wife. And Catharine was more creative and energetic than the previous teacher, so Lizzie's prediction was likely to come true anyway, regardless of the boast.

"It sure will be nice to see what she does with the Christmas pageant this year," Grace said to break the silence. "Always been my favorite gathering of the season."

She wanted to add that Menno always enjoyed it too, but there was no point in dwelling on his passing. He was with the heavenly Father now, and there should be no sorrow surrounding that change of circumstance. Why, to be overly dramatic by mourning his passing would be downright selfish! And Grace had no time for engaging in a pity party, even if her heart ached a little each morning and night when the house was so quiet and still. But the thought of Menno reminded her of a memory, a recent memory.

"You know," Grace said, glancing out the window as a horse and buggy passed by, "I seem to remember your Catharine came visiting my Menno just a few days before his passing."

Lizzie seemed startled by this news. "She did?"

A smile broke onto Grace's face. "*Ja*, indeed." She turned to face Hannah. "In fact, I was with you at the Smart Shopper. When we returned, I found Catharine sitting next to Menno on the sofa. She told me she had come to see you, Hannah, and stopped to visit with Menno while she waited for our return."

"Oh, my!"

Grace could tell from the expression on Hannah's face that she too, felt pride in her great-niece's kindness, but, unlike Lizzie, she wouldn't be comfortable voicing it, especially with other women gathered. A thoughtful gesture like visiting with an elderly man—an ailing elderly man—while waiting to meet her great-aunt was just one of those things that made Catharine such a special role model for the children under her care.

"So much to do between now and Christmas," Mary said, tactfully changing the subject. "You will be coming to the quilting bee, Grace, *ja*? I'm hosting it for the Millers, you know."

"And my Daniel's wedding the Thursday after baptism Sunday," added Esther Wagler, who had joined their small group. "It's to be held at his Beth Ann's family *haus*, of course."

"Why, I remember when your Daniel was as tall as June cornstalks!" Mary shook her head and clicked her tongue, a look of melancholy showing on her face. "And now he's getting married? Oh, help! I know how I felt when my last one married, so I'll pray for you, Esther. It's a bittersweet moment, for sure and certain."

The room became quiet, an unspoken signal that it was time for the pre-meal blessing. Conversations immediately ceased and heads bowed as everyone silently prayed. Almost a minute of silence passed before the bishop lifted his head and, without any further instruction, led the other men toward the table at the far side of the room. Then the women assumed their places at their own table, the one that was set up closer to the kitchen.

Because the *g'may* was quite large, there were always two seatings for the fellowship meal. Usually, the older members and those with small children took the first seating. If there was room, the single men might join that seating. But always, the single women and the women of the hosting family worked during the first seating. It was their role to ensure that the water cups were filled and serving platters kept full. It wasn't unusual for the single women to tend to the men's table, an innocent way of interacting among the men, especially the unmarried ones.

During the meal, the women would catch up with each other, sharing news of friends and family from other church districts or of those who had moved far away. While many of the Amish wished nothing more than to live off the land, honoring God by being stewards of the earth, it was increasingly difficult to supply multiple sons with large enough parcels of land for each one to farm. Every year, more and more families left Lancaster to join other communities in states that offered more land, better opportunities, and fewer tourists. Still, the Amish communities of Lancaster County did not decrease in number. Instead, with their high birthrate and many youth taking their baptismal vows, their community maintained a steady growth.

It was, indeed, a testament to their parents' faith that so many of their children chose to be Amish by baptismal vow and not just by birth. On that one day of the year, pride shone on the faces of the parents as they watched their children take the kneeling vow and become part of their community.

Grace knew that feeling well—the pride of that moment. If only it had lasted. Esther's reminder that baptism was to be held in two weeks seemed to cling to her like a dense fog as she remembered Susan's choice and how it had torn the family, dividing them into two factions. *If only it had ended differently,* Grace thought, *how different my life might have be.*

"Grace?"

She lifted her eyes and stared at Hannah. "Hmm?"

"The platter? Might you pass it down this way?"

Visions of the past retreated and Grace quickly reached for the plate before her. "Oh, help! I didn't hear you, Hannah," she said apologetically as she passed a platter of cold cuts to her. "Mayhaps my hearing's starting to go."

Hannah took the platter and scooped two slices of baloney and one of cheese onto her own plate before passing it along to the woman seated to her right.

The simple fare served at the fellowship meal usually consisted of fresh bread, cold cuts, pickles, pretzels, coleslaw, applesauce, and chow-chow. It was a meal that could be prepared ahead of time and required no cooking, for Sunday was the Lord's Day and a time of rest, even for the family who hosted the worship service. After the meal, the young women would bring out their baked goods, replacing the platters of food with apple, shoofly, or pumpkin pie. Returning to the kitchen, they would replenish the initial platters to serve at the second seating.

On this particular Sunday, Grace felt removed from the conversation. She hadn't left the house much during the previous week and had little to contribute. Instead, she smiled when appropriate and added a little "Oh, my!" as needed in order to appear engaged in the conversation; that way, no one would notice her reticence.

Deep down, however, her thoughts turned back to the earlier conversation with Mary, Lizzie, and Hannah. Was she truly to live the rest of her life alone, with no interaction with her children, grandchildren, and great-grandchildren? Why, Ivan's oldest son, Levi, should be marrying soon. Ivan's second child, sweet Lydia, had just turned twenty! It wouldn't be long before the next generation would all be settling down. Of course, Linda's older *kinner* were already married and had *boppli*, although Grace heard little news on that front. Ever since she had married and moved onto her husband's farm, Linda seemed more and more distant from her family in Akron, clearly preferring the liberal nature of her new church district over her parents' emphasis on the more conservative and Plain lifestyle.

Oh, she thought with a deep ache in her heart, if only she could have done a better job at raising her children! Perhaps then she wouldn't be facing the holidays, the very first since Menno died, alone.

The air in the room suddenly became still and she realized that everyone's head was bowed for the after-prayer. She followed the others' example, thankful for the distraction from the painful thoughts that had crept into her mind. For years, she had learned to compartmentalize things that evoked painful emotions. She had learned to put those emotions and thoughts into a little box, lock it, and tuck it away into the far recesses of her mind. It just wasn't worth it to think about things that were in God's hands and not hers.

"You'll come over later for Scrabble, then?"

Grace turned to look at Hannah. "Scrabble?"

Hannah clucked her tongue and shook her head. "*Ach*, Grace, you must be feeling poorly to forget that we talked about playing Scrabble just last Wednesday! Why, it's my turn to beat you this week!"

Trying to feel less distracted, or at least appear so, Grace gave a little laugh. "Oh, Hannah," she said, dragging out her friend's name in a playful manner. "I'm not so sure that would happen. What has it been? Three weeks since you last won?"

"Six o'clock, then?"

Grace nodded and promised that she'd be there promptly at six. Though she much preferred staying home, she knew it would do her good to spend an evening visiting with Hannah and playing a friendly board game. They'd have decaf coffee and, if Grace was lucky, maybe even some popcorn. Hannah always made the best popcorn, sprinkling a bit of brewer's yeast instead of butter over the popped kernels.

As she walked home from the service, wanting both the exercise and the quiet time, she thought back on the day. The bishop was correct; she needed to turn her complaints and problems over to God in prayer. While her heart would never heal from the loss of her husband, she still had a life to live with her friends and community.

Dear Lord, she prayed as she walked, *I accept this burden of loss and know that You still have plans for me. I have been weak, dwelling on my loss, instead of praising Your gifts. Give me strength to try harder, as Menno always taught me. Through You, I can find the strength to live once again.*

CHAPTER TWO

October 7, 2015

*R*AIN BEGAN TO fall around five in the evening, so Grace wasn't expecting any visitors. Earlier she had eaten a small bowl of homemade chicken soup with a freshly made roll before turning on the propane lantern in the sitting room. With the sun setting earlier each evening, she often sat in her reclining chair and crocheted until bedtime. The quiet of the house felt heavy to her, so she began to hum one of her favorite hymns, "How Great Thou Art." The words and the melody always created a soothing sense of peace within her.

When she heard the knock on the door, she startled. She glanced at the grandfather clock and saw that it was well after seven. For just a brief moment, Grace thought she had imagined the noise. Sure enough, there was a second knock. Someone was visiting, even though one look at the window showed that the rain was really pouring down now.

"Oh, my!" she exclaimed to herself as she set down her yarn and stood up, wondering who could be visiting her on a Wednesday evening and in the middle of a rain-storm, no less.

As she opened the front door, a strong gust of wet wind greeted her even before she could focus her eyes on the figure standing there. "Mary Esh? Whatever are you doing visiting in such weather?" Taking a step backward, she motioned for Mary to enter. "Come inside, dear. You'll catch sick!"

A tall figure in black hurried into the sitting room, shivering as Grace shut the door behind her. "It sure is cold, ain't so?" Mary laughed as she unpinned her black wool shawl and hung it on the metal hook by the door, the drops of rain glistening on the fabric and dripping onto the floor. "Oh, help," she muttered. "Your floor's going to be wet, Grace!"

"Never you mind. Let me fix you a coffee, warm you up inside."

She hurried into her small kitchen and Mary followed her. With expert ease, Grace filled up a kettle of water and placed it on the stove. When she turned the knob, the gas made a soft *poof* and the flame began to burn under the kettle.

"Are you on your way home, then?" Grace reached for the jar of instant coffee from the cabinet and took down two coffee mugs. "You dare not stay long, Mary, what with the rain and all. You know how those *Englische* cars are on slick roads."

"I'll be just fine. It's just a few houses down the road," Mary responded with a dismissive wave of her hand. Her friend reached into the pocket of her apron and brought out a small wrapped package. "The mailman delivered this to our *haus* and it looked important. I wanted to ensure you received it straightaway."

Grace stared at the plain brown wrapping and saw a blurry line of print on the outside of the package. Without her glasses, she couldn't read the words. "Is that for me, then?" she asked, genuinely surprised. No one had ever sent her a gift through the mail.

"I didn't go forgetting your birthday now, did I?"

"*Nee, nee,*" Grace laughed as she reached for the package. Curiosity got the best of her and she opened it in front of Mary. There was no note inside, only something soft wrapped inside white tissue paper. "What in the world?" When she slid her finger along the taped seam of the paper, she glanced at Mary. "This came to *your* mailbox?"

Mary nodded. "Just today. With your name on my address and no return address on it. Must have made a mistake in writing the address, I reckon."

"That is curious," Grace said as she unfolded the tissue paper, the crinkling noise filling the silence of the room. As the layers peeled back, she saw a pretty white handkerchief. The edge was handstitched, and in the lower corner, someone had embroidered a small flower, a purple iris, Grace's favorite flower. "Oh, help," she muttered. "Will you look at this, Mary?"

For a moment, both women admired it: Mary for the fine stitching and pretty design and Grace for a memory that stirred within a little box tucked into the corner of her memory. The white linen. The design of the iris. All so familiar, and yet something she hadn't thought about since she was eighteen years old.

"Such a shame there is no name attached to the gift," Mary sighed.

Grace glanced up, her thoughts broken by Mary's words. Indeed, without an address, Grace could not properly thank whoever sent it. "Now why on earth would someone send me such a treasure?" She looked at Mary, her eyes wide and a puzzled expression on her face.

"There's only one answer to that question," Mary replied as she raised an eyebrow and gave a soft smile. "Looks to me like someone has a *secret sister*!"

As soon as Mary said it, Grace knew that her friend had spoken true. Something inside her chest warmed at the realization that, somewhere in their *g'may* or surrounding community, someone cared enough to send her a surprise. No event was associated with the gift, not a holiday, anniversary, or birthday. Instead, it was one of those gifts meant to touch the heart and let the person know how special she was.

"*Ja, vell!*" She smiled at her friend. "Isn't that just something?"

And for a moment, she stared at the handkerchief, her thumb caressing the flower. Whoever made this had taken a lot of care, for the stitches were small and tight, with multiple colors of purple used to make the flower. The edging was just as pretty. It was a gift she would cherish, although she wondered why anyone would have sent it to her. Who was she to deserve such a special (and surprise!) gift?

Yet there was something familiar about the handkerchief. As she looked at it, forgetting that Mary stood before her, Grace frowned and searched her memory. *What was it? What was nagging at her?* Slowly, as if walking through a misty field, she began to remember. The memory unfolded as she returned to the day she turned sixteen, almost fifty years ago, when someone else had given her a similar gift.

1963

"Happy birthday, Grace!"

She had just awoken, somewhat later than usual, but she knew her *maem* wouldn't scold her. Not today of all days. After all, it was Grace's birthday and a special one at that! Of course, Grace hadn't meant to oversleep, a fact *Maem* certainly knew. Grace was never one to miss chores. In fact, on many mornings Grace woke up earlier than the rest of the household and already had a pot of coffee percolating on the stove when her parents emerged from their first-floor bedroom.

Now, as Grace descended the stairs, she smiled at her younger sister, Anna Mae, who had shouted out the birthday greeting. At twelve years of age, she was becoming a young woman and a good friend, despite the four years' difference between them. "*Danke*, Anna Mae."

Maem looked up from the counter where she was slicing bread for the breakfast meal. Her dark hair, pulled so tight that the part down the middle exposed her pale skin, was already neatly brushed and tucked under her heart-shaped prayer *kapp*. She might be only fifty, but she looked older. Quite a bit older. Yet *Maem* always had a smile on her face. Grace suspected that it radiated from her heart.

"Well, look at you now!" *Maem* said as she turned around and walked toward her daughter. "Sixteen at last! I can scarce believe it!" In a rare moment of intimacy, *Maem* leaned forward and hugged Grace. "Seems like just yesterday you were born. Time sure does pass quick, ain't so?"

Feeling a little embarrassed at the extra attention, Grace wasn't certain how to respond.

"Sixteen?" a voice said from the doorway.

It was Benny, her younger brother. The only one in the family with blond hair, and curly at that! He was also the one who tended to get into the most trouble. At thirteen, his ability to filter his comments hadn't developed quite yet. The most outspoken of the eight children, four of them already married and living with their own families, Benny had a propensity for saying what he thought without caring for the consequences. Grace braced herself for whatever he would say next, for surely it would be sassy. She wasn't disappointed.

"Why, that makes you all grown up! Ready for your *rumschpringe* yet?" He laughed when he said it, those blue eyes twinkling. "Bet you're gonna go to Philadelphia or wear makeup like those Troyer sisters do!"

Maem frowned. "Benny! That's enough."

Again he laughed. "Aw, you know it's true. Emanuel told me himself! He saw those two girls at a diner wearing *Englische* clothes and colored paint on their faces."

Grace tried to hide her amusement with his description of the Troyer twins. "You make them sound like Native Americans going to battle with war paint on their faces!"

"Need I remind you, Benjamin, that gossip is a sin," *Maem* scolded, fixing a serious look on Benny. Whenever she used his full name, the world seemed to stop as that everlasting smile faded from her face. "I'd appreciate it if you focused your thoughts on more godly things. Perhaps you should read some scripture to us while we wait for Emanuel and *Daed* to come in from the dairy barn."

Looking at each other over Benny's head, Anna Mae and Grace suppressed their smiles. Benny, however, found no joy in his assigned task. Reluctantly, he dragged his feet as he crossed the room to where the family Bible was kept by their father's reading chair. He plopped down, sighed, and reached for the worn leather book. "Which verse, *Maem*?"

She tilted her head for a moment as if thinking, but Grace knew that her mother had already selected the verse. The dramatic pause added to the seriousness of her admonition. "I think Ephesians chapter 4."

"The whole chapter?"

"Don't sass me or you will," *Maem* scolded. "*Nee*, it should suffice if you started at verse seventeen. See what you can learn from that today."

Another drawn-out sigh, and then Benny began to read:

"'This I say therefore, and testify in the Lord, that ye henceforth walk not as other Gentiles walk, in the vanity of their mind, having the understanding darkened, being alienated from the life of God through the ignorance that is in them, because of the blindness of their heart: who being past feeling have given themselves over unto lasciviousness, to work all uncleanness with greediness. But ye have not so learned Christ. If so be that ye have heard him, and have been taught by him, as the truth is in Jesus: that ye put off concerning the former conversation the old man, which is corrupt according to the deceitful lusts; and be renewed in the spirit of your mind; and that ye put on the new man, which after God is created in righteousness and true holiness.

"'Wherefore putting away lying, speak every man truth with his neighbour: for we are members one of another. Be ye angry, and sin not: let not the sun go down upon your wrath: neither give place to the devil. Let him that stole steal no more: but rather let him labour, working with his hands the thing which is good, that he may have to give to him that needeth. Let no corrupt communication proceed out of your mouth, but that which is good to the use of edifying, that it may minister grace unto the hearers. And grieve not the holy Spirit of God, whereby ye are sealed unto the day of redemption. Let all bitterness, and wrath, and anger, and clamour, and evil speaking, be put away from you, with all malice: and be ye kind one to another, tenderhearted, forgiving one another, even as God for Christ's sake hath forgiven you.'"

Respectfully, he looked up at his *maem* and raised an eyebrow as if asking her for approval. She merely smiled and turned back toward her task of preparing breakfast for the family. Her point had been made and the reminder of God's Word would hopefully tone down Benny's propensity for trouble, at least for today.

Grace reached out to take the Bible from him. "That was right *gut* reading, Benny. You barely stumbled over any words, and I liked how you emphasized some of them. You almost sounded like a preacher!"

He beamed at her praise. "*Danke, schwester.*" Then, with a glance at Anna Mae, he fumbled in his pocket for something. They shared a secret look. Grace quickly found out why. "Got you something for your birthday, then."

His words surprised her. Birthday gifts were not usually exchanged. Perhaps from parents to children but rarely between siblings. "You did?" She took the small white package that he handed her. "Whatever for?"

Color flooded his cheeks and he shuffled his feet. "It's from Anna Mae too."

Anna Mae grinned and joined them in the sitting area. "Open it."

Grace looked up at her mother. "May I, *Maem*?"

"Of course!" She dried her hands on a towel and walked over to where they stood. "I should like to see this gift too. I knew nothing about it."

"Well, she's sixteen," Benny said. "Figured she's a woman now. Deserves some recognition…even if she might paint her face and go traveling."

Nervously, Grace opened the white tissue paper. Inside was a small box. She frowned, having not one idea what could possibly be in it. Lifting the lid, she saw a folded white handkerchief. Pretty cross stitches lined the edging, and in the lower left corner was an embroidered purple iris. Her favorite flower! In the springtime, she loved running down to the pond located behind the cow paddock where the purple iris bloomed under the shade of the heavy weeping willow tree. It felt magical to push aside the long, hanging branches and kneel near the iris patch. *Maem* let her cut some of the flowers to bring inside the house for the table. Last year, *Maem* even let her keep one in a small cup on her nightstand.

"I…I don't know what to say." Grace looked up and stared at the three pairs of eyes watching her. "It's a lovely gift. *Danke.*"

Benny hooked his thumbs under the straps of his suspenders and tugged at them, smirking. "I bought the handkerchief with my own money!"

"Benny!" *Maem* scolded at his boastful comment.

"It's true!" he sassed back. "Anna Mae did the embroidery. I just don't want Grace thinking I wasn't involved in the gift too!"

Grace gave him a light hug. "Very thoughtful of you, Benny. I'll be sure to treasure it forever." While hugging him, she glanced over his head at Anna Mae and smiled in appreciation. It had been a while since Grace had reflected on how much she loved her family. Each member had his own personality, but at the core of each person was faith in God and love of each other. Her parents had instilled these in their eight children from the very day they were born.

Even Benny, with his rambunctious nature, deep down was a faithful servant of God. Grace had heard it in his voice when he read the morning's verses as *Maem* had instructed. At worship services, he might squirm during the bishop's longer sermons—even Grace had to admit that the bishop tended to drone on a bit long— but Benny still prayed faithfully and, as a rule, wasn't too naughty. Just a bit outspoken, she reckoned.

Grace couldn't recall any specific verse in the Bible about being outspoken, although she knew Proverbs had several verses referring to the wisdom behind holding one's tongue.

Ja, vell, she thought, *he's still young. He'll learn.*

Tucking the handkerchief into the pocket of her work apron, Grace hurried over to help *Maem* with the final preparations for the morning meal. A glance out the window over the kitchen counter told her that *Daed* and Emanuel were headed toward the house from the barn. They'd be hungry, for sure and certain. A good, hearty breakfast and a few cups of hot coffee would keep them going throughout the day.

"*Gut mariye*, Grace!" *Daed* sang out happily. "Reckon that birthday wishes are in order, *ja*?" He loved to tease his children and as a rule was always good-natured, even when disciplining them. As for Grace, he had never needed to speak sternly to her, and their father-daughter bond was rather special, mayhaps the strongest among his daughters.

"*Danke, Daed*," she replied as she set the food on the table. Anna Mae was busy filling up the water glasses, and Benny had already assumed his spot on the bench. "Do you think I look sixteen, then?" Grace asked, slipping into a chair opposite Benny.

Daed spent a moment studying her, as if truly contemplating her question. With a thoughtful tug on his beard, he pursed his lips. "Mayhaps just a little," he quipped. "I think I see a wrinkle or two under your eyes."

Everyone laughed at his gentle teasing and then settled around the table for the morning prayer before the meal.

After *Daed* raised his head, the boys reached for the serving platters and scooped scrambled eggs, bacon, sliced scrapple, and homemade hash browns onto their plates before passing them to the others. The sounds of forks against china and spoons scooping jam out of a jar took precedence over conversation for the first few minutes. Everybody had a hearty appetite, and *Maem's* food was just what they needed to satisfy it.

"Headed to a horse auction this morning," *Daed* said. He glanced at Grace. "Emanuel's going. Thought you might like to ride along."

Maem lifted her head and answered first. "You looking for a horse, then? Something wrong with Roonie?"

"*Nee*, nothing wrong with our horse," *Daed* reassured her. "They have some Belgian mules going up for sale later this morning. One of ours is getting up there in age. Have to prepare for the worst."

"Oh, *Daed!*" Anna Mae cried out. "Not Duke!"

"*Ja*, Duke's given us plenty of years, but I noticed his labored breathing during our last haying. He's old, Anna Mae." His soft and gentle tone did little to calm his youngest child. He returned his attention to Grace, anticipating her reply. "*Vell?*"

Grace wasn't certain how to respond. She'd like to go to the auction; it would be a rare treat. But with Anna Mae still in school and Benny underfoot, that might leave *Maem* in a bind. "May I, *Maem*? I sure don't want to leave you with all the chores."

"I'm sure Benny will be most helpful, won't you now, son?"

The expression on his face said otherwise, but he knew better than to sass his mother in front of *Daed*. On more than one occasion *Daed* had taken Benny behind the woodshed for sassing. "Honor thy father and mother," *Daed* would say as he led Benny out of sight of the other children to discipline him.

"*Ja*," Benny sighed. "Being that it's her birthday and all...."

Two hours later, *Daed* drove the horse and buggy into the parking lot of the auction facility. There were plenty of different auctions held there throughout the year: equipment, horses, carriages, household furniture, even vegetables. Grace couldn't remember ever having gone to the horse auctions. Either she had been in school or *Daed* had taken just Emanuel.

The first thing she noticed was the number of buggies lining the back of the lot, over a hundred of them. Most horses, unharnessed from their carts and buggies, were simply tied to a long rope stretched between the trees. All of the horses nonchalantly ate the hay that had been spread on the ground by the auction staff because the horses would be there for several hours. Some were stealing the hay from each other, causing the occasional indignant neigh from their disgruntled neighbors. There were a number of pickup trucks and horse trailers along the side of the building. Many *Englischers* attended these auctions as they knew that the horses there were healthier and better bred than those outside the Amish communities. Grace was glad that this was a buyers' auction and not one of those horrid ones where trailers came from faraway states to bid on cheap horses to sell to foreign countries for meat consumption. No, these horses were at the beginning of their life spans, not the end.

The second thing she noticed was the tall young man who entered the building just as they approached the door. He was older than Grace, but there was something familiar about him. His green eyes sparkled as he held open the door and took a step back. There was something about the way he smiled at her that caused her to blush and look away. Being noticed by a young man was certainly something new. And on her sixteenth birthday, at that!

Daed grumbled a gruff *"Danke"* at the man and pressed his hand firmly between Grace's shoulders to direct her inside the building. She stumbled over the threshold, but *Daed* caught her elbow to steady her.

"Who was that?" she whispered.

"Menno Beiler." *Daed's* voice sounded none too happy about this particular young man, and for that reason, Grace became curious. After all, *Daed* seemed to like everyone.

"Does he belong to a nearby church district? He looks familiar."

Emanuel snickered under his breath and Grace glanced at him, mouthing the word "What?" Her brother merely shook his head, still smiling as if enjoying a secret joke.

"He lives in another church district but hasn't been baptized yet and most likely won't ever from what I hear of his running round," *Daed* answered her in a firm tone of voice. "And he is no one for the likes of you to share company with, Grace."

Again she felt her cheeks grow hot. She hadn't meant to sound forward or even to show interest in the man. No, she was more intrigued by her father's reaction. Now, however, she longed to glance over her shoulder and sneak one last look at this Menno Beiler. When she did, she saw that he was watching her as well and she quickly averted her eyes. Whatever could he have done to earn such a lack of respect from her father? She wondered.

She knew better than to inquire any further with *Daed*. If there was a story to tell, Emanuel would be the one to ask, later and in private. As her older brother, he'd be the one taking her to and from the youth singings on Sundays, her escort for the first year or so until she started courting young men, those who would secretly ask to take her home. Certainly Emanuel would tell her more about this Menno Beiler, especially if he was someone to avoid.

After her father registered for his bidding card, he escorted Grace toward the front of the building, where folding chairs were set up facing a fenced chute. The horse handlers stood by the heavy door at the far end of the chute, waiting for a horse to be brought over from the holding pen behind the building.

Grace settled into her chair, her eyes wide as she took in the sights and sounds surrounding her. Men were talking in both English and Pennsylvania Dutch. From the way the men were dressed, she could easily tell who was Amish, Mennonite, or *Englische*. It surprised her that so many of the men intermingled, chatting amiably with each other, despite the clear differences in their backgrounds. As horses were brought to the doorway, a handler would hold its lead and halter and run with the horse back and forth in the chute while an auctioneer spoke so fast that Grace couldn't tell what he was saying.

Emanuel laughed at the perplexed look on her face. "Don't even try to figure out what he's saying."

She smiled at his teasing, but her eyes remained riveted on the horses. They were all so beautiful, and she hoped they would be purchased by owners who would take proper care of them. Most Amish men took wonderful care of their animals, but she knew stories of a few who did not. Those were the stories that always seemed to gain the most interest from the *Englischers*.

"The draft horses and Belgian mules should be coming up soon," *Daed* said. "Want a soda pop?" He didn't wait for either Emanuel or Grace to answer as he headed toward the food stand at the other end of the building.

Grace sighed. "I think the auctions must be very scary to the horses, *ja*? They'll be going to a new home tonight."

"Aw, Grace," Emanuel said softly. "Don't get all tender-hearted on us. They have to work too. And I'm not so certain that they have feelings like that."

She shrugged in response. She felt otherwise but wasn't about to argue with her brother.

"Emanuel!" a voice said cheerfully from behind her.

She glanced over her shoulder and was surprised to see Menno Beiler approaching them. Her eyes darted in the direction that her father had disappeared moments ago. There was no sign of him.

"Haven't seen you at the youth singings in a while, Menno," Emanuel replied. "Been keeping busy, then?"

Menno took off his straw hat and ran his fingers through his hair. Grace noticed that the top of his forehead was pale while the rest of his face was tan. Obviously he worked outside. "Oh *ja*," he responded. "*Daed's* keeping me busy on the farm, for sure."

"Me too."

Menno's eyes looked over at Grace. "This is your younger *schwester*, then?"

Grace lowered her eyes. Her cheeks flushed as he stared at her.

"Yes, this is Grace."

"Nice to meet you, Grace." Menno reached into his pocket and extracted a white object. "You dropped this when you stumbled on your way in."

The handkerchief dangled between his fingertips. She gasped, and when he reached out to hand it to her, she took it. "I'm ever so grateful you saw it! I just received it today, as a gift."

Menno raised an eyebrow.

"That's right," Emanuel replied, barely suppressing a smile. "It's Grace's birthday today." He paused. "*Sixteenth* birthday."

She didn't care for the way he stressed her age.

"Sixteen, eh?" Menno slid his hat back onto his head and smiled. "*Ja*, *vell*, you have yourself a *wunderbaar gut* day, Grace." He started to walk backwards, leaving them. "And be careful not to lose your birthday gift again." He winked before turning around and heading in the direction of a group of young men.

"Emanuel!" she whispered when Menno was far enough away. "Who is he?"

There was a twinkle in her brother's eye and she knew what he was thinking. But she didn't care. She wanted to know.

"Menno Beiler. Lives on a farm in Ephrata, I believe," Emanuel responded. "Nice enough fellow, but he's four years older than you and been traveling a bit during his *rumschpringe*. Hasn't been attending church, either."

That would certainly explain why *Daed* didn't care for him. A young man with a questionable commitment to the church, and possibly the faith, would cause such a reaction among most Amish people. She knew she was going to join the church. She'd wait for a year or two before taking the instructional from the bishop, but she was definitely going to become a baptized member of the church.

Who would want to leave and why? she thought.

While she didn't have much interaction with the *Englische*, she certainly didn't like their noisy, fast cars that spooked the horses. And the music? A few times when she had ridden along with *Daed* to get some things at the local hardware store, an *Englische* man would park his car next to their buggy. With their whitewall tires and chrome bumpers, the cars were big, bulky, and ugly, in Grace's opinion. Some drivers played the radio, and the music sounded awful: loud, banging, and incoherent. Sometimes there would be a woman in the car, her hair piled on top of her head and bright paint on her lips.

Grace was unimpressed.

No, the outside world could stay far away from her. She preferred the quiet of the farm, the routine of the day, and the peace of knowing God.

Almost two hours later *Daed* signaled that it was time to leave. After having returned from the food stand with three soda pops—a rare treat indeed—he stayed until the last Belgian mule was auctioned off. While he bid on two of them, he hadn't been very aggressive in competing with the other bidders. At the end of their stay, they left empty-handed.

But Grace had enjoyed the event. It was an experience she would not soon forget, especially the way that Menno Beiler had looked at her and how those looks made her feel. On the bouncy ride back to their farm, Grace sat in the back of the buggy, her chin pressed upon her arm as she gazed out the open back window. In her other hand, she clutched the handkerchief, the one that Benny and Anna Mae gave her with such love and the one that Menno returned to her with such interest, a twinkle in his eyes. And she couldn't help but wonder if she'd ever see Menno Beiler again, perhaps at a youth gathering or a singing in the near future.

It was a thought that lingered with her long after the day had ended.

2015

"Grace?" Mary touched her arm, a gesture that brought Grace back to the present moment. A look of concern filled her friend's face. "You all right, then?"

Color flushed her cheeks. "Oh, heavens to Betsy, *ja*! I was just remembering when I turned sixteen." She touched the little handkerchief. "My *schwester* and *bruder* gave me a handkerchief almost exactly like this. I treasured it for a long time and was mindful not to get it stained." She laughed to herself. "Although I lost it at a horse auction the very day I received it! Can you believe that it happened to be Menno who retrieved it?"

Mary clucked her tongue and shook her head. "If I didn't know how honest you are, I almost wouldn't believe you!"

Grace nodded. "*Ja*, it's true. Oh, I was ever so thankful! Poor Benny would have been upset if I had lost it. He was just so proud of having bought the material." Looking up at Mary, she sighed. "I haven't thought about Benny in a long time." She smiled softly as she remembered her younger brother. "He was quite the handful, I'll tell you that, but such a special boy."

"What happened to him?"

That was the question many people had asked for years after his death. During his own rumschpringe, his propensity for adventure had created a whole new set of problems for the family. He stayed out late, smoked cigarettes, and even came home smelling of alcohol once. But it was his love of racing that got him into the most trouble. With his own horse and hand-me-down courting buggy, he loved to race other boys. Just two months before his seventeenth birthday, he did more than lose the race. This time he was riding bareback through a field. The horse stumbled, and Benny flew onto the ground. Three days later, the family gathered at the side of the freshly dug grave, watching as the men lowered the simple pine casket into the earth.

But Grace didn't share all of that with Mary. Instead, she merely replied, "He died in an accident." She paused, holding up the handkerchief. "The strange thing is that, when no one was looking, I tucked the handkerchief into the casket before they closed it. I wanted the special gift he gave me to stay with him forever."

Mary gave a small gasp.

"I never told anyone about that," Grace went on. "Mayhaps I confided in Menno when we were courting. But no one else knew, and even if someone saw me put it in the casket, that was how many years ago? No one would remember something so insignificant."

"Such an odd coincidence."

Grace sighed and forced a smile.

She missed Benny and his antics. The gift made her wonder what he would be doing now, were he still alive. Surely he'd have inherited the farm, maybe even worked alongside Emanuel, who eventually married and lived there instead. Many families had one or two brothers take over the farm. Emanuel could have used the help, that was for sure and certain. Having five daughters and only one son left Emanuel with long workdays just to pay the bills. *"Ja, vell,* I'm sure that's all it is. A coincidence. After all, the whole *g'may* knows how much I love my purple irises. It's just a lovely gift from a very thoughtful person."

"Indeed it is," Mary said. "And on that nice thought, I'd best get going before Stephen wonders where I am."

Grace fetched Mary's cloak and thanked her once again for stopping to drop off the gift. As she shut the door behind her unexpected guest, Grace stood there clutching the embroidered handkerchief in her hands. Her thoughts returned back to her parents' farm and the happy memories she had of living there. In her mind, she could still smell the fresh-baked bread her mother had made every morning. She could hear the clamor of the cows meandering back to the barn when it was time for their afternoon feeding and milking. She could feel the love that permeated the entire house because her family always focused on honoring God.

Whoever had sent her that handkerchief had done so much more than give her a small gift, she thought when she finally turned around and walked back to her sitting room. They had given her something she had long ago forgotten: the happy memories of her youth.

And for that, Grace said a silent prayer of gratitude to the unknown person, her secret sister.

Chapter Three

*T*HE LARGE, WOODEN quilting frame occupied most of the great room in Mary Esh's house. A variety of plastic and metal folding chairs surrounded the perimeter where the ladies sat, their shoulders hunched over, as they expertly poked a needle and thread through the light-colored pattern on the fabric pulled taut on the frame. Most of the women were the same age as Grace, late sixties and early seventies. Over the years, they had attended many quilting bees and were very familiar with how the event unfolded. After their own morning chores were finished and a dinner prepared for their husbands, they would meet at the house of the hostess. Usually they would quilt from midmorning until noon, when the younger women would serve them a meal. The break was perfectly timed so that the older women could stretch their shoulders and give their eyes a break. Stitching the perfect stitch, tiny and evenly placed, strained their aging vision.

After the meal, the women would return to the frame while the younger girls cleaned up the dishes. By that time, several of the elderly women would begin to excuse themselves and bid everyone farewell. It was time for them to retire home to attend to their chores, as well as a perfect opportunity for the younger girls to take over the quilting under the watchful eyes of the remaining, more experienced women.

Quilting was an important tradition that was passed down from generation to generation—a social event of sorts.

"Such a shame," Mary commented with sadness in her voice. "I heard that your son's bride, Beth Ann, wants a store-bought comforter for her bed and not a quilt." She turned to look at Esther Wagler. "Is that true, then?"

Esther pursed her lips in assenting displeasure. "She's a fine girl. But all these young women now want those store comforters, it appears. They just don't seem to have the appreciation of the love passed on to them when we make them a quilt. In our day, there were no Walmart stores selling ready-made bedding sets."

Mary sighed. "Things were much simpler then."

Esther gave a soft grunt. "Simpler or not, good taste and quality quilting never go out of style, if you ask me!"

"But you said she's a fine girl," Grace said, quick to point out the positive in order to avoid any gossip-like talk. She had been on the receiving end of that too often in her life. Menno always avoided speaking poorly about anyone, and Grace had long ago learned the wisdom in taking such a stance. "I reckon that's much more important than the type of blanket that covers her bed."

"*Ja, vell*, it sure is a shame to have so many young women not learning how to quilt," Lizzie added. She gestured toward the quilt they were working on. "At least Melvin's Rose has enough sense to want a proper quilt and a traditional pattern at that!"

Two women tittered at the comment. Even Grace had to smile. Mary Esh's nephew, Melvin Miller, lived in their church district and had always been known to be a bit on the slow side. When word had initially spread that he was to marry Rose King, everyone fought the urge to comment on such an unlikely pairing. After all, Rose King was a high-energy young woman who worked multiple jobs, including going to market in Maryland three times a week. She was known to be outspoken and quite the go-getter. If Grace had been asked to pick the one person who might want a store-bought comforter, she would have chosen Rose King.

Yet Rose had insisted on a handmade quilt and even sat with some of the older women in the *g'may* to ask for their assistance in selecting the pattern and colors. As a result, her reputation as a fine Amish woman had spread throughout the community almost as quickly as the news of her upcoming wedding to Melvin Miller.

Mary sighed, a wistful smile on her lips. "I remember *my* wedding quilt. The diamond log cabin pattern in blues and creams. It was breathtaking! And the quilting bee? Why, so many women were at the quilting bee, I was overwhelmed!"

Grace had heard Mary speak of her wedding quilt often. She had seen it, and it was indeed beautiful, quilted with the love of many women in the community. If anyone deserved such an outpouring of support,

Mary did, since her mother had died when Mary was ten and her father had not remarried.

"That was quite a day." Hannah sighed at the memory, a happy look on her face. "I was ever so happy to be getting such a *wunderbaar* sister-in-law!"

One of the older women sitting a few seats away leaned forward and peered in Grace's direction. "Did you have a quilting bee, Grace? I've never heard you speak of one."

The color rose to Grace's cheeks. "Oh, my," she said, quickly brushing off the subject as she returned her attention to the quilt, not wanting to draw more attention to herself. "That was so long ago, I scarce remember it!" As she pushed the threaded needle down into the quilt, she said a silent prayer that God would forgive her because, despite her words, the truth was that she *did* remember. But it was a memory she did not want to share with anyone else.

1965

The air in the barn felt still and heavy, the humidity of summer oppressive even though it was after seven o'clock. A few kerosene lanterns hung from black metal hooks screwed into the rafters. The flame gave a soft glow that began to fill the barn with light as the sun retreated behind the tree line. Small groups of young people stood about, chatting and waiting for the singing to begin. Her friend Hannah had yet to arrive, and as the sun continued to sink in the sky, Grace began to wonder if she was coming at all. There was an odd mixture of people at the singing tonight; several were from different church districts. Grace suspected they were cousins of families who lived in her *g'may*. Summer was a time for visiting, after all. They seemed content talking with each other, and for that she was grateful. She wasn't in a socializing mood. Not tonight anyway.

Grace stood alone by the barn door, hoping for a breeze to cool down her damp skin. She loved summertime with the growing crops and the pretty blue skies. However, once the end of July rolled around, the humidity seemed to drain her energy level. Though the days became shorter and shorter, a few minutes each day, the air still remained brutally hot and humid.

At night, she had recently begun to sleep downstairs where it was cooler, dragging her mattress down two flights of stairs and into the basement, Benny and Anna Mae often following her lead. In the dark, cool basement, the three of them whispered into the night until, one by one, they drifted off to sleep.

With Emanuel already married, the three remaining children had grown especially close. Even Benny—who was well into his *rumschpringe* and loving every minute of it—enjoyed spending time with his two sisters.

Tonight, however, he had driven Grace to the youth singing in his courting buggy. But to her dismay, he drove away rather than staying with the other young people. Grace had merely sighed and shaken her head as she walked into the barn. She knew where he was going: racing. The Amish grapevine had picked up on that recent round of gossip a while ago. Unfortunately, because the boys involved were over sixteen and not yet baptized members of the church, there wasn't much their parents, or the church leadership, could do except pray that they would outgrow this dangerous desire to race each other.

"You look like you could use some lemonade there, Grace Mast!"

Startled, she looked up from where she was standing by the barn entrance and was surprised to see Menno Beiler standing a few feet away, two cups of lemonade in his hands. With his straw hat tipped back on his head and his hair clipped just above his eyebrows, she could see his eyes sparkling as he handed one of the cups to her and grinned.

"*Danke*, Menno," she managed to say as she accepted the cup from his hand. She didn't know why but she suddenly felt nervous. Wishing she could still the rapid beating of her heart, Grace tried to project an image of nonchalance, but it was hard with those big green eyes staring at her.

The truth was that she had learned quite a bit about Menno Beiler over the past two years. Initially, when she started attending the youth singings, she never saw him there. She might have forgotten him if it weren't for that handkerchief. If she ever heard his name, she immediately paid attention to learn more about the man with the sparkling green eyes who had stared at her during the horse auction she attended with her *daed* and her *bruder*. She learned that Emanuel had been correct:

Menno had quite the reputation among the youths in their *g'may*.

It seemed that Menno liked fast horses and travel. She had heard tell of bus trips all across America, sometimes for weeks at a time. And his love of racing his horse was also well known. Too many boys took to racing their horses during their *rumschpringe*. At worship service, the bishop spread the word to the parents to control their sons.

There was even a rumor that Menno had dated an *Englische* girl for a few months. Such relationships always made people raise an eyebrow. Although more and more cars were traveling the back roads that wound through the Amish communities, Grace didn't have much opportunity to interact with *Englische* girls. But she knew that they kept their long hair down and wore dresses made of bright colors with too-short hemlines. Some of them even smoked cigarettes, put on makeup, and danced to music.

Grace certainly couldn't imagine what Menno would want with *that* type of girl.

Unfortunately, the stories had lived far longer than his temporary desire for exploring a previously forbidden world. He had taken his kneeling vow the previous year, and despite those eyes that whispered of a desire for mischief, he now lived life in full humility and commitment to the *Ordnung*, the unwritten rules of the Amish community.

In many ways the stories that were told of his initial years of *rumschpringe* sounded far too familiar to Grace.

Now that Benny was sixteen, he seemed to be following a similar journey, hanging with some young men from a different church district that was less mindful of rules and reputations.

Grace thought Menno rather handsome too. His curly brown hair framed his face in a way that accentuated his strong features. He was tall, with broad shoulders and a tan that clearly pointed to a man who enjoyed working in the fields. His black trousers were clean and freshly pressed, by his mother, no doubt. But unlike many of the other young men at the gathering, he had avoided getting hay dust or mud on them. She respected that, for it meant less laundry for his mother. She thought him a conscientious young man for considering his mother's workload.

He reached up and tipped his straw hat back, just enough so he could stare directly into her eyes without the brim of his hat blocking his view. "You eighteen yet, Grace Mast?"

His question made her laugh. "What an odd question!" The truth was that she *had* turned eighteen, and not that long ago. *How did he know that?* she wondered.

With a confidence she had never seen before, he leaned against the door frame of the barn and whispered, "Been waiting for you to turn eighteen, you know. Gonna start courting you if you are."

She couldn't help herself from laughing again. She had never heard such brazen talk! Had he simply asked to drive her home, she would have been flattered and said yes. Now, with the confidence of a lion, Menno seemed definitely out of line with the traditional ways of Amish courtship. Yet try as she might, she had never heard even a whisper of his courting another Amish girl. Just that one *Englischer.*

"What makes you think I'd agree to start courting you, Menno?" she heard herself reply, surprised by her own brazen response.

He winked at her as he thrust his hands into his trouser pockets and started to back away slowly. "The color just rose to your cheeks, Grace Mast. I'm a-thinking you won't say no when I fetch you to ride home in my buggy tonight."

And just like that, he was gone.

Stunned, Grace stared after him, long after he disappeared into the midst of other youths who stood in small groups talking.

That had been the beginning of their courtship.

After every youth singing, Menno Beiler was there to bring her home in his open-top courting buggy. He always made sure to take the long way home—something that Grace was completely aware of but never commented upon—driving carefully down the winding back roads. One of the many things Grace liked about him was how talkative and interesting he was. She often heard from her girlfriends that the boys who brought them home after singings barely spoke at all. No one had ever asked Grace home from a singing before. Not really. Not by way of attempting to court her. Sure, Jake and Abe had offered her a ride once or twice, but they were headed in the direction of her family's farm anyway. Plus they always had their sisters with them. Instead, she usually rode with Emanuel until he himself began courting. Then she simply walked home or rode along with one of her friends.

Suddenly, everything changed. Seeing Menno became the highlight of her week. Whether they were at a youth singing or a gathering, he made it abundantly clear that his intention was to take Grace home afterward. He would always bring her something to drink, stand close to her, and lean down to talk with her during breaks from the singing. Other young men tended to use more discretion, asking their intended in private or when no one was paying attention. Not Menno.

"Been a long week, *ja*?" Menno said as he sat next to Grace on the bench that was set up in the Hostetlers' gathering room. As usual, he handed her a cup, this time filled with meadow tea. He watched as she took a sip, glancing at him over the rim of the cup.

"*Danke*, Menno," she said softly. "Meadow tea is my favorite. Did you try some?" Hesitantly, knowing it could be construed as a public gesture of intimacy, she handed her cup toward him, indicating that he might share the drink.

But he waved off her offer. "I did try some, and it's not quite to my liking," he offered by way of an explanation. He lowered his voice as he leaned closer to her, adding, "Betsy Hostetler doesn't make meadow tea the way I like it. I reckon she boils the leaves way too long."

The serious expression on his face made Grace laugh. She covered her mouth with her hand as she tried to silence herself too aware that people standing nearby glanced in their direction. "Oh, Menno," she finally said, still smiling at his comment. "Now what would you know about making meadow tea?"

Both of his eyebrows shot up and he looked surprised. "Do you think I don't know a thing or two about the kitchen, then?" he asked with a look of mock indignation. Not waiting for her answer, he began to recite his version of the perfect meadow tea recipe. "Rinse the mint leaves under cold water while waiting for a pot of water to boil. One handful for every six cups of water in the pot."

Grace laughed again.

"Once it boils, immerse the leaves and let them soak for seven minutes, not eight like everyone usually does. Remove the leaves and add one cup of sugar, stirring to dissolve before pouring the tea into a cooled container." He paused and tilted his head as if to make certain she was listening to him. How could she not? His recitation was so amusing that now a few other young women were listening and smiling as well. "The cooled container is very important. You see, it helps to bring the temperature down faster while preserving the fresh taste."

"And that's the perfect recipe for meadow tea?" Grace asked.

"Absolutely."

"I shall have to try it, then," she said.

"And I shall have to sample it!" He gave her a quick wink. "Name the day and time, Grace. I'll be there."

She knew she should have been a little less flirtatious with him. The problem was that Menno made it too hard not to be jovial and laugh a lot. He had such a natural demeanor, so easygoing and carefree, that Grace couldn't help but fall into casual conversation with him, conversation that often became teasing and bordered on a cozy familiarity.

At home, though, Grace knew that *Maem* suspected something. She always seemed to be watching Grace, catching her when she daydreamed about Menno. Anna Mae and Benny didn't seem to notice any changes in her behavior. At fourteen, Anna Mae focused on her home vocational studies, while Benny focused too much on enjoying his *rumschpringe* years.

"What are you thinking about, Grace?"

It was early September now and Menno had surprised her with a picnic by the river located on Mills Creek Road. As always, he was impeccably dressed and wore clean boots. He never had any dirt or tears on his clothes or his shoes. She sat on the bench of a picnic table and stared at the water flowing downstream. He perched himself on top of the table, watching her instead.

"Summer goes by so quickly, ain't so?"

He nodded. "For sure and certain."

Grace sighed. "I'll miss summer, I reckon, but I do so love the autumn season and the holidays. Such a happy time of year with baptisms and quilting bees and…" She paused, blushing for a moment. She was about to

mention the wedding season but felt that was too forward. He might infer that she was suggesting something.

"You can say it," he said, smiling.

Catching her breath, she looked up at him, suddenly
aware that he had read her thoughts. As usual, his green
eyes twinkled.

"I like it when you blush, Grace Mast," he teased.
"Your cheeks get such a pretty pink color."

Embarrassed, she pressed her hands to her face as if
hiding her unintentional display of emotion.

He laughed and reached down to pull her hands back.
"Silly Grace," he went on. "You *know* that we're getting
married this November, don't you?"

At this announcement, neither a request nor a proper
proposal, just a casual announcement, she gasped.
"Menno Beiler!"

In one quick movement, he slid down from the top
of the picnic table and sat next to her on the bench.
His one hand continued to hold hers. It felt strange to
have someone holding her hand, his skin soft and warm,
even if she could feel a few calluses on his palm. "Why,
Grace Mast! Did you ever have any doubts?" He clicked
his tongue and shook his head, playfully teasing her.
"Would you think I'd be spending my time with you if I
didn't have that intention in mind?" Then, with a more
solemn tone, he quoted, "'Live joyfully with the wife
whom thou lovest all the days of the life of thy vanity,
which he hath given thee under the sun, all the days of
thy vanity: for that is thy portion in this life, and in thy
labour which thou takest under the sun.'"

She wasn't certain how to respond. Clearly he was proposing to her with the assumption that he didn't really need to ask: he knew she would say yes if he did. And he was correct. But despite his forwardness in the matter, it was something that deep down she had known to be forthcoming. That she *wanted* to be forthcoming.

"I...I reckon I'd best tell *Maem* and *Daed*, then," she whispered.

For a second he seemed to consider this thought. Her parents hadn't hidden their displeasure about Menno's attention to Grace. Her *maem* often scowled when he came to the door, and her *daed* barely said more than a quick greeting that sounded more like a grunt than a "hello." But Grace didn't care. As she sat on that picnic bench holding his hand, she knew she wanted to be known as Menno's Grace for the rest of her life.

"Mayhaps I'd best tell them with you," he said firmly. "If you're to be my *fraa*, Grace, I want to be by your side, through the good and the not-so-good. If they are to be upset or displeased, we will face it together. I would not put you into the lions' den without the protection of angels."

She smiled at his analogy and nodded her head in consent.

When they returned to her parents' farm, Grace noticed that it was unusually quiet. No kittens played in the driveway, and Anna Mae's push-scooter was not in its usual place on the porch. Even Benny seemed to be missing, for his courting buggy did not occupy the open space in the horse stable.

They know, Grace thought.

Inside the kitchen, both *Maem* and *Daed* sat at the kitchen table as if they had been waiting for Grace and Menno to arrive. *Daed's* hands rested upon the Bible, and Grace noticed that he tapped his fingers against its cover. Just inside the doorway, she stopped and pressed her lips together, waiting for him to look up in case he was praying. Rather than look up, he sighed.

"Daed?"

"'Therefore shall a man leave his father and his mother, and shall cleave unto his wife: and they shall be one flesh.'" His words seemed sorrowful. He turned around and stared at her, his eyes flickering only once to where Menno stood by her side. "Marriage is forever."

Swallowing, Grace felt the sudden dryness of her throat. "I know that, *Daed.*"

"And this is your decision, then? Marrying a man with such a past?"

Why are they so opposed to Menno Beiler? she wondered. *Are they unable to forgive his past transgressions during his* rumschpringe? Forgiveness was core to the Amish faith. And, after all, he had taken his kneeling vow. His lust for wandering the country and courting *Englische* girls was long gone. In that moment, she felt anger toward her parents, her father mostly, for their inability to display one of the key values they had preached about so often.

"It is." When she spoke, her tone was stronger than she felt.

Now it was *Maem's* turn. "And it has to be now? You barely know each other."

Grace shifted her eyes from her father to her mother, but she did not respond. How could she possibly explain that although they had been courting only a short time, she loved him? Besides, it was the getting to know each other that intrigued Grace the most. He was, by far, the most interesting young man she had ever met. She suspected a future with Menno Beiler would be far from rote and routine.

"You have your baptism in October and now a wedding to plan in November?" *Maem* shook her head, clearly unhappy with the projected timeline. "We haven't even made your wedding quilt yet!"

"That's not so important, *Maem*."

Menno cleared his throat, indicating that he wanted to speak. He had removed his hat and held it in his hands, before his waist. Grace was amazed at how calm he appeared. "I'm to take over my *daed's* farm, and by spring, I'll have the *grossdawdihaus* ready for Grace to move in. We'll live there until my parents are ready for their life-right."

Just as Menno, the youngest son, would inherit the Beiler farm, one day Benny would inherit their father's farm. Unlike other cultures where the oldest child tended to inherit the bulk of property or investments, the Amish usually let the younger children move into a smaller section or mini-house attached to the main house. When Benny became older and married, he would live in the *grossdawdihaus* with his wife until

Anna Mae married and moved out. By that time, *Maem* and *Daed* would move into the *grossdawdihaus* as their life-right, their right not to worry about being taken care of in their old age. The children would pay their bills and help care for them. It left a strain on Benny, but the other children would help out as well as their parents aged.

"There'll be plenty of time to make a quilt in winter," Menno added matter-of-factly.

"*Nee*," *Maem* said. "There will be no quilting bee in the winter."

Grace caught her breath and stared at the floor. Quilting bees were always such a happy time, one of the bright spots in what usually would be a long, cold, gray winter. Women would gather and share fellowship as they stitched the pattern of the young woman's quilt. Each stitch was made with community love, they would say. When the quilt was finished and the edges bound, it would be folded and neatly stored in the young woman's hope chest until the day she married.

However, Grace hadn't expected Menno to appear in her life, so her hope chest remained empty.

"A young woman must have a quilt *before* her wedding!" With a deep, heavy breath, she looked at her husband and said, "Best be bringing up that quilting frame from the basement. We'll set it up in the empty gathering room."

"*Maem*, are you sure...?"

Her mother pursed her lips and didn't appear very happy. Whether *Maem* was unhappy about her determination to make a quilt before the wedding or the fact that Menno was her selected, Grace didn't know. But she watched as her mother seemed to work out the logistics in her head. "Won't be time to invite other women to help. They'll be busy with preparations for winter and such. We'll just have to make a simpler quilt pattern."

Throughout all of this, *Daed* remained silent. His eyes stared at the wall, focusing on nothing. Grace wished she knew what he was thinking. If she had hoped for a blessing from her father, clearly it was not coming. After *Maem's* declaration of the simpler quilt pattern, her father stood up and headed toward the first-floor bedroom, his Bible clutched in his hands. He paused at the doorway as if he wanted to say something. With his back turned toward them, he remained silent and opened the door. He looked like a defeated man as he passed through the doorway and shut the door behind him.

For a moment, Grace wanted to apologize to Menno for her father's behavior. To his credit, Menno looked completely self-composed. If *Daed* hadn't forgiven or forgotten Menno's *rumschpringe*, Menno was not bothered.

The next few days passed in a whirlwind of activity. After morning chores, *Maem* took Grace to the store to pick out fabrics for the quilt. They had decided on the very simple pattern called Lancaster Diamond. While it needed more quilting, the piecing of the top was simple enough that *Maem* would not need anyone to help her. That's what she said to Grace, anyway. Grace wondered why invitations were not discussed and no extra cooking was planned to accommodate the anticipated guests for a quilting bee. She never thought to ask her *maem*; to do so would be disrespectful. Besides, she was busy piecing the quilt top, and by the weekend, she had finished it. She also had drawn the quilting pattern on it and pinned the batting and backing, so once *Daed* and Emanuel rolled it onto the quilt frame, it was ready to be quilted.

But no one came to quilt.

Every day after morning chores, Grace sat in the straight-back chair and quilted her own wedding quilt. After school, Anna Mae would try to help out by lending a hand for an hour. On a few occasions, *Maem* sighed, and after washing her hands and drying them on her apron, she joined Grace at the frame. But most of the quilting was done by Grace. She suspected that her *daed's* attitude about the upcoming wedding had affected her *maem*, and *Maem* did not have the heart to host a quilting bee or help much with the quilt in the face of her husband's displeasure.

Toward the end of the week, however, an unexpected visitor showed up at the door: Menno's *maem* and sisters. Grace watched with curiosity how *Maem* greeted them, as if they were old friends. The sisters were quiet and merely reached out to shake Grace and *Maem's* hands.

"What a pleasant surprise!" *Maem* said, and she sounded as if she actually meant it. Grace frowned, wondering at this change in her mother's behavior. Both of her parents had been rather quiet since the day they learned of her betrothal. Now, with the Beiler women standing in her kitchen, *Maem* seemed to be her old self.

"We heard there was some quilting going on," Menno's mother said, smiling at Grace. "Is that the wedding quilt, then?" Without waiting for an invitation to enter, Barbara Beiler crossed the room and looked down at the quilt. "Oh my!"

Grace couldn't tell whether she was pleased or horrified.

Barbara waved to her two daughters. "Linda, Bethany, come see!" Obediently, they joined their mother. "It's going to be a beautiful quilt. Such small stitches, Grace. You are a fine quilter, I reckon."

The compliment helped Grace loosen up. "*Danke*, Barbara."

"And I see the colors match Menno's eyes." Barbara nodded her approval. "How sweet."

Grace glanced at her mother, wondering if she had noticed that only green colors, with a touch of cream, had been picked out for the quilt.

Barbara wasted no time occupying the lone empty chair next to Grace. She glanced at her two daughters. "Linda, mayhaps you can find more folding chairs, *ja*? A bride should have help with her wedding quilt, and I'd love to share my love of the Lord while stitching, praying, and sharing fellowship with Grace. Oh, and Bethany, did you bring in that pumpkin bread I made this morning?"

From behind her back, Bethany produced a large loaf of bread wrapped in plastic wrap. "Right here, *Maem*."

Suddenly, the room became full of noise and activity. Barbara Beiler talked as she quilted, often asking Grace questions, and even including Grace's mother in the conversation. The two sisters sat earnestly beside their mother, quilting without adding much to the dialogue with the exception of when Barbara sang a hymn. Grace loved to sing and knew the hymns by heart. Slowly, she began to feel happy, enjoying her makeshift quilting bee, even if only three people attended it. They were three people who loved God, loved family, and, apparently, loved her.

2015

The woman seated next to Grace pushed back her chair and announced that her back ached. Grace looked up, her memory interrupted, and was surprised to see it was almost noon. The younger women were already busy in the kitchen, laughing and chatting with each other as they prepared the meal for the women. She caught sight of Rose King, her pink dress as bright as her smile and covered with a perfectly clean black apron. Even her prayer *kapp* was clean and freshly starched, the two strings hanging down her back with a small, crisp bow at the end.

Grace didn't care for the way the young girls wore their prayer *kapps* nowadays; when she was growing up, she would have been brought before the bishop for such an infringement. But that was then and this was now.

Other women started to stand, collecting their quilting materials: scissors, needles, thread, and thimbles. After the meal, most of the elderly women would leave, Grace among them. Her back ached too and so did her head. This quilt that was being made with community love by so many women would most likely be finished in just two sittings. The memory of her own quilting, fifty years ago, stirred old emotions—disappointment in her parents strongly conflicting with her love for the Beiler family.

Indeed, without the help of the Beilers, it would have taken Grace much longer to finish that quilt. At the time, Grace couldn't help but feel as if she was being punished—for what, she did not know. After all, it was her mother's duty to organize the quilting bee. Since she hadn't, Barbara Beiler, not having heard any news of a quilting bee, had taken it upon herself to show up and provide extra hands to help her future daughter-in-law.

For that, Grace had been most thankful.

Today, Grace better understood why her parents had been so resentful of Menno, but she still questioned their inability to follow their own faith and extend forgiveness to him.

That thought made her head ache.

"You feeling all right, then, Grace?"

The hand on her arm felt soft and light. Grace turned to look at whomever had approached her. Rose King. "Oh *ja*, indeed. Right as rain in spring," Grace said, trying to sound cheerful.

"I'm quite glad you came today," Rose said. She looked over at the quilt and a smile broke out upon her face. "It's so beautiful, isn't it?"

The look of joy and glow of happiness that exuded from the young woman standing before her made Grace feel better. Young love, she thought. God's gift to man and woman. "Your color choices are quite nice for the chosen pattern, Rose. Autumn colors, especially that rich orange block. Reminds me of October pumpkins!"

"Oh!" Rose gasped. "I almost forgot! Stay right here, Grace Beiler."

Like a giddy schoolgirl, Rose hurried through the other women as they made their way to the table. Grace could barely see her as she disappeared into the mud-room. A few moments later, she returned, holding a brown paper package in her hand. With a big smile, she held it out to Grace.

"What's this?" Grace asked.

"I made something for you."

"You did?"

Rose nodded and gently pushed the package into Grace's hands. "Someone left a note in our mailbox. The writer asked that I make this for you and give it to you today."

Perplexed, Grace's mouth fell open as she looked from Rose's glowing eyes to the package and back to Rose again. "Who wrote such a note?"

Rose shrugged. "It wasn't signed, but definitely it was a woman's handwriting."

"Oh, help!" Grace didn't know what to make of this. First the handkerchief and now this? Perhaps Mary had been correct in assuming that a secret sister was behind it all. Carefully, she began to unwrap the package. A few of the other women watched, curious to see what Grace was holding.

As the brown paper fell away, Grace knew right away what she held in her hands. For a moment, she thought she might become emotional. Taking a few deep breaths, she managed to meet Rose's gaze. "Pumpkin bread?" she asked. "Someone told you to make *me* pumpkin bread?"

"Are you surprised?" Rose laughed. And then, just as suddenly, she became somber. "You do like pumpkin bread, *ja*?"

Grace held the pumpkin bread in her hands, staring at it as if it were the most beautiful gift she had ever received. The memory of Barbara Beiler accepting Grace into the family began with the day she had marched into *Maem's* kitchen and told Bethany to fetch the fresh loaf of pumpkin bread she had baked that same morning for everyone to share.

Did she like pumpkin bread?

Lifting her eyes, she looked at Rose and smiled. "Oh, Rose," she said softly. "It's my most favorite kind of bread. *Danke*, dear friend. *Danke*."

It was all Grace could do to remain focused on the singing before the meal. Her mind stayed, instead, on that loaf of pumpkin bread given to her so long ago by Menno Beiler's mother. Who could possibly have known about the importance of that particular gift, fifty long years ago, and how much its memory would mean to her? Especially at a quilting bee?

For the rest of the meal, Grace sat silent, deep in thought, wondering who, indeed, was this very clever and well-intentioned secret sister.

CHAPTER FOUR

October 11, 2015

WHEN SHE AWOKE on Sunday, Grace felt a sense of anticipation, an eagerness that made her feel much younger than her sixty-eight years. Today, three young men and two women were going to accept their baptism and, by taking their kneeling vows, commit to following the *Ordnung*, the unwritten rules of the Amish community that would guide their daily lives. It was an important day for many reasons. For Grace, it brought back memories of her own baptism and how her life had changed when she acknowledged her commitment, not just to the Amish religion and way of life, but to the Lord Jesus Christ.

Only other baptized members of the *g'may* came to this worship service, which meant the smaller children remained at home with an older sibling. Mothers with infants were permitted to bring them, of course. But as a rule, it was a members-only event. Though the service was no different from other worship services, with the exception of a shorter second sermon in order to accommodate the baptism ceremony, it sent a strong signal to the unbaptized that unless they committed to the church, they were not truly a part of the community.

Last year, their *g'may* had only two newly baptized members. This year, everyone was quite excited to see five young adults vowing to become members of the Amish church. Of course, back in her day, there might have been as many as ten accepting the baptism. With more expansive farms then and, ultimately, larger families, there were more young adults in each church district. Joining the church was a rite of passage that very few youths questioned.

Today, the church districts were splintered. Highways cut through districts, and suburban developments intercepted the pockets of farmland. Since Grace now lived on the edge of a developed neighborhood, her *g'may* had more elderly people than families with youth. The district had split three years ago, and the way the lines had been drawn, only a few farms, mayhaps ten in all, remained on their side. Most of the farms, and therefore the majority of the youths, fell on the other side of the newly drawn district line.

There had been a time when the Amish leaders worried about the growth of the church. Because the Amish never evangelized, the only new members were the offspring who chose to accept the baptism. When Grace was growing up, most Amish lived on expansive farms that were handed down from generation to generation. Little by little, as farms were split between sons, diminishing in size while the population increased, more Amish men had to venture out to seek other occupations.

And then that unfortunate movie came out, the one that introduced Lancaster County to the entire country. It was 1985, the year that changed everything in their community. Though Grace had never seen the movie (or any movie for that matter), she'd heard enough to know that it introduced the Amish way of life to the *Englische*. It had even been filmed on a farm in Strasburg, a fact that had many tongues wagging over just how such a thing could have occurred in their area.

The farm had been vacant, and the film crew rented it. Suddenly, the world knew about the Amish, and as a result, curious tourists began to visit the area, attracted by the local prices of goods, substantially lower than their *Englische* counterparts. As word spread, tourists began flocking to the area, big hotels were built, roads became increasingly clogged with cars and buses, and *Englische* developments ate up farmland.

The Amish looked at the tourism as a necessary evil because their local economy had become less and less equipped to sustain their growing population. With fewer farms available, tourism was adding much-needed income for the local population as more Amish began working among the *Englische*. Their exposure to the outside world increased on a daily basis; the convenience of technology and other modern amenities became a necessity for some. And that exposure brought about a decline in the numbers of Amish youth joining the church. Many opted for the less conservative Mennonite church, especially those who had no expectations of being able to own a farm of their own. Others, unable to decide whether to remain within their own *g'may* or join another church, didn't join any church at all.

When baptism day arrived, everyone rejoiced at the entry of new members to their faith. Grace knew that the parents felt pride to see their children bow before the bishop and affirm their faith, something that would have been unquestioned only a few decades ago. She remembered well how she had felt when Ivan, Linda, and Susan had joined the church. It was a testament to their upbringing and a moment of unspoken pride for all parents.

Standing in front of her dresser, she assessed her appearance in the mirror. Her black dress and apron, freshly starched and ironed, were pinned properly, and her prayer *kapp* was positioned flawlessly atop her head so that the heart-shaped garment, smaller than what the younger women wore, peeked over the top of her head. Her eyes lingered for a moment on her face. *Sixty-eight*, she thought. The wrinkles under her eyes and creases in her forehead told the story of many years spent working hard in the garden and helping Menno in the fields. Her age showed, and she felt tired—tired mostly from missing Menno and worrying about her future.

What would she do? Living alone never was part of her vision. She felt as if she had a lot of life left in her. But could she live it without her Menno? Was it possible to live without the man who, for fifty years, had stood by her side through the good and the bad? Did she even want to?

Her thoughts were interrupted by the rapid succession of knocks at her kitchen door. That would be Hannah, eager to get going to the worship service. Hannah and her husband, James, had offered to take Grace with them since the baptism service was being held at one of the large farms, a good two miles away. After Menno died, Grace gave their horse and buggy to Ivan. She was too old to take care of a horse every day, and she didn't fancy the idea of harnessing the horse every time she wanted to go somewhere. It wasn't fair to the horse, Grace had rationalized. But in truth, it was not fair to *her*.

"Coming, Hannah," Grace called out. She shut her bedroom door behind herself, more from habit than necessity, and hurried down the narrow hallway toward the door. She paused to grab her black wool shawl and black drawstring bag before hurrying out.

The sun was barely cresting over the horizon as the horse and buggy traveled down the road. Up ahead, another buggy was headed in the same direction, most likely a neighbor also on the way to the worship service. No one spoke in the buggy; it was too early for conversation. Instead, the horse's hooves beating against the macadam, even and rhythmic, and the gentle humming of the buggy's wheels kept Grace preoccupied.

She listened to the noise, a song in itself, and one that she missed hearing. She watched the horse twitching its ears as if anticipating a command from the driver. James held the reins in his hands, occasionally moving one slightly to keep the horse trotting straight, instead of getting distracted by something along the road.

When the horse and buggy finally turned down the lane to the farm, Grace felt a new wave of peace flow through her. She missed living on a farm: the smell of cows, the sight of silos, and the sounds of the windmill. But, oh, the good memories that came back to her! Memories of early morning milkings, afternoons spent in the garden, and evenings spent looking out across the fields as she sat next to Menno in their rocking chairs on the small porch that Menno had built just for these peaceful respites.

After James stopped, young men hurried to assist the older women as they climbed from the buggy. Grace walked slowly toward the house, staring at the barn. She could hear the cows moving in the rear paddock. One of the cows mooed and she smiled, her mind drifting back to memories of farm life—such *wunderbaar gut* memories of working alongside Menno.

"Come along, Grace!" Hannah called from the doorway.

"*Ja, ja!*" Grace picked up her pace and hurried to join her friend as they entered the farmhouse.

The women were gathering in the large kitchen. They stood in a line, a sea of black silhouettes, greeting each newcomer. Grace made her way through, offering a handshake to each woman while leaning forward to give her a kiss, the typical greeting of the women attending worship service.

Esther Wagler, however, pulled Grace aside.

"I simply *must* speak to you!"

Grace flustered at this unexpected interruption of the typical routine at worship. "I really should greet the other women." Even though Esther, like Grace, was a comparatively young widow, Grace had avoided Esther's attempts to commiserate with her. Though she liked Esther well enough, being in her presence reminded Grace of the open wound in her heart. She knew what people thought when they saw the two women together: widows. It was a distasteful word for Grace and one she was not inclined to accept. Not just yet. At least when she was in the company of married women, Grace could pretend that nothing had changed.

Still, Esther ignored her protest. She pulled Grace away from the line and led her through the doorway of the pantry, far enough so that no one could overhear her.

"I must admit to being curious, Esther," Grace admitted. She hoped no one thought her impertinent. The last thing she'd want to do was offend anyone.

Dismissively waving her hand, Esther slipped a piece of paper into Grace's hand. The touch of the coarse parchment caused Grace to catch her breath and she looked down at it. It was cream colored and folded twice. Hesitantly, she unfolded it and held it at arm's length since her reading glasses were in her bag. All it said was two words: *Song 51*.

"Oh." Her response was nothing more than a whisper.

"What does it mean, then?" Esther asked, peering over her shoulder.

Quickly, Grace refolded the paper and tried to catch her breath. "Why did you give this to me?"

"Why, someone left me an envelope in my mailbox yesterday."

Grace frowned.

Esther continued to explain. "There was a simple note inside that asked if I would give this to you today."

"Where's that note?"

Esther shook her head. "I'm sorry, Grace. I threw it out. I wasn't thinking."

"And I guess it wasn't signed?"

Again Esther shook her head.

Secret sister strikes again, Grace thought. She clutched the paper in her hand and glanced around the room. She half-expected someone to be watching her as if anticipating her reaction. But no one seemed to be looking in her direction.

"*Vell*?" Esther said. "What does it mean?"

Grace tried to remain calm as she responded, "It's a hymn from the *Ausbund*, Esther. Other than that, I don't reckon I know the purpose of the message." It wasn't a lie. She didn't know its purpose. "Now, let's get back into the greeting line. You know how some of those older women get offended, Esther, if everyone doesn't greet them properly."

But as she hurried back to her place in the line, she kept a tight hold on the note. True, she didn't know the purpose of the message. But she knew its meaning very well. And that was something she wasn't willing to share with Esther or anyone else for that matter.

1965

"Hurry up, Grace!"

Grace frowned at her mother calling her from the bottom of the staircase. *Why is she in such a hurry?* she wondered. *Daed* hadn't even come in from the barn yet. Ignoring her mother, she glanced at the small, round mirror that hung on the wall over the basin stand in the corner of her room. It was too small for her to see herself properly, and she worried that her hair wasn't pinned back just right.

"I don't understand why I can't go," a small voice said from the doorway.

Grace looked over her shoulder and smiled at her sister. "You know that it's only for baptized members of the church district," she explained for the fifth time. As a child, Grace had never understood why communion and baptism were members-only services. Later she realized that it was a way of segregating the baptized from the unbaptized, a not-so-subtle reminder to the unbaptized that they were not truly part of the Amish community yet. But she didn't want to say that to Anna Mae; her sister would figure it out on her own, realizing it just like every other person who took the baptism. "Remember that I didn't attend last year either?"

Anna Mae sighed, pushing against the threshold of the door with her bare toes. She leaned her head against the door frame and stared up at Grace. "I'd still like to see you get baptized."

"I'd like that too." Grace turned toward her sister. She never liked seeing anyone unhappy, and in Anna Mae's case, the sight of her sad eyes tore at Grace's heart.

"But the good news is that I'll get to be at your baptism!" She tried to sound cheerful. "Besides, won't it be nice to be alone in the house? How often does that happen?"

Grace couldn't remember ever being alone at the house. With seven siblings, someone always seemed to be in the kitchen or outside in the barn. She wondered what it would be like to actually be alone for a few hours, to do whatever she wanted for just a little bit. Suddenly, Grace almost wished she could trade places with Anna Mae. After all, Benny wasn't home. The previous evening, he had gone out with his friends and never returned, his absence probably the source of *Maem's* irritation.

"I didn't think of that!" The idea of being home alone seemed to perk up Anna Mae. She pursed her lips as she contemplated Grace's comment. "Reckon I'll go play with the kittens for a spell. Maybe read that book Teacher let me borrow."

"Now don't get caught," Grace warned. Sundays were for resting, visiting with family and friends, and most importantly honoring God. Reading a book from school was isolating and, like crocheting and quilting, would not fit into any of those categories.

"Grace! *Daed* is ready now!" *Maem* called out one more time.

With a deep sigh, Grace brushed passed Anna Mae. "Coming, *Maem*," she called.

Grace hurried down the stairs, her footsteps on the wooden floor announcing her arrival. She paused on the bottom step and waited for her mother to turn around and say something, mayhaps to compliment her appearance.

Maem didn't even look at her.

Instead, she was packing items into a box: multiple jars of chow-chow, beets, and applesauce as well as four loaves of fresh bread. Without flinching, her mother lifted the box and set it on her hip. She wore a scowl on her face, and her round-rimmed glasses couldn't hide the disappointment in her eyes.

If only Benny would have come home last night, Grace thought. He was ruining everything of late. And his behavior seemed to exacerbate her parents' negative feelings toward Menno. She knew it wasn't fair, especially because Benny was making bad choices without any influence from Menno. Yet she also knew that it would be disrespectful to bring up the subject to either *Maem* or *Daed*.

"Let's go, then," *Maem* said as she hurried toward the door.

Obediently, Grace followed.

The buggy ride to the Kings' farm took ten minutes. The overcast sky hinted at rain and made everything feel dark and dreary. It mirrored her parents' mood. Benny, the wild child of their family. His approach to *rum-schpringe* had shocked even Grace, especially because he had teased her so much when she turned sixteen.

At first, he attended youth gatherings along with the other young adults. Often he would drive Grace to the gathering, knowing as others did that Menno would bring her home. Of late, however, Grace noticed that Benny slipped out of the gatherings and disappeared. Soon the gossip began to reach her ears that Benny was hanging out with young Eli Troyer and two Mennonite boys who had a reputation for doing bad things: smoking cigarettes, hanging out with *Engsliche* girls, and racing their horses.

The shift in his behavior didn't make anyone happy in the Masts' house. Still, they knew that *rumschpringe* was the time to explore the world and make decisions about the future. Grace knew her parents worried about Benny and prayed that he'd soon calm down and be more responsible.

This, however, was the first time he hadn't come home at all. And the combination of anger and fear created a tense atmosphere in the buggy. Grace was thankful when she saw the mailbox at the end of the Kings' property.

As her father guided the horse and buggy down the driveway, she saw that the turnaround at the Kings' farm was full of black buggies, probably twenty or so. *Daed* parked at the end of the line and went about unharnessing the horse. Normally, young boys were assigned this task, but today there were none in attendance since the younger, unbaptized boys and men were not permitted to attend. *Maem* got out of the buggy and reached for her box of food, leaving Grace to push the front seat forward herself so she could crawl out of the buggy's door. Her mother was already yards ahead, walking quickly down the driveway and, as she approached the house, nodding at the men who lingered near the porch.

Grace had a hard time keeping up with her.

After she entered the Kings' mudroom and unpinned her black shawl, Grace folded it neatly and placed it on top of the others with the black bonnet she had worn over her head covering. She ran her hands down the front of her dress and apron before lifting her fingers to touch her hair, smoothing down any stray strands that the bonnet might have disturbed. Only then did she enter the kitchen and join the other women.

Everything about the gathering appeared the same as it was at every other worship service. There were no extra smiles or words of encouragement. In fact, as Grace greeted the other women, no one seemed to recognize that the day was special, a big milestone in her life. She shook hands with the women, not being given the greeting kiss because, as of this moment, she was not a baptized member. At the end of the line, she assumed her position next to her *maem*.

By the time the bishop and preachers entered the room, Grace felt nervous and wished more than anything that she could speak to Menno. She hadn't expected the baptism service to be so...ordinary. In fact, if anything, the people seemed even more somber than usual.

The bishop and the preachers shook hands with each of the women with a light and loose handshake, Grace noticed, before walking through the room to assume their places in the center. The downstairs had been completely cleared of furniture, hinged walls had been opened, and benches were arranged so that the men could sit on one side while the women sat on the other.

After the church leaders assumed their positions, the women filed into the room and sat down, chair legs and benches scraping on the hardwood floor. Once they were settled, the men entered the house. Grace scanned the line, looking for Menno. When she finally saw him, she noticed that he stared straight ahead, not glancing in her direction. The serious expression on his face startled her. Where was the Menno Beiler who charmed her with his smile and sparkling green eyes? Instead, he never once looked in her direction as he sat down among the other unmarried but baptized men.

After everyone was seated, the men removed their black hats, leaning forward to slip them under their chair or bench. A long moment of silence followed, and then the gentle voice of the *vorsinger* began to sing the first note of the opening hymn. Grace joined the other members as they sang along, some members singing from memory while others, like Grace, glanced down at the hymnal for reference.

After the second sermon the bishop stood before the congregation and asked the three young adults who were to be baptized to come forward and follow him to another room. It would be the last time he would give them instructions about the lifelong commitment they were taking. Should any baptized member decide to leave the religion, he would be shunned and unable to live among the Amish or speak with his family again. If a baptized member broke one of the rules, the same would apply: shunning. All baptized members vowed to live a Plain lifestyle and to reject conformity to the outside world.

For Grace, taking the vow had been an easy choice.

After this last instructional the bishop indicated that it was time for the baptism. Covering their faces with their hands as a sign of humility, those being baptized followed the bishop as he returned to the worship room. Grace managed to peek through her fingers so she could see where she was walking. She noticed her mother watching her, the first indication of any sort of pride from her family.

The three baptismal candidates stood before the bishop, their hands still covering their faces. After a lengthy pause, the bishop spoke, telling the story of Paul baptizing an Ethiopian. It was the same sermon that had been given to generations before and would be given to generations after these candidates had been baptized. Yet Grace felt the power of the bishop's words. For her, it was the first time she had heard them. She imagined she would hear them many more times over the years, but for today, she absorbed each word in a way that gave new meaning to the passage.

When the short sermon was over, the bishop cleared his throat. "If you are still intent on taking this baptism," he said, "then I ask you to kneel before me. If, however, you have any doubts, this is the time to speak up."

There was a lengthy pause.

No one spoke.

"In Matthew 6, the Savior says that no one can serve two masters. Anyone who tries to do so will hate the one and love the other, or he will cling to the one and despise the other." A moment of silence followed, just enough time for Grace to think about the *Englischers'* love of money and how it often created a wedge between them and God.

The bishop continued.

"You are now asked if you are willing to renounce Satan and all of his followers, the dark kingdom filled with deceitful and worldly riches," he said as he stood before the baptism candidates. "To renounce your own carnal and selfish will, lusts, and affections. In doing so, you pledge yourself to be faithful to God, to receive the Savior, Jesus Christ, and to allow yourself to live a life that is led by the Holy Spirit in all obedience to the truth and to remain in this unto death." He paused before he added a simple question, "Can you acknowledge this with a yes?"

Grace nodded her head and whispered, "Yes."

She heard the other two candidates do the same.

"Then speak the confession of faith," the bishop commanded.

Grace had practiced it so much that she knew it by heart. But words escaped her. For a moment, she wondered if the other two had forgotten the words too. And then, in a moment of clarity, she remembered.

"I believe that Jesus Christ is the Son of God," she said softly and heard the others join her. It was easier to remember the words when they said them in unison.

Grace felt someone removing the pins from her prayer *kapp*: the bishop's wife.

"I pray that you will be worthy of God's grace as members of the church," the bishop said. She heard the sound of water as the bishop baptized the person next to her. Then it was her turn.

"Grace Mast, upon your confessed faith, you are baptized in the name of the Father and the Son and the Holy Spirit," he proclaimed. She heard the soft noise of the bishop's fingers dipping into a bowl of water and felt sprinkles of water on her bare head. "Whoever believes and is baptized shall be saved. Amen."

She felt a hand gently remove her own from covering her face and then touch her shoulders, an indication that she should open her eyes and stand. The bishop's wife stood before her and gave her a holy kiss.

Her baptism was over.

She was now officially Amish, not just by birth, but by choice.

When instructed, she returned to her spot. No one said anything to her. She glanced at her mother and noticed that her eyes appeared glassy: the second sign of pride. Knowing that her mother was touched by Grace's baptism made her feel better. Despite his disappearance, Benny hadn't ruined the entire day.

The thought of Benny made her reach into her pocket and touch the handkerchief. She had brought it with her, just in case she became emotional. It comforted her to have it with her as she thought of one day seeing Benny and later Anna Mae take their own baptismal vows.

The final hymn began, and Grace let her voice join the others as they sang:

Eternal Father in the kingdom of heaven
Who rules eternally,
From beginning unto the end,
Who loves us altogether
And gave for us in death
His most beloved Son,
Who deemed us all,
Those who truly know Him,
Yes, who now want to follow Him
By whom we name ourselves,
He alone is the eternal comfort,
Who now builds on Him
Will be delivered from hell.

It is truly a narrow way,
Who now wants to go this heavenly path,
He must surely keep himself
That he does not stumble on the path,
Through affliction, misery, anxiety, and need,
Love must not wax cold.
He must completely depend
On God, wholly trusting in Him.
The Scriptures show clearly and plainly,
Upon God shall man securely build,
He is the rock, cornerstone and foundation,

Whoever builds a house on Him,
No wind will blow it down.

After the rest of the worship service, Grace immediately began helping the other women with preparing the trays of food. There was no chance to interact with Menno, for he was busy helping the men convert the benches to tables for the fellowship meal. But she did steal a glance toward him once or twice. He still looked very somber, and for the briefest of moments, she wondered if he might have changed his mind about marrying her.

Someone touched her arm. "Congratulations," Hannah Yoder whispered to her. She had been baptized the year before and knew how apprehensive Grace had felt.

In response, Grace merely smiled.

"I liked that song they sang at the end of service," Hannah said as she helped Grace set the table with plates, cups, and saucers. "It was different from the one they sang at my baptism."

"Oh?" Grace wouldn't know the difference since she had never attended a baptism prior to today. "I wasn't familiar with it," Grace confided. But she had liked the words. God was the rock, cornerstone, and foundation of her life. The vow of baptism signified her belief in that truth.

Hannah looked over her shoulder and saw her brother walk by. "David? What was that last song?"

"Eh?"

Hannah frowned. "The last song that they sang today. It was beautiful."

"*Ach, ja*," David said, understanding the question at last. He was a very devout young man and could always be counted on to know answers to questions related to the Bible and the *Ausbund*. Why, Grace wouldn't be surprised if one day he was nominated as a church leader. "That song was written in the year 1530," David Yoder said. "It's Song 51 in the *Ausbund*."

With that, David left their side and joined a group of young men while Hannah and Grace quickly finished setting the table. Without the other young women at the service, there was more work for them to do. But Grace didn't mind. She wasn't thinking about work but about the beautiful words that had been sung. *Song 51,* she repeated to herself, making a special mental note to look it up at home so she could memorize those words and sing them in her head forever.

2015

During most of the worship service, Grace could think of nothing else but the note she had placed in her pocket. With the exception of Bishop Yoder and his sister, Hannah Esh, no one from her current *g'may* had attended her baptism. In keeping with her outgoing personality, Lizzie, the bishop's wife, was not one to keep secrets. As for her husband, Bishop Yoder was not one to participate in such trifling games as secret sister. The thought of his doing so almost made her smile. That left the distinct possibility—perhaps the only one!—that

Hannah Esh was the secret sister. But how could she have remembered that detail, the particular hymn sung at her baptism, when it had happened so long ago, especially when Grace herself hadn't thought of that song for a long, long time?

Fifty years had passed since her baptism. So much had happened during that period of time! Her eyes wandered to where Rose King stood. In just a few short weeks, Rose King would become Rose Miller, and so would begin a new journey in her young life, a journey filled with trials and tribulations that the young woman certainly could not predict.

Grace sighed as she thought back over the past fifty years. The years had brought trials and tribulations, yes, but always during the hard times, Menno had stood by her side. She depended on him for strength and support. Now he was gone. With wedding season and then Thanksgiving and Christmas coming up, she missed him more than ever. Often she wondered how she would get through the holidays alone.

But then she remembered the line in Song 51: *He must completely depend on God, wholly trusting in Him.* That was the ultimate purpose of baptism, of committing to the *g'may*. She admitted that she had spent her life depending to a great degree on Menno. Now she had to learn to depend on God alone. Faith and devotion to God would get her through anything, and as long as she leaned on God, she wasn't really alone.

She wondered how her secret sister knew about the significance Song 51 held for her. Even more important,

Grace wondered how her secret sister knew that she needed to be reminded to trust in God.

For the past few months, Grace had remained stoic in her mourning, trying hard to keep her emotions and despair to herself. She knew the consequence of mourning publicly for too long and didn't want to replicate her parents' mistake. But inside, she worried that she wouldn't make it through the holidays without Menno by her side.

When the bishop indicated it was time for the final prayer, Grace quickly followed the others and knelt with her hands covering her face and her forehead bent down toward the seat of her chair. She prayed her gratitude that someone had shown enough interest in her to send her a reminder, that simple slip of paper with those words gracefully written upon it: *Song 51.* No matter how bleak her future looked, Grace knew that with God as her foundation, she could survive.

The reminder was well timed and much appreciated.

When it was time for everyone to rise, she discreetly reached into her pocket and touched the piece of paper. Warmth spread throughout her body, and she smiled as she realized that her secret sister was telling her that everything would be all right as long as she trusted in God.

CHAPTER FIVE

November 2015

*T*HE NEXT FEW weeks seemed to drag for Grace. She knew that many of the women in the *g'may* were busy helping others with preparations for upcoming weddings. Usually there would be two or three weddings in each *g'may* with a few others in adjacent communities. This year, she was invited to only one wedding in her *g'may*: Melvin Miller to Rose King. Outside of her *g'may*, Esther Wagler had invited her to attend the wedding of Daniel and Beth Ann. But Beth Ann's *g'may* was too far away, and Grace did not have a ride, as she reluctantly explained in her letter to Esther.

So while others were busy helping prepare food for the weekly events, Grace sat alone in the house, watching the world through her front window. An arctic blast from the north seemed to hover over the area, and she convinced herself she was almost glad she didn't have to leave the house. But deep down she knew it wasn't true. Early in the morning, she watched the buggies travel in different directions, and on Tuesday and Thursday, she knew where they were headed: to a wedding.

Grace tried to focus on positive things: Winter, the holidays, and her loneliness would end when the warmer weather returned. She would be able to garden and spend time outside, visiting with people who went out for early evening walks. Everyone always seemed much more social in the warmer weather, especially with the longer days.

To keep herself preoccupied, she focused on crocheting gifts for people for Christmas. For the children at the schoolhouse, she crocheted little bookmarks they could use in their devotionals. She chose remnant yarn that she had in a big box in the spare room. A few years back, Menno had tried to clean up that room, organize it, and turn it into a craft room for her. A place for her to sew or quilt or crochet. But then he had fallen ill, and a disorganized room used strictly for storage seemed suddenly very unimportant.

When Grace finished making the bookmarks, she decided to crochet dish towels for the women in the *g'may*. Though they didn't usually exchange gifts, the focus of the holidays being on Christ and not gifts, Grace hoped she might have an opportunity to visit with more families after Second Christmas in January. Once the long stretch of January and February loomed ahead, with no more holidays or weddings on the calendar, she might get more invitations to her friends' houses. It would be right *gut* to have something to give to the women, a small token to express her appreciation for their kindness.

On the Wednesday before Melvin and Rose's wedding, Grace bundled up to brave the cold on her daily walk to the mailbox. She wanted to collect yesterday's mail and put out her own letters for the postal worker to retrieve. When she pulled down the front of the mailbox and started to place her two letters inside, she noticed a letter inside the mailbox waiting for her. Surprised, she reached for it. It was a small white envelope, and she turned it over to look at the return address.

Her breath caught at the familiarity of the street name: it was her own farm in Ephrata. *Ivan*, she thought. *He wrote to me at last!* Feeling like a giddy child, she quickly placed the two outgoing letters in the box, shut the lid, and hurried back toward the house. When she realized that she had forgotten to put up the red flag on the mailbox, she retraced her steps and pushed it up.

Back inside her house, the warm temperature immediately took the chill off her skin. She forced herself to calm down as she hung up her old coat and hurried into the sitting room. The light from the window was still strong enough to allow her to read the letter from her recliner, although she needed her glasses to properly decipher the small handwriting.

She smiled, enjoying the anticipation of reading Ivan's news. She made certain to write to both Linda and Ivan at least once a week. Yet it had been quite some time since either of them had responded. Even then, the letters were brief and not much more than a list of updates, nothing personal and certainly no inquiries into how Grace was faring. Though she knew they were busy, it still hurt that her own children didn't seem to realize how much she missed Menno and how the upcoming holidays made her feel like a heavy weight was pressed against her chest.

Settling into her recliner, she reached for her glasses and braced herself for the contents of the letter. She used her letter opener to slice open the top of the envelope and then removed the single sheet of paper from within it.

Maem,

Danke for your letters. Jane keeps reminding me to write back. With the short days and extra amount of work on the farm, there seems to be no time to finish everything. Levi has been a great help around the farm. Jane has been keeping busy with all the baking for the weddings: six in all between her family and our g'may. Active season this year. Lydia has been helping with the baking, which has been much appreciated by Jane.

I'm glad you'll be sharing Thanksgiving with James and Hannah Esh and her family. We intend to visit with Jane's sister in Pequea. But I've scheduled a driver for December 18th so that we can come to have supper with you. Will just be Jane and me with the younger kinner.

Your son,
Ivan

Grace stared at the piece of paper and tried to digest the contents. Simple. Direct. Brief. He hadn't even asked after her or wished her God's blessing. She tried to remember if he always had been that way, cold and distant, or if everything had changed after Susan left.

Setting the letter on the table, she glanced at the small trifold calendar. Her eyes fell upon November. Next week was Thanksgiving and it fell on November 26th. It seemed that the month had dragged on for quite a long time. She was looking forward to December and the upcoming children's pageant along with the worship service before Christmas.

The children's pageant!

Grace reached for the calendar and flipped the page so that she could look at December. Sure enough, December 18 was a Friday, the day of the Christmas program at the school. She couldn't miss that! She had already made little gifts for the children, her crocheted bookmarks. Yet how could she possibly write back to Ivan and ask him to reschedule his driver? She felt so happy that he had written to her in the first place, never mind that he was coming to visit.

"Oh, help," she muttered to herself, wringing her hands in her lap.

She was still sitting there, pondering what to do, when she heard the door open. "Grace?" a voice called out.

"In here, Hannah."

"There you are," Hannah said cheerfully when she entered the sitting room. "I just heard from John David that he's to be joining us next week for Thanksgiving! And Katie Sue with Mother too!" She laughed. "I just love the holidays, family coming together and all." Sitting on the sofa next to the recliner, Hannah leaned back and sighed. "There'll be so many children at the *haus*! It will feel so much more festive, don't you think?"

Grace didn't feel much like visiting but certainly didn't want to appear rude. "Oh *ja*, indeed," she replied. Her voice lacked the same enthusiasm that Hannah had displayed. Grace glanced at her friend, and when she saw that Hannah had raised an eyebrow at her half-hearted response, she sighed. "I just received this letter from Ivan." She reached for the letter and handed it to her neighbor. "I don't know what to do."

Hannah squinted as she read the small, neat hand-writing. Her eyes flickered back and forth while Grace watched. When Hannah looked up, handing the letter back, she shook her head. "What's wrong with Ivan's visiting you? It's a *wunderbaar* gesture on his part," she said, before adding, "It isn't as if he's been by as much as he ought."

"But the date!" Grace leaned forward and pointed at the date. "It's the eighteenth of December! That's the date of the children's program."

"*Ach*, I see!"

Everyone knew how much Grace enjoyed that pro-gram. Since moving into the little house with Menno, she hadn't missed one performance, even though they had no grandchildren attending the school in Akron. Nor had she ever missed a pageant when they lived in Ephrata, even when her children were small and did not attend school yet.

"*Vell*, let's see," Hannah said slowly, taking her time and drawing out each word. "Mayhaps you could borrow the Eshes' phone and call him. Ivan has a phone in the dairy, *ja*?" Grace could sense the hesitation in her words. Though the Amish were not permitted phones in their houses, most farmers needed to have access to one in order to contact suppliers or receive orders for their goods. In years past, farmers shared a phone in a communal shack located nearby. Today, however, most farmers kept a phone in the barn. But to use a phone for such a personal issue would surely not be considered an emergency!

"Oh," Grace fretted. "I thought of that. I'm just fearful that it will give him a reason to back out of coming!"

"Did he say what time he'd arrive, then?"

She hadn't thought about that. The children's program was held during school hours. With Ivan and Jane bringing the younger *kinner*, they would have to wait until their own school was let out before they came over. Her eyes skimmed the letter once again and stopped when she saw the word "supper." She breathed a sigh of relief. "Suppertime," she said, lifting her hand to cover her mouth. She smiled apologetically, embarrassed at how she had reacted. "I hadn't even thought of that! *Danke*, Hannah!"

With a laugh, Hannah relaxed back into the sofa. "*Ach*, the holidays. Trying to see the different families can certainly be stressful. I understand your worry, Grace. I'd have reacted the same." She sighed and shook her head. "Honestly, as the *kinner* grow and have their own families and now grandchildren having children, it's near impossible to get everyone together at once for Christmas fellowship."

Grace didn't want to think about Christmas. For the past few years, Menno had insisted that Ivan host an afternoon gathering, and although Grace welcomed the chance to see their grandchildren, conversations with Ivan were still strained. Grace wasn't certain she could be so forceful, and Ivan's letter hadn't mentioned anything about a Christmas gathering. Without Menno to insist, Grace had doubts that Ivan would include her in his plans.

"It sure will be nice to attend Melvin and Rose's wedding tomorrow," she said, changing the subject to one that was much more pleasing to her.

"You'll ride with us, then?" Hannah offered.

Grace nodded. Thoughtful Hannah. Always considering Grace's needs when it came to transportation. Truthfully, Grace had intended to hire a driver, but she felt relieved to not have to pay the fee. Many Mennonites and *Englische* offered their services to drive people to places that were too far for them to walk or drive a buggy. But they charged far too much money, sometimes a whole dollar per mile.

"All right, then," Hannah said. "I'd best get back home. James will be looking for me. So much to do, what with the wedding tomorrow and all."

As she shut the door behind Hannah, Grace paused. She felt conflicting emotions, a mixture of joy and dread. Oh, how she loved weddings! But this would be the first one she attended without Menno.

Shutting her eyes, Grace remembered the day fifty years ago when she became Menno's wife. Not once had she considered the fact that one day she might have to relinquish that precious role. Nor had she considered how lost she would feel without it.

1965

As the days before the wedding swiftly passed, Anna Mae commented on more than one occasion that Grace seemed "on the edge" and "nervous." And indeed, Grace felt the fragility of her nerves, caught as she was between her own joy and her parents' displeasure.

Menno spent almost each evening in the kitchen, sitting at the table with her and *Maem*. They spent time making lists of whom to invite and writing out the invitations. It was Menno's job to deliver the invitations while *Maem* focused on making Grace's dress and deciding whom to put in charge of organizing the food.

Whenever Menno arrived, *Daed* would quickly disappear, either into the bedroom or outside to linger in the barn until his future son-in-law left.

On more than one occasion, Grace wanted to ask her mother why *Daed* was so persistent in his disapproval of Menno. However, she knew better than to ask that question. Since she was a little girl, she had been taught that questioning her parents about such issues was improper. She was asked to be very careful about using the simple question, "Why?" As an adult, she came to realize how well she had learned that lesson. She was too intimidated by her parents' authority to ask such a simple question. By the end of today, however, she would answer to a different authority: Menno Beiler.

After Barbara Beiler's appearance at the house to help with quilting, *Maem's* exterior wall slowly began to crumble. Both of Barbara's daughters always accompanied her, and it was clear that the two of them were God-fearing and righteous, intent on walking with Jesus, even though they were not baptized members of the church yet. Still, there seemed to be some issue between her parents and Menno, except it was unilateral: from her parents toward him, not the other way around.

Not once did Menno comment on it.

He always arrived with a smile on his face, his hand extended in proper greeting to them.

The previous two days had been especially stressful for Grace. The neighbors and her two older sisters had come over to help prepare the food. Even her father and brothers helped, perhaps the only event when men would work alongside women in the kitchen. Menno came during the midday, taking a break from his chores at his father's farm, but there hadn't been time to visit. Grace worked alongside the women who were making cheese and bread while Menno helped organize the benches in the large gathering room with Benny.

There was no doubt about his work ethic: Menno knew what hard work was and did not try to shy away from his duties. A few times, Grace caught herself watching him, admiring how he interacted with Benny and Emanuel. If only her father could see what she saw, Grace thought with a heavy heart.

He left in the late afternoon, smiling at Grace as he slipped out the door. Even though he was getting married in the morning, he still needed to help his father with the evening milking. It struck her that the next time she saw him—tomorrow morning—he'd be just moments away from becoming her husband.

She was mistaken.

The clock had just struck eight when they heard a gentle knock at the door. With everything set up for the wedding the next day, the only place for the family to gather was the old farmer's table in the kitchen. *Daed* had been reading the Bible while *Maem* checked through her lists to make certain she hadn't forgotten anything. At the sound of the knock, everyone looked up in surprise. Anna Mae jumped up and hurried to the door.

Grace caught her breath when Menno walked into the kitchen. He removed his hat and seemed nervous about something. For a moment of panic, she feared he had changed his mind. Something like that happened infrequently, but she knew it was not unheard of.

"Might I have a word with you?" he asked, directing the question toward Grace's father.

Grace felt the color drain from her cheeks. Her mother immediately motioned for Anna Mae and Benny to leave the room. Slowly, they retreated upstairs. Even after they disappeared into the darkness on the second floor, Grace suspected they were listening at the top of the stairs.

Menno paced the kitchen floor for a moment, his hands behind his back and a very serious expression on his face. *Maem* and *Daed* watched him, curious about the reason for such an unexpected visit on the night before his wedding. And his peculiar behavior only piqued their curiosity further.

Finally, he stopped and turned to face them.

"I would like you to pray for me," he said, his eyes staring steadily at Grace's father. "I would like you to pray for me that I am as good a husband, father, and, most importantly, Christian as you are."

Astonished, Grace almost spoke up, but she fought the urge to interrupt the moment. Clearly, this was important to Menno. Only once before had she noticed him in such a fervent state of religious reflection, and that was at her baptism.

Clearing his throat, *Daed* frowned. "I am no more so than anyone else," he said modestly.

In a swift motion, Menno moved to the table and sat in the chair next to *Daed's*. He reached for her father's hand. "*Nee*," he said earnestly. "Tomorrow, I am taking on the responsibility of caring for your *dochder*, and I ask for you to pray for me. It is important to me."

There was nothing *Daed* could say to that. How could he deny such a request? Still holding Menno's hand, *Daed* shut his eyes and prayed. Grace saw the intensity with which her father prayed as his mouth twitched a few times during the long silence. When he finished, Menno thanked him, sincere in his gratitude for what *Daed* had done.

Grace wanted to ask Menno before he left why he had done such a thing. His unexpected visit and display of humility and respect certainly caught her off-guard. Even more odd was his request to *Daed*, especially given her father's somber mood whenever Menno visited. But, as usual, she let the question remain unspoken, taking the glow in his eyes as the only answer she needed.

Now, as she dressed in her new light blue dress with white apron and cape, she felt the same apprehension that she had seen in his face the previous evening. After her vow to God to follow the *Ordnung* and renounce worldly pleasures, standing before the bishop and promising to honor and obey Menno for the rest of their lives would be the next most important vow in her life.

Weddings were always held in the bride's house, so when she went downstairs, she walked into a kitchen and gathering room already set up for the service. Throughout the previous week, *Maem*, Anna Mae, and Grace had scrubbed the rooms so that the woodwork shone and the windows sparkled in the sunlight. Emanuel, Benny, and *Daed* had removed most of the furniture and dismantled the hinged walls between the large gathering room that was reserved for worship services and the rest of the downstairs.

Over three hundred people would show up for the service and fellowship, staying well into the evening, only a few leaving for afternoon chores. Because the day was so long, the women would serve two meals, taking turns at replenishing plates of food and pitchers of iced tea and water so that everyone had a chance to both help out and enjoy the day.

The only decorations would be the different foods covering the tables: plates of fresh bread and rolls, dishes of salads, vegetables, and meats, and large bowls of room-temperature mashed potatoes and applesauce. And then there was the dessert table. The women engaged in friendly, unspoken competition over which dessert the bride would select, each woman secretly hoping it would be hers. Between cakes and pies, there was always plenty to tempt even a nervous bride on her wedding day. Other than the food, however, there would be nothing extra—no table linens, flowers, candles, or music—with the exception of the singing of hymns throughout the day. It would appear like any other fellowship gathering.

Of course, Menno and Grace would sit at the special corner table, reserved specifically for the groom and bride. A lot of people would pause before them, offer a congratulatory handshake, and then move on to eat more food and visit with friends and relatives, some of whom they may not have seen in years. That was the only aspect that set the event apart.

"Grace," her mother called over to her. She was working alongside Emanuel's wife as they organized the counter so that arriving guests knew where to leave their contributions to the wedding meal. "Help Anna Mae with the *Ausbunds.*"

Obediently, Grace hurried over to where her younger sister stood next to several wooden crates, each packed with the black hymnals. Anna Mae had been tasked with setting one on each chair and upon the benches for the worship service that would precede the actual wedding ceremony. Anna Mae smiled at her but said nothing as Grace began to help her distribute the remaining books.

While Grace hadn't expected a fuss, she had hoped that her mother might say something—anything—to acknowledge that this was not an ordinary day. She tried to think back to when her older sisters had married. *Had* Maem *behaved in the same manner?* She pondered. But her memory failed her. After all, she had been not much older than Anna Mae at the time, and she was certainly unaware of how nervous her sisters must have felt. Instead, she remembered looking at them, admiring their light blue dresses and feeling slightly envious that they were *real* women now.

When the *Ausbunds* were distributed, Grace set the top back on one of the boxes and bent down to lift it. It would need to go out to the bench wagon that was parked beside the barn. But Anna Mae blocked her path. She glanced over Grace's shoulder, making certain no one could overhear, and then with a big smile, she whispered, "You look so pretty, Grace."

The color immediately rose to Grace's cheeks, but with the crate in her hands, there was nothing she could do to hide her reaction. Anna Mae giggled and hurried away, her own cheeks growing crimson.

No one had ever told Grace that she was pretty. It wasn't something Amish people said to one another. The sinfulness of vanity meant avoidance of compliments, especially about people's appearances. In fact,

Grace had never even considered whether or not she was attractive. Her community considered a person's righteousness and humility of much greater importance than looks.

Yet even as she reflected on this reality, she knew that she had been drawn to Menno initially for two reasons: his self-confidence and his attractiveness. Perhaps that was why her parents showed little enthusiasm for their marriage. Had she sinned in being more drawn to those attributes than to the more important ones? That thought troubled her and she looked up, staring at nothing in particular.

"Grace?"

Startled, she almost dropped the crate when she heard her father say her name.

"You all right, then?" he asked, reaching out to take the crate from her.

Immediately she noticed a change in his demeanor. He appeared calmer and more relaxed than in the days leading up to the wedding. "I'm fine, *Daed*." She tried to smile. "*Danke*," she added, indicating her appreciation for his taking the crate.

He returned her smile and then did something she had never seen him do: he winked at her. That one gesture told her all she needed to know: her father finally approved of her marriage to Menno Beiler. Stunned, Grace stared after him as he carried the crate out of the house. He had a slight spring to his step as he handed the crate to Benny and pointed toward the barn. "And after returning that crate," her father instructed him, "fetch the other ones from Anna Mae and put them on the wagon too."

Without argument or a sassy comment, Benny did as he was told.

Standing there, looking around the room at the organized chaos, Grace began to see things in a different light. Women worked in the kitchen, laughing and talking with each other. Outside the window, she could see that men gathered by the barn while young boys directed arriving guests so that they could park their buggies and unhitch their horses. As people entered the house, they smiled and greeted one another, shaking hands and occasionally glancing in her direction.

Indeed, she had not expected a fuss, but all of these people *were* fussing to make certain that *her* day was special. All of this was in celebration of her marriage to Menno.

Shortly before nine o'clock, the women began to assemble. Grace assumed her regular place among the unmarried women for the very last time.

During the worship service, she found that she could barely focus on the songs. Her stomach felt fluttery, and she couldn't help but glance over at Menno a few times. He was the vision of serenity. It wasn't the first time she had seen him like this at worship services, and his attention to the words of both the songs and the sermons touched her. She realized that his devotion at worship and his unexpected visit last night may have been what broke down her father's resistance.

That thought calmed her nerves.

During the last song, the bishop exited the room. Without being told, Menno and Grace stood up and followed him. This was the way of the Amish, as it had been done generation upon generation. The bishop took them upstairs into one of the bedrooms. He gestured for them to sit on the edge of the bed. Grace felt awkward when she brushed against Menno and quickly moved a little farther away. Out of the corner of her eye, she thought she saw him suppressing a smile.

For a few long seconds, the bishop paced before them, his hands clutched behind his back. With his long white beard and balding head, he looked stern and extremely serious. Grace knew him to be very conservative and unwilling to bend rules or authorize much change in the *g'may*. She was glad that he didn't see Menno's reaction just moments before.

"I needn't tell you the serious nature of the commitment you are both making," the bishop finally declared. "In a few minutes, you will be joined together as man and wife for the rest of your earthly lives. There is no greater love on earth than that of man and wife. Menno, you will provide for Grace and your *kinner*." He paused and Grace thought Menno nodded his head. "Grace, you will care for Menno, raise your *kinner*, and support his decisions." Another pause. She wasn't certain whether she should say something or nod, so she simply nodded.

For the next fifteen minutes, the bishop recited scriptures about the significance of marriage in the eyes of God. There was a fervor about his mini-sermon as he instructed them in their marital duties. Grace found herself listening more to his tone than his actual words. He almost sounded as if he were trying to scare them, and the butterflies returned to her stomach.

Yet Menno remained calm as he paid complete attention to the bishop. Color rose to Grace's cheeks, and she tried to focus on what the bishop was saying.

When he finished, they both affirmed their commitment to each other, and the bishop, satisfied, indicated that it was time to rejoin the congregation downstairs for the actual wedding ceremony. The staircase of her parents' house had never seemed so long and narrow to Grace. She reached for the railing and stumbled, immediately feeling Menno's hand on her elbow. She wanted to turn to him, to thank him, but she knew better. She needed to walk straight ahead and keep her eyes on the bishop. There would be time later to tell him how much she had appreciated his gesture.

They followed the bishop and stood before the congregation, neither one looking at each other, for they faced the bishop. The room was quiet, at least two hundred people watching their backs. Grace stood to the left of Menno, a symbolic expression of the place she would sit beside him at the kitchen table and in the buggy.

After clearing his throat, the bishop leveled his gaze at Menno. Once again, Grace was stricken by how stern the bishop appeared. His eyes narrowed as he began to enunciate the wedding vows.

"Can you confess, brother, that you wish to take this, our fellow sister, as your wedded wife, and not to part from her until death separates you, and that you believe this union is from the Lord? That through your faith and prayers you have arrived here?"

Menno responded with a simple "*Ja.*"

The bishop turned his attention to Grace. "Can you confess, sister, that you wish to take this, our fellow brother, as your wedded husband, and not to part from him until death separates you? That you believe this union is from the Lord? And that through your faith and prayers you have arrived here?"

She bit her lip and nodded her head. The word seemed stuck in her throat until she finally forced out a soft "*Ja*" in response to the bishop's question. Unlike during her baptism, she felt uncomfortable with everyone staring at her.

"Since you, Menno Beiler, confessed your wish to take our fellow sister to be your wedded wife, do you promise to be faithful to her and to care for her, even though she may suffer affliction, trouble, sickness, weakness, despair, as is so common among us poor humans, in a manner that befits a Christian and God-fearing husband?"

Once again, Menno clearly enunciated his answer: "*Ja.*"

The bishop returned his gaze to Grace. "And you, Grace Mast, you confessed that you wish to take our fellow brother to be your wedded husband. Do you promise to be faithful to him and to care for him, even though he may suffer affliction, trouble, sickness, weakness, despair, as is so common among us poor humans, in a manner that befits a Christian and God-fearing wife?"

"*Ja,*" she managed to say.

The bishop stepped back and gestured toward Menno. "Extend your right hand to each other." When they did so, he covered their hands with his and said, "The God of Abraham, the God of Isaac, and the God of Jacob be with you both and help your family come together and shed His blessing richly upon all of you. Now go forth as a married couple. Fear God and keep His commandments."

And with that Grace and Menno were married.

At the ending of the ceremony the bishop asked everyone to kneel for a final prayer. Grace knelt beside Menno and shut her eyes, praying that God would be with them in their life together, especially during the hard times that they would undoubtedly experience. She wanted to be a good wife and mother, to make Menno a happy husband, and to please God in the process with her devotion to Him.

When it was time to stand, she felt Menno help her by holding her elbow. Again she blushed, certain that some of the worshippers had witnessed that display of intimacy. Yet, she reasoned, now that they were married, no one could complain of any indiscretion.

As she stood there, smoothing down the front of her dress, she sensed his eyes upon her. With everyone moving around, setting up the tables for the feast, Grace felt safe to look at him. Those green eyes sparkled and he smiled at her, everything about his presence absorbing her into him. For a moment, she forgot that other people were around. It was as if they simply evaporated.

He leaned forward and whispered, "I knew I was gonna marry you that first day I saw you at the horse auction."

Her mouth opened in surprise at his words.

And then, just briefly, he brushed his hand against hers.

She felt her heart flutter and had to catch her breath. Without a doubt in her mind, God had led her to this man. She loved him and knew that he loved her.

For the rest of the afternoon and into the early evening, guests continued to arrive at the Masts' home. To accommodate the people who arrived later, having traveled to multiple weddings in a single day, women continued to work in the kitchen, ensuring that plates of food were refreshed often.

During most of this time, Menno and Grace sat at the corner table, the place of honor for the groom and bride. The other single women sat next to Grace while the single men sat next to Menno. People approached the newly married couple in pairs, offering their congratulations and blessings for a happy marriage.

There were brief breaks when Menno would lean over to say something to Grace, but there was never enough time to truly engage in any conversation. But underneath the table, he held her hand, his thumb gently caressing her skin. When people approached, he might squeeze her hand lightly as if giving her an extra boost of support. In all, Grace guessed that over four hundred people came to the wedding fellowship, although not all at one time.

When the sun started to sink just over the tree line, some of the young men and women disappeared outside. Grace realized that she was no longer one of them, and even though she wouldn't have wanted to go, she never would be able to again. But she knew that they would be outside, talking under the cover of darkness. New relationships might be formed as a result of her wedding, since families came from different church districts, which meant some youths met for the first time. It wasn't unheard of for a couple that met at a wedding one year to be married the following one.

By the time the remaining guests began to leave, it was already dark. Lanterns were hung on the sides of the buggies so that cars could see them on the roads. Menno went outside with the other men, offering to help harness horses to buggies for some of the elderly guests. Grace offered to help in the kitchen, but her mother shooed her away.

"Make certain you had enough to eat," she told Grace. "I have some extra plates set aside for latecomers who were hungry."

Grace laughed. "We've been eating all day. Why would I be hungry?"

For a moment, her mother stopped working and frowned. Then, as she realized the merit in Grace's statement, she laughed too. Lifting a hand to her forehead, her mother shut her eyes and shook her head. "Oh, Grace, what a long few days it has been!" She dropped her hand and looked at her daughter as if seeing her for the first time. Something softened in her expression. "It was a right *gut* day, ain't so?"

Grace nodded, too moved to express her feelings with words.

"I have something for you," her mother went on. She glanced over her shoulder at the other women who were working. "Reckon they can do without me for a moment, *ja*? Come with me, Grace."

After lighting a small lantern, her mother led Grace upstairs and into the back bedroom, the only bedroom that wasn't used. While it was pristine, being cleaned weekly even though no one slept there, it felt empty without any clothes hanging from the hooks on the wall. Against the wall, there was one small dresser. Her mother set the lantern on top of it and opened one of the drawers. She searched through several items before she found what she sought: a book.

"There it is!" She smiled as she turned around and handed it to Grace.

It was small with a light blue cover. When she opened the book, the pages were blank. Puzzled, Grace looked at her mother. "What is it, *Maem*?"

"A five-year journal," she said. "When I married your *Daed*, your *grossmammi* gave me one just like this. A different color, I recall. But she told me that it was a wonderful gift to write down one or two little thoughts each day. And I have. Every night, before I go to bed, I write in my own diary. Little things: about worship service, if someone visited, what the weather was, if one of my *kinner* took ill. On days when I feel a little overwhelmed—and you will too, Grace, believe you me—it's soothing to look back at some of the old passages. In times of hardship, reflect on the past and remember all of the good that God has given us." She gave a little laugh. "Why, I can go back to read about the day you were born!"

Grace held the gift in her hands, amazed at the revelation her mother just shared with her. To learn that her mother kept a journal for all those years! She had never known. Truly, her mother had just given her a very valuable gift. Grace could almost envision herself writing entries in her journal about her life with Menno. "Oh, *Maem*," she breathed. "This is truly special. *Danke* ever so much!"

She couldn't wait to show it to Menno. On her way down the hall, she paused and put the journal in her bedroom on the nightstand. She stood for a moment, staring at the room. Years ago, she had shared a room with Anna Mae. That had been when her older sisters and Emanuel still lived at home. When they married and moved into homes of their own, Grace moved into an empty bedroom.

Now she would share the bedroom with Menno, but only on the weekends, until the spring when she would move to the Beilers' farm. She never understood the reasoning behind that tradition, but she never thought even once of asking why.

"Grace!"

There was an urgency in the voice that called out to her.

"Grace! Get downstairs quick!"

Clearly, something was wrong. She hurried down the stairs and, at the last step, paused. Most of the guests were gone. However, a small group of women hovered over her mother, who sat slumped in a chair, her hands covering her face. Her shoulders trembled, racked with grief.

"What's happened?" Grace asked, desperate to find out what had caused her mother to cry when, just moments ago, they had shared a special moment in the upstairs bedroom.

Outside the window, she saw something flashing: red and blue lights. There was a police car in the driveway. In the headlight beams, she saw a group of men huddled together. Immediately she recognized Menno's form. He had his arm around another man: *Daed*.

"Please," Grace pleaded as she looked from one person to the next. "Tell me."

The women looked at each other as if urging someone to speak up. Her mother's sobs became uncontrollable and Grace went to her, comforting her as best as she could. Rubbing her back, Grace tried to soothe her, but her mother remained inconsolable.

The door opened, and when Grace looked up, she saw Menno leading her father inside, the bishop and two preachers following close behind. Her father appeared in the same condition as her mother, his cheeks streaked with tears and needing Menno to support him.

Grace caught Menno's eyes and, without a word, questioned him by raising her eyebrows.

He merely shook his head, his own cheeks drawn and pale.

The bishop stepped forward and placed his hand on her mother's shoulder. "God will get you through this," he said. "I would like us to gather in prayer."

Grace watched as the other women quickly took chairs that had previously been folded up for storage and put them into a semicircle. The remaining people, twelve in all, moved toward the chairs. The bishop helped her mother to a chair, freeing Grace to hurry to Menno's side.

"Menno? What's happened?"

He nodded to one of the preachers to assist her father to a chair and took Grace by the hand. He led her outside into the cold November air so that they could talk in private. She rubbed her arms and waited for whatever news he had to share with her. And when he told her, she forgot about being cold. Her gasp of disbelief created a burst of steam that clouded her vision. Or was that the tears that sprang to her eyes?

"Benny?" she cried.

Menno stood before her, silent in order to permit her time to process what he had told her.

"He's dead? That cannot be! Why, he was just here!"

Menno reached out and pulled her into his arms.

"This doesn't make sense." She clung to Menno's shirt and cried into his shoulder.

"Shh, Grace," Menno whispered, rubbing her back in the same manner Grace had tried to comfort her mother just moments before.

"How?" Grace managed to ask.

Menno didn't respond right away. He seemed to be gathering his thoughts. When he finally answered, his voice was soft and he spoke slowly. "He must have left with the other young men. They went racing, Grace."

"Racing?" She pulled back and looked at him, stunned at that one word.

"Apparently so." He paused, and she knew that he was trying to find the right words to provide her with more details. "They were riding bareback, Grace, through a field. His horse…Jacob Miller was there, and he said Benny's horse stumbled. Mayhaps there was a hole or a dip in the field. When Benny fell…"

He didn't need to complete the sentence.

Grace let out a sob, permitting Menno to hold her once again. The depth of her sorrow was so great that she barely thought about the fact that this was the first time he had held her in his arms. The need for comfort and understanding outweighed her discomfort with the unfamiliarity of his embrace.

November 19, 2015

Just as Grace expected, the wedding was filled with guests, many of whom traveled from afar. There were even guests from Ohio and Indiana. The Esh family was large and, as a result, had spread out to other states with more affordable farmland. Grace couldn't help but think back to her own wedding and the tragic events that had unfolded that evening. Her mind wandered away from the sermons and songs as she remembered the sad news that had infringed on her wedding night.

For the three days following her wedding, Grace had done her best to comfort her parents and younger sister while Menno worked beside Emanuel in the dairy before returning to his family farm to help with chores there. He'd return in the evening to again help with the cows.

Over six hundred people visited during the first two days, coming to the house to view the body and pay their respects to the family. Several women of the *g'may* organized the food so that Grace could stand near her parents. The condolences began to sound repetitious to her. After all, how many different ways can a person say, "Benny walks with God now," and "He's in a better place"?

The one thing Grace did not hear was anyone questioning the reasons behind the accident. Faith in God meant never asking that question, and she chastised herself for even thinking it. Long after his casket was lowered into the grave, her white handkerchief with the purple iris tucked beside him, she often reflected on how the happiness surrounding her wedding day had been destroyed with one bad decision that had, apparently, been part of God's plan. That's what she had been taught her entire life.

But now, as she sat on the hard bench watching Melvin and Rose exchange their vows, she wondered what lay ahead in their future. What did God have planned for the newly married couple? Would the painful events overshadow the joyful moments? And what, Grace wondered, was the point of it all? Just like many other Amish couples, they would have babies, work hard, worship even harder, grow old, and then meet their Maker.

"What profit hath a man of all his labour which he taketh under the sun?" she thought, the scripture taking on a new meaning for her as she sat there, wondering not just about Melvin and Rose's future, but also about her own. *"One generation passeth away, and another generation cometh: but the earth abideth for ever. The sun also ariseth, and the sun goeth down, and hasteth to his place where he arose."*

Her thoughts were interrupted when the bishop indicated that it was time for the final prayer. She knelt and placed her hands over her face, resting her forehead on the bench seat.

Lord, she prayed, *if it is Your will, bless Melvin and Rose with a long and happy life. Save them from the hardships and heartaches so many others experience. And I pray for the strength to find myself in this new life without Menno while remaining your ever-faithful servant.*

With the service over, a new energy permeated the room as it was transformed from a room of worship into a room for fellowship, celebration, and feasting. Grace wandered to the side, hoping to stay out of the way as the others worked. She noticed Esther, Mary, and Lizzie standing on the other side of the room, near the kitchen, so she started to walk there.

Someone tugged on her sleeve.

Surprised, Grace turned around and did not see anyone there, until she looked down and saw one of the Yoder children, Lizzie's granddaughter, standing before her with a sheepish grin on her face.

"Why, look at you," Grace said, forcing a smile for the blond-haired little girl. "My, my, how you have grown! I remember when you were just born!" Her tone of voice was a pitch higher in the manner that adults tend to talk to small children. Yet it exuded warmth and kindness that caused the girl to giggle and roll her cheek against her shoulder in delight. Then she pulled a small package from behind her back and handed it to Grace before she skipped away, quickly disappearing into the gathering crowd.

"What's this?" she asked out loud, even though no one stood before her. Obviously, her secret sister had struck again. Grace glanced around the room, hoping to spot someone watching, but no one seemed to be paying attention to what just happened. Returning her attention to the package, wrapped in white tissue paper, Grace decided to open it. Right there. It wasn't just her curiosity about the contents; it was a need to figure out who was sending her these gifts!

The paper crinkled as she slid a finger under the pieces of tape, lifting up the back of the wrapping. Carefully holding the paper in one hand so that it didn't fall on the floor, she withdrew the item inside. And when she saw it, she gasped.

The entire room evaporated from her consciousness as she was transported back to her own wedding day, to the very moment when she stood beside her mother in the glow of a lamp in that back bedroom. She felt the happiness and joy the gift had brought to her heart fifty years ago. Forgotten was the misery and pain of the loss that, at that moment in time, had yet to happen.

She held the gift, clutching it to her chest, her eyes misty as she enjoyed feeling eighteen and happy once again. The memory felt real, perhaps the first time she had had such a sensation of elation since long before Menno passed away. And in her ears she heard the voice of her mother as *Maem* had handed to her a special gift, one almost exactly like the little blue journal that Grace now held in her aging hands: *"In times of hardship, reflect on the past and remember all of the good that God has given us."*

The merit of her mother's sage advice, offered fifty years ago, was just as applicable today. Over time, Grace had sometimes forgotten to practice that advice. Yet the gift, an innocent gift given by a secret sister who most certainly could not have known of its profound significance, reminded Grace that God loved her and had indeed provided her with a good life. She just had to focus on *those* events and memories instead of the painful ones. The only problem was that Grace wasn't certain she knew how.

Chapter Six

*O*N Thanksgiving morning, the sun shone outside, a welcome change from the previous overcast days. Grace stood at the front windowsill, her fingertips lightly pressed against the white-painted wood, lifting her chin so that her cheeks could feel the warmth. She shut her eyes and stayed there, enjoying the peaceful moment.

The previous day, she had dug out all her old diaries. She sat on the sofa, the diaries spread out around her. They represented her fifty years with Menno. Ten five-year diaries in all, with only one incomplete: the final year of her most recent one. She had stopped journaling when Menno first took ill. At the time, she abandoned the diary with complete consciousness, justifying it because his care took precedence over anything else in her life. In hindsight, she knew the real reason why. Subconsciously, she hadn't wanted to write the entry that would, undoubtedly, reflect the worst event in her life: his death.

While she read them, she found herself smiling at the short entries. She could remember writing many of these entries, and the memories that flooded back, especially about the children when they were younger, made her forget, even if for a short while, the pain of loss.

At eleven o'clock, she wrapped her black shawl over her shoulders, pinning it with a large safety clip, before picking up a small box from the table and carrying it to the door. She had offered to bring some food to Hannah's house for the Thanksgiving meal: cookies, two pumpkin pies, and some canned beets from her pantry. Balancing the box on her hip, she managed to open the door and step outside.

If the sun had warmed her face earlier, the reality of the cold air on her face hit her the second the door shut behind her. Luckily, Hannah lived only two houses down the road. The walk in the brisk air would do her some good, anyway, she rationalized as she fought the urge to return to her house and not go at all.

Each step toward Hannah's house separated her from those diaries, the happier memories that she needed to hold on to at the present moment. Instead, she was reminded that, on the first important holiday since Menno's death, she was not going to be sharing her meal with her family. Instead, she would be the widow invited to the neighbors' house, the pity guest who got to watch the Yoder family enjoy each other's company.

Stop it, she scolded herself. *Be thankful for the invitation and rejoice in the love of God.*

Several buggies were already parked in the driveway, the horses standing inside the large garage that had been converted into a stable. The gate was open and she could see them watching her, their ears twitching as they ate their hay. She missed having a horse and buggy, but she had made the right decision to give it to Ivan's family. They needed it and could take proper care of it, especially during the cold winter months.

"Come in, come in," Hannah said, opening the door even before Grace knocked. She had been waiting for Grace to arrive. "It's right cold out. Come and let me take that box from you, now." Without waiting, Hannah took the cardboard box from her hands and passed it to one of her granddaughters.

"Danke," Grace said, feeling a little less like a pity guest when she saw the big smile on Hannah's face. Such a genuine welcome warmed Grace's heart. Truly she was thankful for having such a good friend and neighbor as Hannah Esh.

Grace's eyes glanced around the room and took in the sight of nearly thirty people sitting on a variety of chairs in the large gathering room. Wooden and metal folding chairs were set up along the perimeter of the room. Mostly older people sat there while the younger women busied themselves in the kitchen.

She recognized several of the men and women who sat on the chairs, their feet crossed at the ankles and most with their arms folded over their chests. The women mostly sat on the far side and talked among themselves, some of them crocheting. Grace noticed Hannah's oldest daughter, Katie Sue, talking with Hannah's mother, Miriam, who, despite her age, appeared alert and in great health.

"Go take a seat now," Hannah urged, nudging Grace in their direction. "You know my *maem*. She's been asking for you all morning!"

Obediently, Grace walked through the room and in the direction Hannah indicated. Several children ran by, their feet bare, for they had left their shoes at the front door, which Grace noticed as she tried to navigate around them. From the kitchen came wonderful smells: turkey, ham, bread. A long table was set up in the living room, a much larger room than typical for most *Englische*-converted homes. The entire atmosphere began to relax Grace, and she realized that she truly felt joy at sharing this special, if not bittersweet, fellowship with Hannah and her family.

"Why, Grace Beiler!" An aged, weathered hand reached out for hers. Grace accepted it, the coolness of Miriam's thin skin a reminder of how Menno's hands had felt just before he died. But Miriam still had a spark of energy and life in her eyes. "You've been hiding in your *haus*, then!"

Grace greeted Katie Sue before sitting next to Miriam. "You look well," she said to the older woman. In truth, she did. With the exception of the clacking of her false teeth and the deep wrinkles under her eyes, Grace never would have known that the woman who sat before her was almost ninety years old.

"Feeling well too," Miriam said cheerfully. "God has blessed me with extra time for another holiday gathering. Can't beat that."

Both Grace and Katie Sue laughed at Miriam's upbeat attitude.

"Hear tell that you have a new great-grandchild over at the old farm," Katie Sue said.

"Soon, but not yet." Grace looked around the room and realized that Miriam's attitude was one that she needed to adopt: feeling blessed, rather than accursed, for having survived Menno. With Menno gone, maybe now she could try to mend broken fences with Ivan. His upcoming visit would certainly provide an opportunity to do so. She missed being around young children, hearing their silly questions and watching their eyes brighten as they learned new things. And reading those diaries had reminded her that she still had family, even if Menno walked with Jesus.

Miriam continued to talk, unaware that Grace had drifted off into a daydream. "Wish He'd bless me with ninety more years," the older woman said in a saucy way. "Want to see what happens to these great-grand-*kinner*. Why, when I was growing up, things were so different. Weren't hardly no cars on the roads at all! And those picture films! We didn't have to worry about our youth sneaking off to see them fancy painted women!"

While she listened to Miriam share stories from when she was younger and comment on how much things had changed, Grace couldn't help but smile to herself.

Miriam's words made Grace try to remember how much things had changed since she had been a young child and later a mother. Despite their age difference, Grace's memories of her own childhood were similar to

Miriam's. Now, as a grandmother, she suddenly saw the world with a different set of eyes. By the time her grandchildren were her age, life would be different indeed. Certainly things had changed since her own children had grown up.

Things did change. And when change started, it seemed to take on a life of its own.

In the fifty years that she had been married to Menno, how much their world had transformed! Ephrata and the surrounding towns had grown from small rural farming communities to more metropolitan areas, both from tourism and suburbanites. The strict conservative bishops and preachers from her youth had died and been replaced with new ones, men who recognized that some compromises were needed in their lives. Telephones began to show up in shops and barns. Kerosene lanterns were replaced with battery-operated lamps. Youths accepted jobs in the world outside their religious confines.

Such change happened so gradually that, until Miriam mentioned it, Grace hadn't really given it much thought.

For the next hour, Grace visited with other guests, most of them related to Hannah or her husband. Most of all, though, she enjoyed watching the children. She watched the little ones running back and forth, playing with toys and laughing. The sound of laughter brought back memories of her own children during a period of her life that, despite some pain, was the happiest of times.

1966–67

The blood in the toilet told Grace all she needed to know: the baby was gone. It was her second miscarriage since their marriage, almost twelve months ago. Unlike her first pregnancy, her second one had been kept secret from Menno. She didn't want to get his hopes up only for him to be disappointed again. It was better that only she suffer rather than her dragging him into the despair of losing a second baby.

Still, as she sat on the floor with her arm across the top of the toilet and her forehead pressed against the side, she felt the tears streaming down her face.

All she desired was to give Menno that one gift all men wanted: a child, preferably a son. While every parent wanted a healthy infant, for the farming family, a son as the firstborn would make the joyous event even more special. Boys grew into men, and men worked alongside their fathers in the fields and dairy.

Even more, she wanted a baby for herself. She wanted to be a mother. She wanted to be a mother to Menno's baby so that she felt settled and part of the Beiler family. It had taken Grace a little bit of time to adapt to living at the Beilers' farm. She certainly couldn't deny that she missed her own family, especially when she quickly learned that there were many ways to live, even among the Amish.

Barbara Beiler ran her family with an iron fist when it came to discipline and respect; but she also gave her children the right to decide about their own futures and the right to make choices in life. Menno was a perfect example. During his *rumschpringe*, he seemed to be on a wild journey in life. Barbara had let him make his own choices, offering him love and support even if she hadn't quite understood his reasons. Now that he had settled down, and with Grace, definitely a favorite of hers, Barbara could breathe a sigh of relief that Menno had come back into the fold.

What remained unsaid was that he too could have been a casualty like Benny.

Without doubt, the pain and suffering within Grace's family lingered far longer than most people permitted. Birth, life, and death were inescapable. After the proper period of mourning, life continued for everyone else. After all, life was God's will. So was death, she reminded herself.

Uncertain what to do, she finally decided to reach out and flush the toilet. Tears streamed down her face as she worried whether or not that was proper. By her calculations, she had been a little over nine weeks pregnant. Maybe ten. Now, as of just a few moments ago, she wasn't pregnant at all.

She wondered when the baby died. *Was it today? Was it yesterday?* She worried that it was something she had done. Try as she might, she couldn't think of anything unusual such as reaching up to a top shelf or bumping into something like a counter or table. Like Benny's death, there was no explanation for why her baby was gone.

God's will.

Tears streamed down her cheeks.

"Grace?"

She wiped her face with the back of her hand and struggled to her feet, hoping her cheeks weren't too red or her eyes too puffy. "I'm in the bathroom," she called back, trying to sound natural. After running cold water from the faucet and splashing it on her face, she took a long look in the small mirror over the sink. While she may have masked her swollen eyes, she couldn't hide her sorrow. Plus, she really needed to lie down for a while. The cramps in her stomach hadn't gone away after her body released what had been her baby.

When she left the bathroom and entered the kitchen, she saw him seated at the kitchen table, reading the newspaper. He glanced up and smiled at her. "There's my Grace," he said and reached out his hand for her to take. "I'm finished with my chores for the morning. Thought we might take a ride over to your parents' and see how your *daed* and Emanuel are doing with the haying."

She couldn't imagine facing her mother right now.

"I'm not feeling so well," she said, her voice soft and her eyes downcast. "Mayhaps I might need to rest a spell."

The gleam in his eyes, so hopeful, indicated that he wondered if she might be trying to tell him something else.

"It's not that," she mumbled. "Stomachache is all."

He pulled her into his arms and gently sat her on his lap. One of the things she had grown to love about Menno was how affectionate he was in the privacy of their small house. He treated her with tender care and thoughtfulness, never shy to reach out and touch her or hug her. Of course, in the company of others, he remained very standoffish and reserved, for public displays of affection were not allowed and could be cause for a stern lecture from their bishop.

"Grace," Menno said, forcing her to meet his gaze. "It will happen when it happens." "What if it doesn't happen?" she whispered, hoping that her voice didn't quiver. "What if something is wrong with me?"

He laughed, a comforting sound. "There's nothing wrong with you. In fact, I think you're as near perfect as any person could be." Then he leaned over to kiss her cheek. The whiskers on his chin tickled her skin. That was one thing she wasn't used to: his mustache-less beard. Even though she knew that married Amish men must grow a beard, she missed his clean-shaven face. He looked much older with his beard. "Now let's get you tucked in for a nap, *ja*? And I can even fetch you a cup of tea."

"Meadow tea?" she asked, a gentle smile on her face as she tried to sound appreciative of his offer. "Warm?"

"Warm."

By the time their first anniversary arrived, Grace fretted that she still had not conceived since her second miscarriage. Menno seemed unfazed by the fact that, unlike most newly married couples, they were not celebrating their anniversary with a baby in their arms. In moments of great panic, Grace did her best to emulate his steady calmness. It didn't always work.

Spring arrived and brought a new hope that life was forming within her womb. Once again, she kept the news to herself so that she didn't raise false hopes in her husband. This time, however, when several weeks turned into months and she felt the need to pin her dress a little looser around her midriff, she felt, in her heart, that God had blessed her at last.

Sitting outside at the picnic table under a large oak tree, Grace set down the pants that she had been sewing for Menno. She shut her eyes and lifted her face to the warm breeze. She liked working outside during the warmer months, especially since their house was so small. The vibrant colors created a prettier backsplash than if she merely sat inside. Besides, she wanted to see the growing cornstalks as they waved in the breeze and smell the comforting, familiar scent of farm life.

One day, she thought, as she rested her hand on her stomach, this farm would be the backbone of this baby's life. As Menno's parents aged and his younger sisters married, they would eventually move into the smaller house so that Menno and his family would live in the larger dwelling. It was the normal cycle of life on an Amish farm.

"Grace," he said as he slid onto the bench beside her.

She hadn't heard Menno approaching from the barn. Smiling, she opened her eyes and turned to look at him. His short-sleeved work shirt was dirty on the front with a small tear at the seam of his collar. She made a mental note to fix that right away. "It's a beautiful day, *ja*?" she said.

He remained silent, his eyes studying her face. She wondered what he saw. Did he see how hard she tried to please him? How much she loved him? How happy she was to be his wife?

His hand brushed against her knee and she jumped, startled at his touch in the open where someone might see. A quick glance toward the larger house comforted her that no one was outside to witness him touching her.

"You seem quite content these days, my pretty *fraa*," he said, leaning his head toward hers so that she could hear his words spoken softly. "I was wondering..."

She fought the urge to smile, enjoying the curious expression on his face. "Wondering...what, Menno?"

Hesitantly, he lifted his hand and touched her stomach. His eyes remained on hers as he caressed what was clearly a small, rounded bulge. "I was wondering if there was anything that mayhaps you wanted to tell me."

Her cheeks grew hot and she knew she could contain her secret no longer.

"Would that please you?" she asked teasingly. "If I had a secret to tell?"

He raised his eyebrows, amused at her coquettish question. "That would depend on the secret. If it was a good secret..."

She couldn't contain her delight any longer. "What if it was the best secret, Menno? The very best in the world?"

"Grace Beiler!" he laughed, clearly understanding her cryptic question. "The best secret in the world?"

Clearly not caring if anyone saw, he pulled her into his arms and hugged her. His arms held her tight and he even kissed the side of her head, careful not to dislodge her prayer *kapp*. "What a *wunderbaar* gift God has bestowed upon us!"

His happiness was contagious and she laughed with him, tears of love clouding her vision. After eighteen months of marriage and two miscarriages, she was finally going to be a *maem*.

Extracting herself from his embrace, she looked into his eyes. "God's will," she whispered.

Menno nodded his head. "That it is, *fraa*. That it is." He leaned back so that he sat beside her, his elbows on the table, and gave a deep sigh. "Do you know when the *boppli* might come, then?"

That was the question, indeed. From what she figured, she was at least four months along, so that would mean a Christmas baby. Still, she couldn't be that certain. She'd have to leave it to God to decide. Like all of the Amish women, she would give birth at home, most likely with Barbara Beiler and a neighbor aiding in the delivery. Some of the women were beginning to rely on midwives to help with the birthing process, but most continued the traditions of their ancestors.

"December, I reckon."

He nodded his head as if in approval.

In truth, it was a good time of year to have a baby. With less work on the farm, Menno could spend more time around the house and make certain Grace didn't go into labor alone. And certainly Anna Mae would come to stay with them for a few weeks. Younger sisters often aided their older ones, although Grace had never been asked because her older sisters lived far away and there were plenty of younger sisters-in-law who lived closer to them.

"*Vell*," he finally said. "I'm glad there are no more secrets between us." He glanced at her, his eyes sparkling and a hint of a smile on his lips. "Even the best of secrets."

"I shall remember that," she responded.

For the rest of July and August, she felt in wonderful spirits. Her energy remained high, and she worked alongside the others in the garden. She even helped with the haying. At her parents' farm, working in the fields had always been a welcome change for Grace. She loved the smell of fresh-cut grass, walking behind the cutter with a rake to spread out the cuttings in order for them to dry. When it came time to bale the hay, she didn't mind helping to stack the bales on the wagon.

Menno drew the line at that, though.

"Grace, you should help my *maem* in the kitchen today," he said when she came out to the barn, ready to go to work in the field. She noticed that his younger siblings glanced up, as did his father. "Bethany and Linda will help Thomas today."

And so the rest of the Beilers slowly began to understand that a new addition to the family would soon be born.

At the next worship service, Grace wondered if other people would notice, her parents in particular. Since

Benny's death, they had changed. Not for the better. Even with the birth of Emanuel and Katie's baby last year, her mother and father were visibly distant, mere shells of their previous selves. In fact, despite Menno's constant consideration in helping Grace's parents with their farm, the atmosphere at the Mast household remained morose.

Grace hoped that a new *boppli* might help rouse her parents from their depression so they could return to the land of the living.

In greeting her mother at the worship service, Grace felt shocked at realizing how old she looked. Her hair seemed thinner, her posture drooped, and there was a vacant look in her eyes.

"Are you feeling *vell*, then, *Maem*?" Grace asked.

"I reckon."

Grace looked around for Katie, her brother Emanuel's wife. Their baby, a little boy named Nathaniel, might cheer up her mother, she thought. "Did Emanuel and Katie come, then?"

A simple shrug was the only response that her mother gave.

As much as Grace tried to engage her *maem* in conversation, most of the responses were short and nondescript. The other women who stood nearby may have noticed, but no one seemed to dwell on it. After all, what could anyone else do about God's decision to call Benny home?

"I don't understand," Grace said to Anna Mae after the service and in between fellowship seatings. "I would think that little Nathaniel would cheer them up."

They stood to the side, away from the other women so that no one could overhear their conversation. Anna Mae looked as distressed as Grace felt. Now that she was a young woman in her *rumschpringe*, she understood much more of what was going on around her, especially at home.

"*Maem* refuses to pick up the *boppli*," Anna Mae whispered. "Emanuel thinks it's because of Benny, Nathaniel being a boy and all."

Grace looked shocked. Was it possible that her mother was rejecting her own grandson? "I can hardly believe you!" But she did. Anna Mae was never one to tell tales.

Her sister nodded her head. "It's right *gut* that your Menno comes to help Emanuel. I don't know how he'd manage working the fields and haying without your husband. *Daed* seems to have aged and barely gets through the morning milking before he is back inside, either reading the Bible or taking a nap."

Looking over her shoulder, Grace tried to find her father. When she did, she couldn't help but sigh. He sat at the table, looking down at his plate and not engaging in conversation. He wasn't even sixty years old, yet with stooped shoulders and a drawn face, he too looked much older. As she started to return her attention to Anna Mae, she noticed the bishop, ever so watchful over his flock, staring at her father too.

Grace nudged her sister and, with a slight tilting of her head, indicated that Anna Mae should look toward the bishop. They both knew what his attention focused on their father meant.

Amish mourning was short-lived. Life had to go on. After all, their faith was based on understanding and accepting God's will as well as the fact that earthly life was only the entrance into a heavenly one. To mourn so long meant a lack of faith. For the bishop to notice that almost two years after Benny's death, the Masts were still mourning certainly meant one thing: he'd be visiting with them during the week. A long discussion would ensue in order to reconfirm their faith in God's will.

Later that evening, when Grace mentioned to Menno her observation about her parents and the bishop, he remained thoughtful for a moment before nodding his head. "It does go against the faith to mourn for so long, I reckon," he finally said. "Are they questioning God's reasons for taking Benny? Do they not believe that he is in a state of bliss awaiting the second coming of Jesus Christ? Doesn't the Bible tell us that 'the sufferings of this present time are not worthy to be compared with the glory which shall be revealed in us'?"

She remained silent. She knew what he meant: the Bible said that suffering on earth was temporary, for God's kingdom would bestow glory and joy on righteous believers. For a moment, she felt ashamed of her parents for having put themselves in this position. Surely the bishop's calling upon them would not only help them through their grief but also restore their faith.

"Man was made to suffer, Grace," Menno continued. "It is through our faith that we are able to return to our daily tasks and maintain a state of well-being."

Later that evening, as she wrote in her diary before retiring to bed, she wanted to comment about Menno's statement. All afternoon, she had thought about his words. While she knew he was right, she wondered if she would have the strength to regain such a state if one of her own children perished. According to Scripture, suffering was part of life. Ever since Eve took the forbidden fruit and offered it to Adam, both men and women suffered. Yet the Bible also clearly stated that glory lay ahead for all believers in Christ. And, she pondered after writing in her diary, God had sent His own Son to suffer alongside mankind in order to take on the burden of sin.

Ashamed or not, Grace still felt compassion for her parents' grief. She suspected their anguish didn't stem just from the fact that since Benny was the son intended to work alongside Emanuel on the farm, his death meant ongoing hardship for the entire family. No, Grace suspected that her parents blamed themselves for not raising him properly. Not one of their other children, eight in all, had behaved so rebelliously. Surely they worried that they had been too permissive with Benny. Perhaps they even felt that he might still be alive if they had disciplined him more.

What they failed to see was what Grace observed: Benny had been a spirited child and an even more rambunctious young man. While it was true that their father didn't take Benny out to the woodshed as often as he had her older brothers, Jacob, Jonas, and Emanuel, Grace suspected that Benny's penchant for unruly behavior could not have been cured by the rod; it was engrained in his personality.

During the next few months Grace learned that her suspicions regarding the bishop's concern for her parents were well founded. Word circulated through the Amish grapevine that the bishop was counseling them. Sometimes Grace overheard conversations after worship gatherings, whispers that included phrases like "lack of faith" and "church discipline." She did her best to ignore such speculation as she prepared for the upcoming season of communions, baptisms, and weddings.

As a young married woman, regardless of her delicate condition, she would play a pivotal role in assisting at these events in the *g'may*. She would cook food to be served at fellowship and help clean the bride's home. During the weddings, she would work in the kitchen, taking shifts with the other women. And by the time her second anniversary arrived, the season would slow down and all eyes would focus on the approaching holiday.

Christmas had always been Grace's favorite time. As a young girl, she had loved the little pageants held at the schoolhouse for the parents and grandparents of their church district. The children stood at the front of the school, reciting scriptures and singing songs about the birth of Jesus Christ. She could well remember how long they had practiced under the guidance of their teacher.

On the day of the event, her mother ensured that all of her children were dressed in freshly laundered and ironed clothes. She always had the girls wear dark green dresses and the boys wear newly made white shirts. Everyone's hands would be inspected to make certain their nails were clean. She would also study their faces, especially Benny's, so that her children would look their best at the program.

Grace couldn't wait until her child was old enough to go to school and perform in such an event. While pride was frowned upon in the Amish religion, Grace knew that there was more than one parent in the audience who needed to ask for forgiveness in their evening prayers on those nights.

Even though her siblings weren't in the school, Grace convinced Menno that they needed to attend. He smiled and obliged her without any question, understanding the joy of such a wonderful evening, especially one that was so close to both Christmas and the anticipated due date of their first child. It would also be a welcome distraction from the scuttlebutt circulating about her parents.

Lanterns lit up the windows of the schoolhouse. Over twenty buggies were parked along the side of the building, the horses tied to a rope that hung between the corner of a hitching post and the large oak tree by the playground. Menno tied the horse before walking around the buggy to the left side in order to help Grace step out. Her stomach protruded from beneath her black shawl and she placed her hand upon it.

"Moving around, then?"

She shook her head as she took his arm so that he could lead her toward the front door of the school. "*Nee*," she admitted. "Been quiet today."

The inside of the school appeared to be packed with the families of the *g'may*. When Menno and Grace entered, the people at the back of the building greeted them with cheerful smiles and extended hands. Unlike worship service where the people were more somber, for worship was not meant to be a social occasion, this event was a celebration of Jesus Christ's birth as well as a recognition of the hard work accomplished by the students and their teacher.

A few men stepped aside to make room for Grace to pass through, and one of the women offered her a seat. Grateful, Grace accepted it.

The students stood at the front of the classroom, their eyes shining and their smiles bright, as they waited for their teacher to indicate that they should begin. The older students stood in the back row and the younger ones stood in the front. Grace thought she counted twenty students. In their *g'may*, the farms were spread out so far that there were two schoolhouses, the other one a bit farther away and bordering on another church district.

The teacher stood in front of her students and smiled at the parents, grandparents, and friends. "*Wilkum* and *danke* for coming to our school program." Behind her, the students beamed. "We would like to start by having a moment of prayer." Silence fell over the group as they prayed.

Grace prayed for the children and their parents, for her unborn baby and her husband, and for her mother and father, who needed the strength of God to get through this difficult time in their lives.

The students began by reciting scripture, retelling the story of Joseph and Mary traveling to Bethlehem for the Roman census and describing how, despite Mary's condition, no one would provide them shelter for the night. One little girl got tongue-tied as she talked about the innkeeper who offered them his stable for shelter, and the audience collectively suppressed their amusement at her expression, so serious and determined to correct her mistake. When she did, she grinned, her two front teeth missing.

By the time the scripture reading was over and the students began to sing "Silent Night," Grace's favorite song of the holiday, she felt the dampness on her dress. It took her a moment to realize that even though the one-room schoolhouse was warm and she was perspiring, the dampness on her clothes was of a different nature.

Her water had broken.

With a slight intake of breath, she looked behind her, trying to find Menno in the shadows. He stood beside one of his cousins who lived on a neighboring farm. At first, he didn't see her staring at him, as he was watching the program so intently. She loved that he could be teasing and playful at times, but when it came to reverence for God and Jesus Christ, nothing could distract him. She had first witnessed this side of him at her baptism and then at their wedding. Throughout the past two years, she had learned that Menno was unlike most other Amish men who adopted an all-around stern, serious demeanor, a demeanor that permeated their entire lives, not surfacing just at worship. While his own demeanor was more jovial and easygoing within the confines of their personal lives, Menno's devotion to God could not be questioned.

He must have felt her eyes on him because he glanced at her. Seeing that she was staring at him, he tilted his head as if asking her if she was all right. Grace shook her head from side to side, her eyes wide and the color drained from her already pale cheeks. Menno seemed to realize immediately that whatever was wrong, it had to do with the baby.

She waited until the song was over and took advantage of the brief pause before the next song to get up, holding her dress tight around her waist and making her way toward the back of the school. Menno helped guide her out of the building, wrapping her shawl around her shoulders as they carefully walked down the three cement steps.

"I think the baby's coming," she whispered in the darkness.

He didn't ask any questions as he guided her back toward the buggy. Silently, he helped her step up and settle on the seat.

It was only when he was driving her back to their farm that he managed to find words. "Are you in pain, Grace?"

"*Nee*," she said, too embarrassed to speak about the wetness on her dress. "I just know."

He questioned her no further, and they rode the rest of the way to the farm swiftly and in silence. She waited, almost impatiently, for any sign of a contraction. None came. She prayed with her eyes shut that her baby was all right and that the birthing would be free from complications. Without even asking, she knew that Menno was praying for the same things.

The farm was dark and Menno held her arm as he guided her up the walkway to the porch.

"Easy now," he said, adding in a serious tone, "can't have you slip, fall, and have our baby on the porch."

His words caught her off-guard. As she visualized such a scenario while trying to imagine why he would say such a thing, she started to laugh. Her laughter seemed to shift the weight within her belly, water leaking and then stopping in short intervals. She grabbed his arm, laughing even harder as she realized what was happening: the baby's head was pressed down and blocking her water from fully breaking. But her laughter had caused the baby to move, just enough.

"Oh, Menno," she said, her laughter dying down. "I cannot believe God has blessed us with such a *wunderbaar gut* gift, a *boppli* just in time for Christmas."

"God is *gut* indeed, Grace," he replied, guiding her through the doorway and toward their bedroom. "Now, if you can stop laughing at me, I'd like our baby born in a bed, all proper like. Let's get you situated so I can fetch my *maem*. Just remember, Grace, that whatever amount of pain we suffer in this life, it will not compare to God's glory and blessings which only He will reveal to us..."

She started to smile at his attempt to offer her support for what was yet to come. Like any first-time mother, she was nervous about childbirth. His words were a soothing balm to her nerves and helped alleviate her fears.

The following day, twelve days before Christmas and after almost sixteen hours of labor, their daughter Linda was born, the greatest Christmas gift God could have bestowed upon the couple.

2015

When everyone was seated at the table, Grace saw James Esh look around at the faces before him. Normally a quiet man, certainly in comparison with his brother-in-law, the bishop, James cleared his throat and spoke to those gathered around his table.

"What a glorious sight to see so many of us gathered together to share our gratitude to God and to each other on this Thanksgiving," he said, his voice surprisingly loud for a man who rarely spoke. "We have much to be thankful for: our family, our friends, our health, and, most importantly, our ability to worship God without fear of persecution, unlike our forefathers."

His eloquence surprised her and she found herself leaning forward, eager to hear what James would say next.

"Over the past four hundred years, our ancestors have struggled and suffered so that we could be gathered here today in fellowship, to give thanks for the blessings of the Lord upon our lives." He paused and looked around the room once again. His eyes rested on Grace's when he continued. "Despite hardships in all of our lives, we *must* remember what the Bible says: 'The sufferings of this present time are not worthy to be compared with the glory which shall be revealed in us.'"

Had she heard him properly? Grace frowned, wondering if she had imagined what James just said. And had he been staring at *her* when he said it? By the time she realized that she had not misheard him, the rest of the people sat with bowed heads in silent prayer to thank the good Lord for the bountiful meal set before them.

But Grace was still in shock.

Romans 8:18 had been one of Menno's favorite scriptures. He repeated it often, especially in times of crisis. When she had discussed her parents' inability to move beyond Benny's death, hadn't that been the exact scripture he quoted to her? When she had given birth to Linda, hadn't that been what he was telling her? In fact, whenever they faced hardships or tragedy, whether in their lives together or within the community, Menno was always the one who offered this scripture as a means to comfort her...and help her move on with life.

Her thoughts were so jumbled by that realization that she could barely taste any of the food on her plate. She needed to know why James had selected that scripture to recite over the Thanksgiving table. Was it because of Menno's passing, or was it a random coincidence?

She knew she couldn't wait until the end of the meal to ask James; so, pushing back her chair, she excused herself from the table. As she headed for the downstairs bathroom, she paused at the end of the table and leaned over James's shoulder.

"That was a beautiful verse you recited," she said in a soft voice. "What a right *gut* reminder for all of us on this Thanksgiving Day."

He wiped at his mouth with the back of his hand and then reached into his back pocket. "Wouldn't have thought of it but one of the *kinner* gave me this here note," he replied. He glanced at her before handing it over. "Now that I think of it," he went on, scratching his cheek by his graying beard, "mayhaps I misread that." He chuckled and returned his attention to his plate of food.

Her hand shook as she held the piece of paper. It was folded in half with the words *For Grace at Thanksgiving* written on the outside. When she unfolded it, the very verse that James had recited was handwritten on the inside. Certainly, that could be interpreted in two different ways: Had the sender of the message meant that he should incorporate that verse over his blessing at Thanksgiving, or that he should give the paper to her instead?

Either way, the message was clear: move on.

Who was this secret sister who seemed so intent on piecing her life back together, as if sewing together fabric squares to make a complete, if not necessarily pretty, quilt top?

CHAPTER SEVEN

December 2015

 OR THE NEXT week, Grace kept herself tucked
away in her home, alternating between reading
the Bible and poring through her diaries. She read
through the months following Linda's birth, groaning
out loud despite being alone, when she remembered
those sleepless nights she went through during the first
few months. She smiled when she read the entry about
Linda's first steps, a moment that had delighted her then
but, in hindsight, had altered her life. Once Linda began
to walk, Grace never had another moment of peace as
she was constantly chasing after her.

She remembered her third miscarriage, just twelve
months after Linda was born. In the diary, she had indicated the moment with a simple comment regarding
feeling ill and taking to bed for a few days. But when
Grace read the date, she remembered far too well how
the familiar stomach cramps had come, and shortly after,
she had recognized the signs of the loss of another life
that had been growing inside of her. Once again, she
had spared Menno the knowledge of what happened, not
wanting to share the emotional pain she felt at the loss.

Setting aside the diaries, Grace leaned her head back against the recliner to rest her eyes. Those little books represented fifty years of life. *Her* life. It was like reading a familiar story, a story she didn't want to keep reading because she knew the eventual outcome. Still, she could hardly put them down, even though she knew what came next at every turn of the page.

The year following her third miscarriage, Ivan was born. Soulful, quiet Ivan who even as a toddler spent his time observing nature and people. Grace often wondered at the differences between Linda and Ivan, the former quite headstrong and the latter more reflective. During that time, Anna Mae came to stay with her under the guise of helping with the young children, but Grace knew the truth. She remembered the conversation as if it had been just a few days ago.

"They just go through the motions," Anna Mae had complained. "No matter how much the bishop counsels them, they cannot accept the fact that he's gone."

Grace worried that they'd be shunned, for she knew how strict and conservative their bishop was. However, before that happened, he passed away and a new bishop was chosen by lot from the existing preachers. Fortunately for her parents, the new bishop had focused more on acclimating himself to his role as church leader than on her parents' continued mourning of Benny's untimely death.

After four years and one more miscarriage, Susan arrived, and a month earlier than expected. Difficult, willful Susan, who cried with every bout of colic for months on end, rarely slept, walked too early, and screamed far too loud. She tried to emulate her older sister, Linda, but the age difference was too great for theirs to be a tight sisterly bond.

With three small children and only one at school, Grace had her hands full indeed. Yet she never complained. She doted on her children, teaching them verses from the Bible and visiting with Menno's parents on a daily basis. They had moved into the smaller section of the house after Ivan was born and both Linda and Bethany had married. Barbara always had fresh-baked cookies or canned fruit waiting to serve Grace and the children.

While her children were young, Grace leaned strongly upon her faith in God and her love for Menno to help give her strength. She had needed it, for a series of hardships still lay in her future. In 1973, just after Susan was born, her father died. Her mother followed two years later after a bad bout of pneumonia. And before all that, Anna Mae married a young widower and moved to his farm in a western region of Pennsylvania, leaving Grace to deal with the complicated decline of their parents' health and, ultimately, their death.

Without Anna Mae to help her, both physically and emotionally, Grace found that the days were never-ending, and a feeling of being overwhelmed became her constant companion. With the children too young to help Menno with chores, Grace often awoke early to accompany him to the dairy barn. She'd help him with the morning milking, feeding, and turnout. Long days of hard work passed, and before she knew it, the seasons changed and she had yet one more miscarriage.

For a while, she blamed herself. She worked too hard, helping Menno and raising the children. With so many miscarriages in her past, she feared she wouldn't bear any more children for her husband and took as much comfort as she could in the three whom they had conceived.

So when James was born almost four years after Susan, Grace rejoiced in her newborn infant. How could she not? Linda and Ivan were at school during the day and Susan occupied herself following Menno around the barn. Alone in the house, Grace sat in the recliner, holding that special baby and loving him with as much love as a mother could possibly give.

Her other children taught her the breadth of her love, but it was James who taught her the depth.

Where has time gone? she wondered, her heart feeling heavy. She craved, just once more, to hold an infant in her arms—not just any infant, but one who came from the love she shared during her lifetime with Menno. It wasn't fair that time passed so quickly. It seemed as if Grace barely blinked her eyes before Linda took her kneeling vow, married, and moved to another town, almost thirty miles away. Four years later, Ivan followed suit and moved into the *grossdawdihaus* with his new bride, Jane. Susan didn't hesitate to take her kneeling vow, either.

Then one day, with all the children grown up and gone, Grace looked around her as she stood in the main kitchen of what used to be Barbara Beiler's house. The house was quiet, save for the ticking of the grandfather clock. And in that moment she realized that time stood still for no one.

The realization struck her to the core. She knew then that she was in the midst of the cycle of life. Each day was a gift that, if she chose not to make the most of it and enjoy it, she'd never get back again. She began to fret about how time passed so quickly and she had no way of stopping it. And indeed, it seemed to hurtle ahead, faster and faster, until Menno's death. And now? She felt as if time stood still.

A sudden rapping at the glass pane of her front door startled Grace from her memories. She hadn't been expecting anyone. With it now being December, the shorter days and longer nights meant fewer visitors, especially with the brutally cold arctic air that had descended upon them right after Thanksgiving.

Quickly, Grace swept the diaries back into the cardboard box in which she stored them. She tucked the box next to her recliner before hurrying to the front door to see who had come calling.

"My word!" Grace blinked as she opened the door to welcome the bishop and his wife. "Come in, come in!" She waved her hand eagerly as she stepped backward to make room for her unexpected visitors to enter her house.

The bishop stepped inside before his wife and stomped the thin layer of snow from his boots before he stepped off the welcome mat. He left his black hat upon his head and tugged at his white beard that grew past the first button of his black jacket, which he promptly unbuttoned. With his blue shirt and black vest, he fit the perfect image of an elderly Amish man, especially a bishop, who often worked during the day and visited members of the *g'may* at night.

"You staying warm in here, Grace? It sure is cold out there!" Without being invited to do so, the bishop hung his coat and hat from a peg in the wall near the door.

"So I can feel…just from having opened the door!" As if to emphasize the cold temperature, she rubbed her hands on her arms. The entry area was much colder than the small sitting room, for she had the kerosene heater running in order to ward off the cold. "What on earth brings you both out on such a frigid night, then?"

Lizzie quickly removed her shawl and hung it beside her husband's coat. "A little something landed in our mailbox." With a curious look in her eyes and a slight smile on her lips, she reached into her cloth handbag and extracted an envelope. She held it up for Grace to see, a mischievous gleam in her eyes. "I reckon you must know that it isn't from us."

Grace gasped. Another letter? She could hardly guess what this one contained. "This is too much!"

Lizzie handed the envelope to Grace. "I've heard about this secret sister of yours! It's flooding the Amish grapevine!"

David grunted and glanced away.

Ignoring her husband's reaction, Lizzie continued, "I don't care what people say! I think this is a lovely gesture, although I do wonder who the person is!"

Grace took the envelope in her hands and stared at the handwriting on the front. She thought it looked feminine, but certainly not from an older woman. It appeared to be written by a younger hand. And in no way did it resemble the handwriting from the previous packages.

"Why, I have no idea, of that I'm certain! I do hope that you weren't inconvenienced by coming out here. This certainly could have waited until our next service." Then, realizing they were still standing in the entryway, she gestured toward the sitting room. "*Vell* then, please sit down. I made some fresh sugar cookies earlier and I have some coffee. It's instant, you know. Go make yourselves comfortable and I'll bring it into the sitting room if you'd like." She didn't wait for their response as she hurried to put the cookies on a tray and heat up some water on the stove.

While she waited for the water to boil, she fingered the envelope that she had shoved into her apron pocket. Her curiosity was definitely piqued and she fought the urge to open it. But as she was beginning to learn, any item sent to her from this secret sister was best opened in private.

She made the coffee and carried the tray into the room, being extra careful as she crossed the threshold so she didn't spill any. Setting the tray onto the small table by the sofa, she fussed over her company as she passed around the mugs and the plate of cookies. Only when they were served did Grace take a seat in the recliner next to the bishop in the old wooden rocking chair. Lizzie sat on the small sofa, the mug of warm coffee balanced carefully upon her knee.

"Now do tell," Lizzie gushed. "Who do you think it is?"

"She said she didn't know," David Yoder snapped at his wife. While the bishop was a patient man with the rest of the church members, it was a well-known fact that Lizzie could try his patience. "If she knew, she'd have answered you before, don't you think?"

Again Lizzie ignored him. "And what is she sending you now?"

How could Grace ever begin to explain? How could she possibly talk about all of the gifts, the reminders of her past that somehow gave her hope for the future? Besides, she wasn't partial to sharing so much information, at least not with Lizzie, who tended to show no discretion when talking to other people.

"Oh, little things," Grace said vaguely.

"I heard about the handkerchief," Lizzie continued. "And the pumpkin bread."

"*Ja*, there were those things, indeed."

David frowned, his eyes crinkling into small half-moons on his deeply wrinkled face. "Lizzie, best to leave private matters to private people!"

The rebuke worked, and reluctantly, Lizzie left the subject alone.

"Have you been visiting much, Bishop?" Grace asked, happy to change the subject.

"Oh *ja*, mostly with the older folks." He leaned forward. "You should come sometime with us to the retirement home. Eli King is always in want of good company."

Grace wasn't certain if she could stand going to the retirement home. Back in her day it was the children and grandchildren who took care of aging parents. Now it was becoming more common for the elderly, especially the infirm, to be put in a special retirement home that catered to the Amish and more conservative Mennonites. Perhaps even she would end up there, Grace worried.

"Eli King? Why, I recall that I was baptized at their farm," Grace heard herself say.

"Oh?" Lizzie reached for one of the cookies, obviously more interested in the previous conversation—or at least her attempts to pry information from Grace. Since she had been raised in a different church district, she wouldn't know about Grace's baptism and most likely wouldn't care where *any* member of the *g'may* was baptized.

Despite being older than both Grace and Lizzie, David, however, still had a keen memory. "That's right. I remember it well," he said thoughtfully. "It was a few years after my *schwester* Martha was baptized." He hesitated, the emotion draining from his face as he mentioned his younger sister. Grace lowered her eyes, remembering all too well the pain the Yoders felt when Martha passed away as a young mother, shortly after her second child was born. She hadn't recovered from a difficult childbirth, and shortly after she died, the infant passed away too.

Grace had been pregnant with Linda at the time. Martha's passing and the infant's death had a profound impact on her. It had taken all of Menno's patient coaxing to convince her that she simply must trust in God. Only with his support had she been able to attend the funerals.

"The Lord giveth and the Lord taketh," David said somberly, referring to the death of his sister Martha. "It is by the Lord's plan we live, not our own."

"His plan," Grace repeated.

David sipped at his coffee.

"It's a lot different today," Grace said softly, "with all that new *Englische* medicine and vaccinations. Helps the *bopplis* and *kinner*, that's for sure and certain. And our midwives are much better educated."

"True, true," David said, his broad chest rising and falling as he took a deep breath. "But regardless of that progress, the ultimate results still depend upon His will," he added.

Lizzie shook her head and clicked her tongue. "Our biggest problem today is the accidents on the roads!"

Neither David nor Grace responded. Their silence hung heavy in the air, but Lizzie didn't seem to notice.

"Why, those *Englischers* with their fast cars and no regard for Plain people! Wasn't it just last summer when two young ones were killed when a truck ran into the back of their buggy at a stop sign?" She looked at her husband and then back to Grace. "Hmm? And so many youth aren't even joining the church, either! Why, I heard tell that in a family of ten, one or two often don't join the church at all!"

"Lizzie…" David's voice was low, as if warning her.

Despite the way her breath caught in her throat, Grace forced a smile and stood up. "Mayhaps I might fetch you some more coffee, *ja*?" She reached for their mugs and hurried into the kitchen. For a few moments, she stood at the counter, gasping for air as she willed her heart to slow down.

Whether it was because Lizzie forgot or merely chose not to remember, those two comments had cut through Grace. Besides her multiple miscarriages in between Linda and Ivan, Grace still harbored the pain of losing both Susan and James. How could Lizzie have been so insensitive to speak as carelessly as she did, when surely she should have remembered Grace's losses?

1995

Grace stood by the kitchen sink, pretending to wash the dishes. At that very moment, she wished she could be anywhere but there. In all the years she had been married to Menno, she had never heard him so angry or using such a harsh tone. She wished she could shrink or simply disappear. To hear him raise his voice was one thing, but it was quite another to know that his anger was directed at Susan.

"I absolutely forbid it!" he yelled for the third time.

Without turning around, Grace could picture Susan, standing stoically as she faced her father. Pretty little

Susan who used to bring Grace flowers from the back meadow and cuddle on her lap in the evening to listen to a bedtime story. How was it possible that her special child, her dear sweet daughter of both her body and heart, was having this conversation—*nee*, this argument!—with her father?

"I'm doing it, *Daed*."

He slammed his hand against the tabletop and Grace jumped.

"*Maem*!" Susan suddenly said, turning her head to glare at her mother. "Speak up for me!"

"Leave your *maem* out of this!" Menno said in a low voice.

Grace shut her eyes and prayed for God to guide her through this situation.

"*Maem*?"

As if an invisible hand guided her, Grace felt herself turn around. Menno glowered at Susan, his green eyes flickering toward Grace as if daring her to speak at all. Her mouth opened and the words that came out seemed to come from another person.

"I stand behind your *daed*, Susan," she heard herself say.

Susan's mouth dropped open, clearly stunned by her mother's announcement.

Menno's dark glare returned to his daughter. "I am the head of this household, and you may not straddle the outside world while living under my roof."

"You straddled the world!"

At this insolent remark, even Grace spoke up. "Susan, that is not any of your business."

Susan shot a dark look in her direction. "You married *Daed*, even if *your* parents didn't like him." She gave an angry laugh. "They thought he was *wild*."

"Your father is a righteous man." Grace lifted her chin, her voice stern and sharp. "He has proven himself to honor God and the church in ways you have no right to question."

"If you decide that this…this *decision*…is more important than your vow of baptism, you know the consequences." Menno paused as if trying to find the courage to speak words that he surely never thought would slip past his lips. "The bishop will shun you, and you will not be permitted to return to this house or family."

Wincing at his words, Grace looked away.

Menno's voice grew stronger. "'And be not conformed to this world: but be ye transformed by the renewing of your mind, that ye may prove what is that good, and acceptable, and perfect, will of God.'" He stood up and took a step toward Susan, his tall frame looming over her. "If you would go against your vow to God, a vow that you took just last year, to renounce worldly goods, you will not be welcomed here. You cannot serve two masters, Susan."

"I confessed that Jesus Christ is the Son of God," Susan retorted. Behind her, the kitchen door quietly opened and James slipped inside. Grace saw him standing in the shadows, obviously having overheard Menno's loud words before entering. "Nothing has changed. I still believe," Susan added.

"You are breaking the *Ordnung*."

"I love him."

Menno shut his eyes. Grace felt the pain that he felt, Susan's confession like a knife cutting through their hearts. It was painful enough to have a child refuse the baptism, but to take it and then leave the community? And for the love of a non-Amish man?

"You barely know him," Grace whispered.

"Oh, *Maem*," Susan said, her voice pleading for understanding from the one person whom, apparently, she had presumed would defend her. "The world isn't like it used to be. It's changing, and it will change the Amish. You too will be forced to conform to the world. Will you shun yourself then?"

Menno moved his body so that he stood between Grace and Susan. "I will not have you speak to your *maem* in such a way. I have no choice, Susan, but to speak with the bishop tomorrow. When his decision is made, you will leave this house until you see the error of your ways and repent."

Even though he tried to shield Grace, she couldn't help but see the defiance in Susan's face.

When did she change? Grace wondered. Only last year in October, Susan had taken the baptismal vow. She spent the winter working at market three days a week, and when spring came, she seemed relieved to cut back, since her help was needed on the farm. In the summertime, she used to spend quite a lot of her free time with her friends at different church-sponsored youth activities. And then autumn arrived.

As the leaves changed on the trees, something began to change in the house as well. Susan started to stay out late, and Grace presumed that she was courting a young man. In the mornings, Susan seemed sullen and often unusually quiet. Grace didn't ask, and thankfully, Menno didn't notice—until the night when the lights of an *Englische* automobile shone down their driveway, lighting up their bedroom through the window.

"What on earth?" Menno asked, tossing back the covers and dressing as quickly as he could. He motioned with his hand for Grace to stay put before opening their bedroom door and disappearing into the darkness.

That had been two weeks ago.

Now, in afterthought, the change that had previously seemed so sudden was clearly more apparent.

"I can do better than that," Susan said. "I can leave tonight."

Grace made a motion to step forward, reaching out her hand. "Don't do that, Susan; it's dark and the roads…"

Menno lifted his hand, stopping her from continuing. Grace stepped back, ever obedient to her husband. If only he would let Susan sleep on this decision, spend time talking to the bishop, perhaps things would work out. After all, her own parents had eventually forgiven Menno for his wild *rumschpringe*. He had explored the world and dated that *Englische* girl. The only difference was that once he had decided to join the church, Menno had held tight to his vow of honoring God, living Plain, and avoiding sin as much as any righteous man could.

Susan's decision was quite different.

Without waiting for a response, Susan climbed the stairs, stomping her feet heavily on each step. Neither Menno nor Grace moved from where they stood, listening to her shuffling around her room overhead. Once, Grace thought she saw movement from where James stood, but all that was left was an empty space, the shadowy outline of his form already gone. She prayed that he had returned to the barn and not witnessed that scene.

The door that separated the main house from the *grossdawdihaus*, the house where Ivan and Jane resided, opened and Ivan entered, a concerned look on his face. "Everything all right over here?" He looked from one parent to another. "*Daed*? *Maem*?"

Grace didn't dare to answer.

Susan came tromping down the stairs, dragging her small suitcase with her. She let it bounce on each step, the noise loud in the quiet of the room.

Stepping forward, Ivan reached for his younger sister's arm. "*Wie gehts*?"

"I'm leaving," she said, anger in her voice. "I've made a mistake, and *Daed* says I am no longer welcome in this house."

Ivan looked over at his father.

Menno remained silent.

Ever sensible, Ivan tried to intervene. "Whatever is going on, I suggest taking the time to talk further. It's dark outside, Susan. And the roads are icy."

Sidestepping her brother, Susan headed for the door. She grabbed her heavy black jacket and slipped her arms into the sleeves. The determination on her face made her seem like an entirely different person than the daughter Grace had raised. "I would have thought, *Maem*, that you, of all people, might have showed more understanding instead of always being so obedient and submissive to *Daed*."

And then she was gone.

Ivan ran his fingers through his hair, stunned by what he had just witnessed.

"We shall never speak of this again," Menno said in a strange voice. "She has made her choice and done so willingly. A vow to God is not something to be taken lightly and broken so easily." Then, with hunched shoulders and vacant eyes, he turned away from them and walked toward the stairs. He ascended slowly, each step seeming forced and painful.

"*Maem*? What happened here?"

Grace didn't want to disobey Menno. "Ivan, I'd best not be talking about such things." After all, Menno had been very clear that Susan's departure was not to be discussed further. Nervously, she glanced toward the now empty staircase. In the distance, she could hear the sound of a horse and buggy. The noise distracted her for a moment.

Ivan approached his mother and placed his hands on her shoulders, forcing her to look at him. "Why did Susan leave?"

"It's...it's not my place..."

To her surprise, Ivan shook her. Just once. But it was enough to snap her out of her stupor.

"An *Englischer*," she whispered. "She's chosen to leave because of an *Englischer*."

She thought she saw Ivan catch his breath. He too knew the seriousness of Susan's choice. Grace saw his expression change as he digested this information. "That's insane," he said, lowering his voice. "Why would she do such a thing?" He lifted his eyes and met Grace's. The realization finally hit him. "She'll be shunned!"

As far as the Amish community was concerned, once the bishop declared her shunned, Susan would no longer exist. It would be as if she had died.

Grace shut her eyes tight, fighting back the tears.

"But the bishop hasn't talked to her yet?"

Grace shook her head, opening her eyes and letting the tears fall.

A puzzled expression crossed Ivan's face. "Then why did she leave tonight?" He glanced over Grace's shoulders toward the window. "It's dark and freezing out there! Where does she think she's going?"

"Ivan…"

He narrowed his eyes and stared at her. "You let her leave. You could have stopped her, spoken to *Daed*, made her stay." He started toward the door, and Grace knew his intention was to retrieve Susan.

"Don't!" she called out. "Your *daed* has spoken, Ivan. You cannot go against him in this matter."

At the door, his hand upon the handle, he looked over his shoulder at her and frowned. If he wanted to say something, he didn't. But Grace didn't need to hear the words from his lips. She knew what he was thinking, regardless of his silence. He felt anger toward her for not taking Susan's side. She always stood by Menno's decisions, obeying her marriage vow that she would submit to her husband. Instead of saying the words, words that would wound her, Ivan merely shook his head, grabbed a coat that hung on the rack by the door, and disappeared through the doorway.

Turning away from the door, Grace lifted her hands to cover her face, unable to stop herself from sobbing. She managed to sit in a chair at the table and held her head in her hands, her tears now falling freely down her cheeks as she realized the impact of the exchange of words as well as what had been left unsaid.

Silently, she prayed that God would give her stronger shoulders in order to carry this burden. She prayed that she would forgive herself for not having defused the situation, for not having spoken up or calmed down either one of them. Instead, she had stood by and let Susan leave without any idea of where her daughter was going.

What have I done? she asked herself.

She prayed harder, asking God to show her how to find a way to face this without asking that ever troublesome word: *Why?* She had to believe in God, trust in His plan, and follow His will. In her mind, she tried to seek comfort by reciting part of the verse from the song sung at her baptism:

It is truly a narrow way
Who now wants to go this heavenly path
He must surely keep himself
That he does not stumble on the path
Through affliction, misery, anxiety, and need.

While that verse had given her comfort in the past, this time it did not. The realization shocked her that after all these years, when tragedy struck, she still found the urge to question God. Was her faith that fragile? Did she not truly believe?

"Grace," Menno called from the top of the staircase.

She glanced at the grandfather clock, the light from the kerosene lantern illuminating the two hands. How much time had passed? How long had she been sitting at the table, alone and praying?

"Come to bed, Grace."

His voice sounded defeated. She sensed that he needed her to help him just as much as she needed God to help her. As she arose from the table and started walking across the kitchen, she heard the sound of a horse and buggy racing down the driveway. Pausing in midstep, she tilted her head and listened. Surely that was Ivan leaving to retrieve Susan, she thought. But then why was the noise increasing as if approaching the house instead of leaving?

"Maem!" Ivan called out as he flung the door open and ran inside. His cheeks lacked color and his eyes grew wider when he saw her standing at the bottom of

the stairs. "*Maem*, you'd best sit down," he said firmly. Without waiting for her response, he led her to the table.

"What's going on now?" Menno started down the stairs in time to see Ivan kneel before Grace, holding her hands in his. "Ivan? I said we weren't to speak of this anymore."

Ivan ignored his father. "I went after Susan," he said slowly.

"Don't mention her name in this house!"

Ivan took a deep breath. "I didn't get far." He paused, glancing momentarily at his father with a stone-cold expression on his face. "James..."

The mention of her youngest child caught Grace's attention. Suddenly she felt more alert as she stared at Ivan. "What about James? He was just standing there..." She pointed toward the shadows where she had seen him. But it hadn't been "just"; it had been well over thirty minutes ago.

"He must have gone after her too," Ivan whispered, his voice cracking with emotion. He paused, trying to catch his breath as he whispered, "There was an accident on the road."

"James?" Quickly, Grace tried to stand up as if to make her way to the door, but Ivan forced her to remain seated. She turned her face toward her son's and asked the question to which, from the expression on Ivan's face, she knew she didn't want to hear the answer. "Is he all right?"

Menno hurried across the room. "What did you say?"

Ivan answered both of their questions with silence.

Grace reached for Menno's hand, not caring that tears once again streamed down her cheeks. *Dear Lord*, she prayed silently, *protect our son James. Shield him with Your loving hand.* Through the window, she could see the flashing of red lights. In the distance, she heard sirens, faint but present. The flashing lights grew brighter, and she knew that a police vehicle was approaching the house.

"Go away," she whispered. Then, looking up at Menno, she pleaded with her eyes. "Tell them to go away."

The stoic expression on his face reminded Grace of her baptism. Not once had Menno looked at her. Instead, he withdrew into himself and focused on something else. Over the years, she had learned that in those moments apart, he was reflecting on God, especially during times of crisis and hardship.

Releasing her hand, he walked toward the door, greeting the police officers standing on the other side, hats in hand, as Menno opened the door to invite them inside. Grace barely heard what they said, their voices sounding distant and far away. Nothing made sense to her. Why had Susan left the house at night? Why had James gone after her? Why would God let a car hit her son?

And there it was.

The question.

The one word she had refused to ask after all these years: *Why?*

The world seemed to spin. She started to push against Ivan before the spinning increased and darkness clouded her field of vision. Light-headed, she put her hand on Ivan's shoulder to steady herself, looking over his shoulder at Menno. He stared at her, the most sorrowful look in his green eyes that she had ever seen. Gone was the sparkle. Gone was the glow. Instead, what she saw was a dull look of defeat. It was the last thing she saw before she fainted.

2015

"Oh, Grace," Lizzie said as she placed her hand on Grace's shoulder. The pressure of the gesture startled Grace and she turned around to face her friend, the bishop's wife, who had followed her into the kitchen. In the dim light from the lantern on the counter, Lizzie's face with her downturned mouth and raised eyebrows expressed how terrible she felt. "I'm ever so sorry. I…I didn't know, not everything anyway."

Grace wanted to tell her that it was fine, but the truth was that it wasn't.

In one night, twenty years ago, she had lost two children: Susan to the world and James to God. How could anyone accept such tragedy with unwavering faith? Menno's response to all of the upsets and tragedies during their fifty years of marriage had been to turn to God. With her husband's constant support and devotion to God guiding her along their long journey together, she had managed to get through each progressively worse event. Now that he was gone, she found herself faltering as she fought the urge to ask those unanswered questions.

All of her life she had followed what was taught at home, school, and church: "Nay but, O man, who art thou that repliest against God? Shall the thing formed say to him that formed it, Why hast thou made me thus?"

From her parents' initial inability to accept Menno, to forgive him of what, in hindsight, were small infractions during a young man's *rumschpringe* before he accepted Christ as his Savior; to Benny's death on the night of her wedding; to the many miscarriages she had suffered; to the loss of two of her grown children, Grace wanted to ask, "Why?" She wanted to talk with someone and be reassured there were reasons for all of the sadness. Yet she never had and most likely never would.

Reaching up, Grace covered Lizzie's hand and said the words that had followed her throughout her entire life: "It's all right."

She knew that Lizzie hadn't meant to stir up so many memories when expressing her opinion of the biggest threats to the future of the Amish. When she replayed Lizzie's words and tried to remove her personal emotions from the equation, Grace knew that her friend spoke the truth. Her own family statistics played into Lizzie's theory.

"Come, help me carry the coffee," Grace said. "I left the tray in the other room."

Almost thirty minutes passed before the bishop signaled that it was time for the visit to end. He stood up and extended his hand to shake Grace's, thanking her for her hospitality and wishing her God's blessing. Lizzie followed him, talking some more about their upcoming visit to see several of the older patients at the retirement home on Wednesday and inviting Grace to join them.

"*Ja, ja,*" Grace said in a noncommittal way. A retirement home was the last place she wanted to visit, especially just a few weeks before the holiday. Her spirits were already down enough. To wander the corridors of institutional housing? To see aging parents, basically abandoned by their children and grandchildren? No, Grace didn't care for that idea at all. Despite how her life had turned out, Grace had not been raised that way.

As she shut the door behind the Yoders, she leaned against it, engulfed in her thoughts. The grandfather clock chimed from the sitting room. Eight o'clock. For no particular reason, she decided to leave the coffee cups and plates in the sitting room. She'd clean them in the morning. Instead, she turned the knob on the propane light in the sitting room so that the gentle hissing ceased, the light along with it. Carrying the kerosene lamp to light her way, she walked the short hallway into her room before she remembered the envelope in her pocket.

Her secret sister.

Grace had forgotten the initial reason for the Yoders' visit: to deliver the envelope.

Setting the lamp on her nightstand, Grace sat on the edge of the bed. She pulled the envelope from her front pocket and stared at it. Nothing unusual stood out, no markings or postage. Just her name: *Grace Beiler.* Once again, she tried to analyze the writing, staring at it to see if she recognized the penmanship. *Female,* she thought. *Definitely a female.* But it was different from the other packages and letters. For a moment, Grace wondered if her secret sister might be trying to disguise her handwriting on purpose.

Inside the envelope was a rectangular piece of paper. It was small, lavender in color, with little white flowers bordering the edges. In block letters, someone had written the words "1 Peter 4:12–13." While she had read the entire Bible many times throughout her life, Grace didn't know that verse off the top of her head and contemplated waiting until the morning to return to the sitting room and retrieve her Bible. But curiosity outweighed practicality, so she picked up the lamp and returned to the dark room she had just left.

Once she settled back into her recliner and situated her reading glasses on her nose, she reached for the weathered, leather-bound Bible that had carried her through so many years. It felt warm in her hands, like an old friend. For a moment, she remembered how she had reacted to Lizzie's comments that evening and felt guilty. How many times had she turned to this book, a place that offered comfort and hope during days of distress? Who was she to think that her life should lack suffering when so many others around her endured much more adversity and tribulation?

"Beloved, think it not strange concerning the fiery trial which is to try you, as though some strange thing happened unto you: but rejoice, inasmuch as ye are partakers of Christ's sufferings; that, when his glory shall be revealed, ye may be glad also with exceeding joy."

She reread the verses, not once but twice. It was as if the secret sister could read her mind! Grace sat there, her mouth opened slightly, not caring that the room grew cold and the flame of the lamp flickered because the wick was too low. The words resonated in her head as if she heard them for the very first time.

All these years, she had been so afraid to ask, "Why?" while all along, what she should have been asking was "Why not?"

If Peter had preached this to followers of Christ in the years immediately after his resurrection, then those people had questioned their faith too. She suddenly understood that part of being a Christian included dealing with fiery trials and suffering the pain of unanswered questions. Perfection in faith was an ongoing struggle, not a smooth journey, simply *because* Christians were human.

She was not alone.

And in her hands she held the answers to all of her questions. Through Scripture, the verses and wisdom that were the Word of God contained in the book within her hands, she could find her answers. For years, she had read and reread the many books of the Bible. She remembered her mother reciting Proverbs to teach her and her siblings lessons in life. She remembered sermon after sermon in which the bishop and his preachers referenced the Bible before relating it to issues within the community or in the world outside.

But tonight, perhaps truly for the first time, the Bible spoke to *her*. It was as if God wanted to personally comfort her.

The realization hit Grace as she sat there in her recliner, the open Bible on her lap and the piece of lavender paper still in her hand. Long after the light flickered down to a mere wisp of a flame, Grace stayed there in awe of the important lesson she had learned tonight, one that she suspected Menno knew but hadn't shared with her. It had taken the simple scripture reference written by an unknown hand to make the message clear.

And for that, Grace said a prayer of gratitude for her secret sister, whoever she was.

CHAPTER EIGHT

December 16, 2015

Wɪᴛʜ Cʜʀɪsᴛᴍᴀs ᴊᴜsᴛ under three weeks away, the market was bustling with people even on a midweek morning. Hannah and Mary each pushed a narrow shopping cart down the aisles while Grace followed behind, carrying a small plastic basket as she navigated through small throngs of people. She hadn't really needed much food, perhaps just some fresh vegetables. The little chest freezer in her small laundry room was packed with meat and vegetables for the winter. On the wall over it were four shelves, each brimming with homemade canned food: applesauce, beets, chow-chow, tomatoes, even cauliflower.

But Hannah and Mary insisted that she accompany them.

Grace knew they wanted to get her out of the house. She had relented because she wanted to pick up a few items for Ivan's visit.

Ever since moving to this community, Grace had dreaded going to market. Unlike at the farmhouse where the closest market was located along a winding back road and free from *Englischers*, the market nearest her present home was a large discount shopping center; the parking lot was filled with dirty minivans and pickup trucks. Even though most of the people who patronized the store were locals, Grace could still feel their eyes glancing at her, as if she were some oddity on display.

She disliked that feeling.

Over the years, the gaping stares from strangers only got worse. The more the builders developed the land, promising a perfect country life to the families living in suburbia, the more the area became exactly what the new residents sought. And Grace was trapped living in a section of Akron, just bordering Ephrata Township, that straddled two divergent cultures. That translated into more interactions with the *Englische* as well as the inappropriate gawking of strangers, especially tourists.

She'd never get used to it.

"Grace? Grace Beiler?" someone called out.

She stopped walking and turned in the direction of the voice. A young woman walked up to her and extended her hand in greeting. It took Grace a second to recognize her. "Catharine Yoder?" Grace shook the hand, startled to see the schoolteacher standing before her. Since Catharine lived with her parents, Grace wondered if she was shopping for her mother. "Is your *maem* along with you, then?"

Catharine shook her head, her big chocolate-brown eyes shining and a warm smile on her face. "*Nee*, I'm alone today," she replied, her voice full of cheer. "Picking up some dry goods to make more sugar cookies for the school program." She hesitated and leaned closer to Grace. "You will be coming, *ja*?"

"Oh, heavens to Betsy," Grace said, laughing just a little that Catharine would think to ask such a question. Of course, with this being her first year teaching, Grace thought, the young teacher might not realize how much the school program meant to her. She reached out and touched the young woman's arm. "I wouldn't miss it for the world!"

Her answer pleased Catharine, and she almost bounced on the balls of her feet, her joy so apparent. "*Wunderbaar!*" she exclaimed. "The students have something special planned. I know my *grossmammi* is curious as all get-out to know what it is!" There was a playful gleam in Catharine's eyes that made Grace smile, for she could well imagine. Lizzie Yoder loved insight into any news that other people didn't know. If lying weren't a sin, Grace suspected Lizzie might be apt to tell people she already knew what this surprise was.

"Speaking of my *grossmammi*," Catharine said, a more serious look upon her face, "there is a group of people headed to the retirement center this afternoon to visit with Eli King and Jane Hostetler. I wonder if you are going?"

The retirement center. There it was again. Lizzie had mentioned it the other night after her unexpected visit at Grace's house. Now, once again, the weekly visit to the retirement center was an issue staring her in the face. Grace fumbled for words, but her tongue seemed tied as she tried to come up with a response.

"*Ja, vell*," she said slowly. Oh, how she didn't want to go! The glow on the young woman's face was more than Grace could take. In Catharine's eyes, Grace saw hope and love, complete faith for the future, all the things that she had felt so many years ago. How could she possibly say no? "I reckon I could join them...," she finally admitted.

Catharine returned to her joyful self. "Oh, that's right *gut*, then. I'll be certain to stop by my *grossmammi's* and tell her you'll be joining the group."

With a big smile and a light bounce to her step, Catharine continued down the aisle, pausing briefly to greet Hannah and Mary before she turned the corner, disappearing as she headed down the next aisle.

Oh, to have that energy! Grace thought with a slight bit of envy, even though she knew it was a sin. She missed feeling young and animated, the prospect of raising her young children with the future wide ahead of her. She missed the country, living with the smells and sounds of the farm that engaged her senses and filled her with love for God's creation. And more than anything, she missed being a part of a family: *her* family.

2010

The smell of fresh-baked bread and sugar cookies permeated the air of the kitchen. Grace leaned over one of the loaves and inhaled deeply. She shut her eyes to truly absorb the yeasty fragrance of what she considered a symbol of love for her family. Nothing said "I love you" louder than fresh-baked goods.

It had been fifteen years since they moved into the *grossdawdihaus* so that Ivan could raise his family in the main house. Besides, with both Susan and James gone, they had no need for the larger house anymore. Returning to the small home where she had started her marriage with Menno brought back bittersweet memories. Her familiarity with the house provided her with comfort, while the realization that this would be the last stop on their journey together gave her sorrow.

"*Mammi* Grace!" a little boy's voice called out as the door flung open. The noise of boots being kicked off and coats dropped on the floor was quickly followed by the patter of bare feet.

She smiled and turned around, lowering herself to embrace her five-year-old grandson, Samuel. Behind him, his older sister Barbie followed, holding the hands of Ivan's youngest child, two-year-old Benjamin. All three children were dressed alike, the boys' shirts and Barbie's dress a pretty dark blue. Jane had a tendency to ensure that the children wore the same colors, especially the younger ones. While she claimed it made laundry days easier, Grace never understood that argument. Instead, she secretly wondered if the real reason was that Jane wanted her clothesline to look pretty with the same-colored clothing fluttering in the wind to dry.

"What a pleasant surprise!" Grace said. She glanced up at Barbie who, at seven years of age, should have been in school. "You're home early, then?"

"*Maem's* not feeling well," Barbie said, her eyes downcast and her voice soft.

Immediately Grace looked concerned.

Jane was almost nine months pregnant with her and Ivan's sixth child. Their oldest son, Levi, worked alongside Ivan, while their oldest daughter, Lydia, would not be called to stay home since her studies were more advanced than Barbie's. Grace wondered why no one had come to fetch her to help or watch the children.

"Is she all right, then?" Grace asked.

Barbie nodded in her typical shy manner. "She's sleeping."

Samuel stood on his tippy toes, and with his nose pressed against the edge of the counter, he peered at the cooling rack filled with still-warm cookies. "Are those there sugar cookies, *Mammi* Grace?"

"Hmm," Grace quipped, putting a finger to her cheek as if pondering the answer to his question. "I do believe they are, Samuel. And I don't quite think I can eat them all by myself. Do you know someone who might be willing to help me?"

Without hesitation, Samuel raised his hand and jumped up and down. "Me, me, me!" His brown eyes sparkled as his curly brown hair flopped onto his forehead.

Little Benjamin imitated his brother and lifted his pudgy arm into the air too. Only when he tried to jump up, he stumbled and fell down.

Laughing, Grace opened a cabinet door and pulled out a plate so that she could serve the children some cookies. "What would winter be without warm sugar cookies?" she said cheerfully. "Why, I can't think of a time when we didn't have sugar cookies in the colder weather."

Without being told to do so, the children sat down at the table, Barbie helping Samuel to crawl up and sit beside her on the small bench. She kept her arm around his waist so that he wouldn't fall. Quietly, the three of them waited to be served, Samuel bouncing up and down in anticipation.

He reminded Grace so much of Benny that some-times she got confused. Her grandson's outgoing behavior and tendency for sassiness stood out among the other grandchildren, that was for sure and certain. She often watched young Samuel and smiled, remem-bering some of the antics of her younger brother when they were growing up. And, of course, little Benjamin did everything he could to emulate Samuel.

Grace suspected that Ivan and Jane would have their hands full when those two boys hit the sweet age of sixteen.

After the children finished their snacks, Barbie car-ried the plate to the sink while Grace wiped the cookie crumbs from the tabletop. Meanwhile, the boys scram-bled into their coats and boots, eager to play in the snow. In their hurry they left the door open, despite Grace's calling out for them to close it.

"Those boys," she said, shaking her head and clicking her tongue in mock disapproval. On the surface, she knew that she had to play the role and instill good manners by feigning concern over their lack of consid-eration. But deep down, she adored her grandchildren

and secretly delighted in the younger two being so mischievous. The gust of cold winter wind began to fill the
room and she shivered, quickly crossing the floor to
shut the door.

Then she turned her attention to Barbie. Grace put
her hand on her hip and sighed. "Reckon I should go
check on your *maem, ja*? If she's feeling poorly, mayhaps
you and I should make supper tonight, do you reckon?"

Barbie gave a simple shrug of her shoulders, still too
young and insecure to know how to respond to such
important questions. For a long moment, Grace stared
at her, realizing that she was growing up before her eyes.
It didn't seem so long ago that Barbie had been born. A
pretty baby with the same color green eyes as Menno,
petite little Barbie was soft and sweet. She had been
named after Menno's mother, but within a short period
of time, it was clear that the name was the only thing
the grandchild shared with her paternal grandmother.
As she became a toddler and then a young child, her
personality more reflected Grace's at that age. Or, Grace
thought with a sad feeling in her heart, her dear sister
Anna Mae's.

"Let's go, then," Grace said, trying to stop the lump
from forming in her throat at the thought of Anna Mae.

She missed her sister. Throughout the early years of
her life, they had a special bond. When Anna Mae met
Jonas Wheeler, the widower with two young children,
an instant spark flamed up between the two of them.
He was in Lancaster visiting with an old friend, or so
he had claimed. Grace suspected he was looking for a

new mother for his children. The farming community where he lived didn't have as many prospective brides as Lancaster County. As for Anna Mae, Grace wasn't certain if she fell for Jonas or for the two children.

Their courtship had been brief and mostly through letters. But when he wrote with the proposal, Anna Mae quickly responded. Within a few weeks, she stood outside the Beilers' house, her three packed bags on the driveway as she waited for the hired driver to pick her up.

Grace had stood there with her silently. She was unable to form any sentences that could possibly express how much she would miss her dear sister.

It had been Anna Mae who addressed the issue. "I know you're upset that I'm going so far," she said. "But I truly prayed about this, and I know that God wants me with Jonas and his *kinner*. We can write to each other and mayhaps visit each year." The idea sounded fine, but the reality was that it was too hard to leave farms to go visiting for more than a few hours at a time. Who would tend the livestock?

That had been the last time she saw her sister.

"*Mammi* Grace?" Barbie tugged at her arm. "You all right?"

Grace smiled. "*Ja*, I'm right as rain. Just thinking about my younger sister. Mayhaps your *maem* will have another *dochder* so you can have a special *schwester* like I did."

Barbie seemed to ponder this thought for a while. Then, with a curious tilt to her head, she pursed her lips and asked, "Where's your special *schwester* now?"

"Oh," Grace responded, quickly trying to think of the right way to explain this to her granddaughter. "She's in a very happy place. She's with Jesus now."

"Why?"

Why? Grace thought. That was a good question indeed. And one that she often *wanted* to ask, but unlike Barbie, she felt she was not *permitted* to ask it. The last thing she needed was to face reproach from the bishop for daring to ask for explanations. She knew what his counsel would be: a stern lecture regarding her faith. "Nay but, O man, who art thou that repliest against God? Shall the thing formed say to him that formed it, Why hast thou made me thus?"

Faith didn't ask why or demand explanations. Faith accepted God's decisions and moved on without looking back.

"She became sick," Grace finally responded, deciding the truth was the best way to approach little Barbie's question. "And sometimes when you are sick, you join Jesus. In heaven."

"Where is heaven again?"

Grace laughed at the innocent question. "Heaven is where God lives. I'm quite sure that Anna Mae is happier there than here, Barbie. There is no sadness or sorrow in heaven."

"So she won't ever come back?"

With a serious expression on her face, Grace shook her head. "Oh no. But one day, we will join her again...if we follow God's commandments, pray, and live our lives in faith."

"What about my *daed's schwester* Susan?" Barbie asked, the innocent look in her eyes almost catching Grace as off-guard as the question. "*Aendi* Susan? Is she with Jesus too?"

"No, dear. She just lives far away." Inhaling deeply, Grace shut her eyes and fought the pounding of her heart. Susan. If only she knew that her words were true. Surely word would have reached them had something happened to her. Certainly the community would not have kept such news from them. Besides, not a day had passed in the fifteen years since Susan left that Grace did not pray for her well-being. True to Menno's word, no one ever mentioned Susan's name again, at least not in his presence. But Grace still wondered and worried about her youngest daughter.

Now, she was surprised to hear Susan's name come from her granddaughter's lips. *Where would Barbie have heard about Susan?* There was only one person who would have talked about Susan, and that was Ivan. Yet obviously Barbie had overheard only bits of conversation, for she didn't seem to know where her *aendi* was. Did Ivan? Had he received word from her daughter? The thought made Grace's heart skip a beat, a conflicting mix of emotions hitting her at the same time: hope for Susan's health, and dread that the old wound would be reopened. Quickly, Grace prayed that Barbie would not speak of Susan again. All it would take was one mention of her name in front of Menno and the tension would rekindle. From the very beginning of her shunning, Menno had kept his resolve that the family was to have nothing to do with her. Even at James's funeral, Susan was forced to stand at the back of the graveyard and not among her family.

That had been the last time Grace saw her, and with so many people around her, she had not dared to approach her.

To suddenly hear Susan's name spoken aloud, and so innocently at that, made Grace curious. What was Susan doing now? Where was she living? Did she have children whom Grace would never know?

It had been fifteen years since they had heard from her. Two letters. That was all they had received. One letter arriving shortly after she left informed them she was safe and living in Philadelphia. The next letter a few months later told them she married the *Englische* man. After that, silence. Whether Susan stopped writing or Menno was taking the letters from the mailbox so that Grace wouldn't be tormented with the desire to respond, Grace never knew.

What she did know was that Menno had been serious when he told her and Ivan that he would not hear his daughter's name spoken in the house again. Not once in fifteen years had Menno even mentioned his third child, Susan. For him, life went on. He had been able to compartmentalize the memories, lock them in a little box that he too had stored deep in the recesses of his mind.

Grace tried to follow his example, but each night, at the top of her little diary entry, she'd indicate a number. It stood for how many days since she had last heard from her daughter. Last night she had written 5426 in the upper corner of her entry. She paused when she looked at it, thinking it an ugly number, symbolic of hidden heartache and false bravado for the sake of Menno and the *g'may*.

Still, she began to wonder why, exactly, Barbie had mentioned Susan's name. There was only one person who would dare to mention her, and Grace couldn't even begin to speculate as to what might have precipitated such a discussion. As she opened the door into the main house where Ivan and Jane lived, she quickly prayed that word of this would not make its way back to Menno.

Inside the house, Grace found the curtains drawn and the breakfast dishes still piled in the sink. From the looks of it, the floor hadn't been swept in a day or two, and toys were scattered in all directions.

"Oh my," Grace gasped as she assessed the chaos in the room. "What's happened here?"

Barbie shrugged.

Taking a deep breath, Grace knew what needed to be done. "*Vell*, best be tackling this mess right away," she said. "Fetch me the broom, Barbie, and then I'll ask you to put the toys away. We'll make this right as rain for your *maem*."

An hour later, the kitchen was put back in order, and while not necessarily cleaned by Grace's standards, it was presentable enough if someone were to stop by unexpectedly. Grace had always kept an orderly house and wondered about Jane's inability to do so. Certainly

Ivan must mind coming home to find everything in such disarray. Something was clearly wrong.

"Now I think I'll go check on your *maem*, then," Grace said, more to herself than to Barbie. "See if she's awake yet and mayhaps would like some soup."

Unlike most Amish farmhouses, the main bedroom was on the second floor. Grace remembered having to walk up and down that staircase multiple times a day, especially when she had small babies. She even knew that the fourth step would creak when she placed her foot upon it.

Yes, she knew every inch of this house. Some of her happiest memories as well as two of her worst ones had occurred while living here. Still, it felt like home, and she wasn't certain she'd ever get over that feeling.

Knocking at the door to the main bedroom, Grace waited an appropriate amount of time before she opened the door and peered inside. Sure enough, Ivan's wife lay prostrate in the bed, a simple white sheet covering her.

"Jane?" Grace approached the bed. "Jane? Are you feeling poorly, then? Shall I fetch the doctor?"

The young woman shifted her head to stare at Grace, her dull eyes trying to make out who stood before her. Her forehead was dotted with beads of sweat and her eyes lacked any luster or glow. Immediately Grace panicked for the unborn child.

"Barbie!" Grace called out. The little girl appeared within seconds, and Grace knew she must have been lingering in the hallway. "I want you to fetch your *daed*."

She kept her voice calm so that the child needn't suspect Grace's worry.

Once Grace heard the little girl's footsteps clamber down the stairs, she hurried to the bedside and sat on the edge, reaching her hand out to touch Jane's shoulder. Her skin felt clammy under Grace's fingertips.

"Jane? Jane, dear?" she said softly. "Can you hear me?"

Jane moaned and tried to shift her head to look at Grace. There were dark circles under her eyes and her skin was drained of any color.

"Ivan will be fetching the doctor," Grace continued in her soft voice. She didn't want to instill panic in her daughter-in-law, but Grace had lived long enough to know that something was wrong, and most likely with the baby. "How long have you been feeling poorly, then?"

Jane merely shook her head and shut her eyes.

Certainly this hadn't been an overnight occurrence, Grace thought. For a moment she felt anger at her son. Why hadn't he called a doctor? Why had he left his wife to suffer? Why had he not come to ask for help? Drawing in deep breaths, Grace tried to shake those emotions. Anger would not help the situation. Her main concern needed to be Jane and her unborn baby.

While she waited for Ivan to come, Grace fetched a wet washcloth from the upstairs bathroom and gently dabbed at Jane's forehead. She prayed to the Lord to take care of the young woman and baby, if that was, indeed, His plan. She prayed that Ivan made the right choices in providing care for Jane, and she prayed for the strength to be of help during this time of need.

A few minutes later, she heard the sound of heavy footsteps on the stairs. Not just one pair but two. Certainly Menno had joined Ivan to see what was wrong. Grace looked over her shoulder at the two men standing in the bedroom doorway.

"You'd best be calling for a doctor, Ivan."

"A doctor?"

Grace fought the urge to snap at him. Was he truly that blind? "Your *fraa* needs some medical care. She's ill."

Ivan removed his straw hat and ran the back of his arm across his forehead. "She said she wasn't in labor," he mumbled.

Behind Ivan, Menno took one look at the sick woman in the bed before he turned and started down the stairs. Grace knew he was headed back out to the barn to use the phone in the small office. Menno would call a doctor and soon, she prayed, all would be well.

She stayed with Jane until the doctor arrived. During that time, she could hear the men pacing the floor downstairs, their voices low when they spoke. Keeping the cool cloth on Jane's forehead, Grace continued to pray. Only this time, she added a special prayer that Menno and Ivan wouldn't get into an argument. *Please, Lord,* she prayed, *keep the two of them focused on helping Jane and not on how negligent Ivan has been.*

The doctor entered the room and took almost no time to assess the situation. Grace stayed in the room as decorum demanded and also in case the doctor needed assistance. He was a familiar face to many of the Amish families in the church district, as he was one of the few doctors who made house calls specifically for the Amish. Grace knew that his knowledge of their culture as well as their religion came in handy when he treated his Plain patients.

"Well," he said after he had examined Jane. "I'm of the opinion that the baby is in distress."

"She's in labor, then?"

The doctor nodded. "It appears so. But the baby isn't in the correct position. I've delivered many babies and encountered this before. The baby needs to be turned around. Its heartbeat is very faint. If she doesn't deliver this baby soon…" He let his voice trail off, not needing to complete the sentence.

"I'll tell Ivan, then."

The doctor nodded his head as he rolled up his white sleeves and assessed the room. Like most Amish bedrooms, there wasn't much to it. Just a bed, nightstand, and one small chest of drawers. Their clothing hung from hangers on hooks on the wall. "You know the drill, Grace. Hot water, clean towels, and lots of prayers."

Down in the kitchen, Grace hurried to the stove and opened the cabinet next to it where the pots were stored. Her mind reeled at the possibilities. If the baby didn't turn, it could die. Perhaps the umbilical cord was wrapped around its neck. In turning the baby, one of the limbs could be injured. And if Jane didn't deliver the baby soon, both were at risk of dying.

Menno and Ivan watched her, neither one uttering a word. By Grace's actions, they knew what was happening.

Grace didn't trust her tongue to speak kindness toward her son, so she remained silent, not knowing how to speak without snapping at him.

It was Barbie who spoke up.

"Is *Maem* going to be all right, *Mammi* Grace?"

Oh, help! Grace turned to face her granddaughter. Had the men been so oblivious to the seriousness of the situation that they had not sent her outside to watch the two smaller boys? While the pots of water heated on the stove, Grace walked toward her and knelt down on the ground so that she could look Barbie in the eye. "The doctor will help your *maem*," she said. "But you can help your *maem* too."

"How?"

"Prayer is always a good start. And mayhaps you could keep an eye on Samuel and Benjamin so that they are occupied until the doctor finishes?"

Barbie nodded her head.

As Grace started to stand up, she heard Barbie's voice ask another question, the one she dreaded and feared the most.

"And *Maem's* baby? If she's a girl, will we name her after *Aendi* Susan like *Daed* wants?"

Grace froze.

A heavy silence fell over the room. She didn't dare look in the direction where Ivan and Menno now sat at the table. Without even glancing at him, she felt the immediate tension from her husband. Grace bit her lower lip and took a deep breath. *Guide me, Lord*, she prayed.

"You'd best go check on your *bruders* now," she finally said and continued walking toward the mudroom where she knew spare towels were kept.

No sooner had Barbie left the house than the arguing began. Grace shut her eyes, listening to Menno as he spoke, rather harshly, to his son.

"Susan? How would my *grossdochder* know about Susan?" Menno's voice was low and cutting, not a hint of his usual kindness. She had only heard him use that tone once before: the night Susan left and James died.

Ivan wasted no time in responding. "I'm a grown man, *Daed*. I can make my own decisions now."

Grace took a step into the room, her arms laden with towels. She stared at Ivan, suddenly realizing that he had been in contact with Susan. He knew about her well-being and her life. Oh, the questions she wanted to ask! But one look at Menno and she knew better than to speak up.

His eyes narrowed and his lips pressed tight together as he too realized what Ivan's words meant. "She is still under the ban," Menno reminded him. "You risk it yourself if you are communicating with her."

"Times have changed, *Daed*. It's not like it was when we grew up and certainly not as strict as when you were young. The bishop has given me permission to stay in touch with Susan." Ivan glanced over at Grace. "And she'll be coming for a visit next month."

The calmness in Ivan's voice surprised Grace. While Menno's words were angry and strong, Ivan merely replied without any emotion. Clearly he had given a lot of thought to this. And at age forty-one, with six children and over two decades of living the Plain life faithfully, Ivan deserved to be heard. For one brief moment, Grace held her breath, hopeful that Menno would back down. It had been fifteen years, fifteen very long years, and Grace wanted to see her daughter again.

But when he slammed his open hand onto the table and stood up, that hope quickly faded.

"She took a vow!" Menno shouted. "She broke that vow and the hearts of every member of this community!"

Ivan didn't even flinch.

"There are rules for a reason. And breaking a vow, a *sacred* vow to God, is incomprehensible. She is the worst kind of sinner, and the bishop should realize that!" Menno stood up, the chair falling over behind him. He kicked it out of his way as he took a step backward, still glaring at Ivan. "'When thou shalt vow a vow unto the LORD thy God, thou shalt not slack to pay it: for the LORD thy God will surely require it of thee; and it would be sin in thee. But if thou shalt forbear to vow, it shall be no sin in thee. That which is gone out of thy lips thou shalt keep and perform; even a freewill offering, according as thou hast vowed unto the LORD thy God, which thou hast promised with thy mouth.'"

Unmoved, Ivan immediately responded, "Jesus associated with sinners. 'I came not to call the righteous, but sinners to repentance.'"

Grace could hold her silence no longer. "Ivan! Menno!" She stood there holding the towels and facing the two men who clearly had forgotten her presence. "Need I remind you that Jane is in a difficult way? She needs our prayers and not to hear you arguing. If you want to be calling from Scripture, let me share one with you! 'How forcible are right words! but what doth your arguing reprove'?" She shook her head, disappointed in both of them. Such bitterness between the two men and at such a stressful time. She needed their cooperation and Jane needed their prayers. "Now, I must take these towels to the doctor, and I ask the two of you to carry the water upstairs once it has boiled. Keep bringing up new boiled water until the baby is born. And then pray! Pray, Ivan, for the life of your wife and unborn child." She didn't wait for a reply as she turned and hurried up the stairs.

For the next three hours, she stood by the doctor's side, fetching whatever he needed and holding Jane's hand when pain came. When the baby was finally delivered, Grace breathed a sigh of relief and said a silent prayer to God, thanking Him for sparing the lives of both the mother and the infant.

"A girl," the doctor said. He smiled at Jane. "You have a daughter."

But Grace saw something in his eyes. Unlike his smile, his eyes held no expression of joy. She waited until the doctor handed her the baby, wrapped in a clean white towel so that he could return his attention to Jane while Grace cleaned the infant. With her back turned to Jane, she unwrapped the infant and dipped a clean cloth in warm water.

For a moment, she startled. The baby's face was beautiful, a miniature angel in her arms, with a small puckered mouth and a slightly upturned nose. Her coloring looked good; she had pinked up right away. But it was her limbs that caused Grace to catch her breath. Unlike other babies, this infant's arms and legs were smaller. She was, indeed, a dwarf.

Oh Lord, she thought. *What trials continue to plague this family. Give us the strength to provide the support Ivan and Jane will need to raise this child.*

As if in response to her prayer, the infant opened her mouth and out came a small cry. The noise sounded like a kitten mewing, and Grace gave a soft laugh at the sound. The baby waved her short arms as she cried, a reminder to Grace that she had a job to do. "There, there," she cooed as she gently wiped the baby clean. Her heart opened and she knew that God answered her prayers, for her shock dissipated and she knew, without any doubt in her heart, that she loved this child.

Swaddled in a clean baby blanket, the baby stopped crying. Grace laid the infant next to Jane. "She's beautiful," Grace said. "A true gift from God."

Though tired and weak, Jane smiled as she held the bundled baby in the crook of her arm. Letting Jane enjoy this moment, Grace hurried out of the room to alert Ivan that he had a new daughter. She didn't dare tell him about the dwarfism. Let him find out after seeing that angelic face and hearing her sweet cry.

Only when Ivan left the room did Grace turn to Menno. The scowl on his face told her that he was still dwelling on Ivan's defiance of his wishes. Oh, she wanted to speak out and to tell him what she thought.

But she knew better than to contribute to the argument. The Bible and the *Ordnung* were quite clear; women were to accept the authority of their husbands, no questions asked.

She cleared her throat and sat down at the table beside Menno. "The child is a blessing, Menno," she said slowly. "God has sent us a special child to tend, a unique *boppli* who will teach us many lessons."

Her words caught his attention and the scowl was instantly replaced with concern.

"Is the *boppli* healthy?"

Grace nodded her head, but slowly. *"Ja,* healthy. But short-limbed."

Something deflated in Menno. His shoulders sank and the corners of his mouth drooped.

"Now, Menno," she said in a soft voice. "They'll be needing our help. It's not as if this doesn't happen. Why, the Troyers who have the harness store—they have two short-limbed *kinner.* They both help at the store and live normal lives. Just takes some adjustment, is all."

He exhaled and bowed his head. "Stronger backs," he mumbled. "Always pray for stronger backs."

Ivan and Jane named the baby Verna, realizing, Grace thought, that naming her Susan would be unthinkable now. No one ever spoke about the baby's extra-short limbs. If the older children noticed, they knew better than to ask questions. As for the younger ones, Grace suspected that they didn't know the difference.

In the weeks leading up to Christmas, Grace helped Jane as much as she could. She'd watch the younger boys while the older children were at school, and she made both dinner and supper for their family. Yet she could sense something was wrong; there was a coldness in the air that didn't come from winter. Menno and Ivan barely spoke to each other, and little by little, Grace sensed some of the same reserved detachment from her son as well.

What on earth could I have done to upset him? she wondered. She knew she couldn't ask Menno, for he was still stewing over the fact that Ivan had disobeyed his wishes by communicating with Susan. And Ivan's aloofness kept her from inquiring of him directly.

It was the evening of the school program when everything came to a head. Jane had stayed home with the baby, being that she was still under four weeks old. Grace bundled up the two smaller boys while the older children dressed themselves for the short walk to the schoolhouse. Ivan walked ahead, carrying Benjamin in his arms, clearly making a statement with his physical distance from the rest of the group. While the children didn't notice it, Grace certainly did.

As with every school program, the one-room schoolhouse was crowded. There were drawings on the walls and small, cutout snowflakes stuck onto the windows. It made for a festive environment, and with Benjamin sitting on her lap, Grace felt a surge of holiday cheer.

Even though the programs tended to be the same each year, Grace still found great joy in listening to the students recite the story of Jesus's birth and sing songs, both from the *Ausbund* and from their Christmas songbook. Some years, there was a variation to the program, one or two of the older children reciting a poem or short story they had written. But Grace knew that the most important aspect of the program was that the children understood the importance of Christmas, the day their Savior was born.

The performance was short, limited to just one hour. But the sky was already gray by the time they started the walk home. Their boots crunched on the packed snow along the side of the road and their breath clung to the air like little puffs of smoke. Samuel liked breathing heavily so that he could see it.

Earlier, Grace had cooked a nice meal for the whole family. Christmas was just ten days away, and she felt a celebration was in order. Not only had Lydia and Barbie worked hard for their holiday program, but Grace also felt that a nice family gathering might loosen the tension that still hung in the air. While she knew she had to accept Menno's word as the authority, she also knew no one could accuse her of disobeying him by hosting a family meal.

Since Ivan and Jane's kitchen was larger, Grace had planned to have the meal at their table. Already it was set with Barbara's old china, each place setting neatly aligned atop freshly pressed white linen. Only something was different when she walked into the kitchen to finish the final preparations for the meal. She couldn't quite put her finger on it.

Jane sat in a rocking chair, nursing Verna, a crocheted blanket covering the baby to keep her warm. Lydia and

Barbie helped Grace in the kitchen while Levi played checkers with Samuel, Benjamin sitting next to them, his eyes wide as he watched the game.

"Now, I know I counted properly," Grace said. "But my word! I have an extra place setting!" She laughed to herself, quickly counting the plates on the table, "Six… seven…eight…nine…ten." Ten? What had she been thinking? "Oh, help," she said, embarrassed at her mistake. "I must be *ferhoodled*! I did put out one too many settings." She reached over to remove one when Ivan spoke up.

"Leave it, *Maem*."

Grace froze, her fingers just inches from the plate.

"I asked Jane to put the extra setting there."

And at that, she knew. Without any further words, Grace understood that Susan was in the house. Dropping her hand to her side, Grace stood up straight and faced her son. "Do you really think this is appropriate, Ivan?" she whispered, loud enough that he could hear. "Must you challenge your *daed* in such a manner? And before Christmas too?"

"This is my *haus*, *Maem*," Ivan said, not a hint of defiance in his voice despite the disregard for his father's authority in his words. "And she is my *schwester*. She needs our help. I will not turn my back on her."

"Where is she?" Grace asked, uncertain whether she asked out of curiosity or alarm that Menno would now walk in. "Your *daed* will not stay if she's here."

"Then he'll be welcome to leave."

He was putting her in a difficult spot. Once again, she was being forced to choose. *Oh, how can Ivan do this to me!* she thought. "I will have to go with him."

Ivan lifted an eyebrow as if to question her on the validity of her statement.

It happened simultaneously. Menno entered through the door that connected the two houses as soft footsteps came down the staircase. Grace stood there, her heart pounding and her palms sweating, as she looked first at her husband and then at her daughter, a daughter she barely recognized.

Now thirty-seven years old, Susan had short hair with bangs covering her forehead. She wore a dress that didn't fit her thin frame, and Grace suspected that it had been purchased just for this meeting. She looked tired, dark circles under her eyes telling a story that Grace did not want to hear. Fifteen years had passed, and just one look at Susan told Grace that her daughter had faced tremendous hardship. The fight in her was gone, replaced with defeat.

Susan paused on the bottom step, her hand on the railing. She met Grace's look and started to say something.

Menno interrupted. "Grace, we must leave now."

For a split second, Grace hesitated. She looked once more between the two of them: her husband and her daughter. In forty-five years of marriage, she had never once defied him. The thought crossed her mind that mayhaps, just this once, she should.

"Maem," Susan said, her voice cracking. "Please!"

"Grace!"

And in that moment, Grace knew she had only one choice. She could not go to Susan. To do so would be to break two vows: one to follow the *Ordnung* and the other to obey her husband. Lowering her head, she turned away from her daughter and avoided looking at the children. Slowly she crossed the room and followed Menno back through the door that led to their house. But she knew at that moment that she had left a piece of her heart in Ivan's kitchen.

2015

When she returned home, carrying her two bags of groceries, Grace noticed something white stuck on the window of her front door. As she neared it, she saw a package on the doorstep. Shuffling the two bags so that she could search for her key, she looked at the envelope and saw her name written clearly in block letters. She felt almost giddy for a moment, knowing without a doubt that her secret sister had struck once again.

Once she had opened the door, she set down the two bags and returned to remove the taped envelope before bending down to retrieve the small package. With her hip, she pushed at the door, making certain that it shut all the way. Whoever had written her name had a very different style of writing. Grace studied it, delaying the opening of the envelope so she could enjoy the anticipation.

The package was a plain white box. It wasn't wrapped, and she could easily lift the lid. For a moment, she debated which to open first: the box or the envelope. Finally, she decided on the envelope and slid her finger along the back fold. Inside were two pieces of paper: one a cutout snowflake and the other a folded piece of paper. She fingered the design of the snowflake, recognizing it as something a child would make at school. Yet the detail to this particular cutout was certainly made by an adult. The cuts were neat and even, completely symmetrical.

Curiosity got to her and she set aside the snowflake. The folded piece of paper was next. Taking a deep breath, she flipped it open and stared at the words. Once again, like the envelope, the words were written in block letters.

What is winter without…

That was all it said. She frowned, completely puzzled by the meaning of the message. *What is winter without snow?* she thought. Well, that made some sense. But it didn't mean anything to her. Every one of the other gifts had signified something, an event in her life. This one, however, did not.

She set the letter next to the snowflake and reached for the small white box. The contents jiggled as she slid it across the table and fumbled with the top. But when she opened it, she caught her breath. Sugar cookies! The box was filled with fresh-baked sugar cookies!

"Of course!" she said out loud, a bemused smile on her lips. She repeated that phrase over and over again during the cold weeks that led up to the holidays. As Christmas neared, she baked a sheet of cookies almost every day for her children, and later her grandchildren, until that one Christmas when Susan appeared on Ivan's doorstep.

But who could know such a thing?

Now she began to wonder. Could her secret sister be one of the children? Perhaps Ivan? After all, he had written to her after several months of silence, and he was bringing the family to her house in just two days. Certain it must be Ivan, Grace found a new hope that the relationship severed five long years ago would be repaired.

CHAPTER NINE

December 16, 2015

*T*HE DRIVER PARKED the van in front of the retirement home so the passengers could exit right at the front door. Grace took a deep breath, gathered her belongings, and climbed from the van. Standing on the cement walkway outside the entrance, she looked up at the two-story building. The institutionalized appearance of the home, so crisp and angular, felt cold to Grace, like a harbinger of death. In truth, she knew that each person who lived in the home would never again live elsewhere. At least not on earth.

All morning she had dreaded the visit that Lizzie's granddaughter had unknowingly guilted her into joining. For weeks, Lizzie had been asking her to join the Wednesday group. For weeks, Grace made up excuses. She never liked visiting the home when Menno was alive. Now she avoided it because she knew that in a few years, this could very well be *her* home.

"You ready, then?" Lizzie asked as she started toward the entrance. Grace gathered her strength and followed the rest of the group into the building, careful not to get hit by the spinning doors.

The first thing she noticed when she stepped into the lobby was the smell. She remembered it from previous visits, back when Menno came to visit members of the church district. He too had been a part of the Wednesday group. And he often asked Grace to accompany him. While she usually declined, there were a few times he made her go, telling her it wasn't proper for him to always be visiting the people without her.

The odor was a mixture of bleach and something else she couldn't identify. It was the scent of clean, but not the clean that usually permeated Amish homes. To Grace, it smelled distinctly like a hospital, full of *Englische* people dressed in green scrubs or wearing white coats. Here, however, the people who greeted the group were dressed in regular clothing: the men in nice suits and the women in dresses, mostly patterned, although some were Plain.

Grace had always suspected that their attire was strictly because of the residents and visitors, most of them being Amish and Mennonite. She wondered what the workers wore at home. Did they wear jeans and sweatshirts? Did the younger women wear makeup? She never did ask, although she wanted to know the answer.

Recently, there were only two people from their district residing in the home, but several of the women who had ridden along in the van had other family members residing there. Lizzie took charge and instructed those without family members to split up. Half of the group would visit Eli King while the other half would visit Jane Hostetler. Reluctantly, Grace followed Lizzie and Hannah, the three of them assigned to visit with Eli, while the rest of the group walked down a different corridor.

Oh, how she hated the sights and the sounds. Grace tried to stare straight ahead and not peek into the rooms with open doors. But curiosity got the best of her. An Amish man, most likely in his late seventies, sat in a chair, staring at nothing with his mouth hanging open. In another room, an elderly woman lay in her bed, covered with a white sheet as she slept. Grace heard a faint voice from another room, the voice calling out a name over and over again.

How cruel, Grace thought, that these people were left here alone and not surrounded by family at the final stages of their lives.

"Ah, here we go," Lizzie announced. She walked right into the room, obviously having visited Eli King before this day. Her familiarity made Grace feel guilty. Even if she lived alone, she was luckier than most to still be able to do so. If she became incapacitated or in need of round-the-clock care, she would have no choice but to stay at such a facility and, most likely, be in want of company.

"Eli!" Lizzie said, her voice loud enough so that the older man could hear. "Eli! You awake, then?"

He blinked his eyes and lifted his head, staring at the three women. Clearly he had been napping. He moistened his lips and cleared his voice before he said in a raspy voice, "Well, if I wasn't before, I sure am now!"

Lizzie laughed and set her large purse on the window ledge. Immediately she drew back the blinds so that sunlight could stream in. "It's too dark in here!" she announced. "You need some sunshine, Eli! Will do you good!"

He waved his hand at her dismissively, which only made Lizzie laugh again.

Grace watched this exchange, feeling a new admiration for her friend. Lizzie was completely at ease as she bossed Eli around, helping him to sit up and readjusting the pillows behind his head. She tried to coax him out of bed to sit in his wheelchair so that they could wheel him down the corridor to the large gathering room where other residents with more mobility often sat and played games.

Again he waved away her suggestion.

"Aw, now, Eli! You can't just sit in your room all day!"

"Why not? There's nothing out there but a bunch of old people playing checkers or Scrabble. Checkers bores me and those Scrabble tiles are just too small to see anyhow!" he snapped back, his feistiness surprising Grace. Suddenly, as if noticing them for the first time, he turned his attention to Hannah and Grace. "Who's that there?"

Lizzie leaned over so he could hear her better. "You know my sister-in-law, Hannah. She's been here before to visit you. James's Hannah?"

He seemed to study Hannah for a moment until he recognized her. "*Ja, ja*, I remember James Esh." He turned to look at Lizzie. "And Hannah is David's *schwester, ja*?"

"That's right, Eli," Lizzie replied. "And we brought Grace Beiler with us today. You remember the Beilers, don't you?"

"Hmm." He lifted a shaky hand to his chin and rubbed it as he thought. "I reckon I do. Menno Beiler. A right *gut* man! Helped me once with some field work when my boy was taken ill." He stared at Grace. "Why didn't he come with you?"

Lizzie tapped him on the shoulder and frowned. "Now, come on, Eli, you know that he passed."

Another long-drawn-out moment before the realization struck him. "I reckon I do, now that you mention it. Why, he was young!"

Grace almost smiled at Eli's comment. Menno had been anything but young. A lifetime of working on the farm and in the elements had aged him far beyond his years. Yet to Eli King, who was probably close to ninety, she imagined that Menno did seem a lot younger. Besides, Eli had been at the retirement home for a while now. For several years, he had bounced around from one child's home to the next until his care required round-the-clock attention. His children simply could no longer care for him, and after much discussion with the church leaders, they moved him here.

Eli pointed at her. "You're still a young one too," he said thoughtfully. "Mayhaps time to find yourself a new husband." He perked up, lifting his hand to his hair to smooth it back, as if he might be a candidate. Any thought of Grace being offended by such a comment disappeared when Lizzie scoffed and tapped him again on the arm, causing Eli to laugh.

For the next hour, the three women sat in the room, visiting with Eli while they crocheted. In fact, Grace found herself relaxing as she listened to Lizzie prattle on about anything that came to her mind. Eli teased her and made jokes, sometimes repeating himself. But the way his aged blue eyes took on a new life made Grace change her mind about the retirement home. While it was true that the residents were facing imminent death, whether through sickness or old age, and they either didn't have family or couldn't be taken care of by them, they could still experience joy. Eli King proved that. And in feeling such joy, he gave it back to the three women seated before him.

It dawned on her that she was no better off living independently than the residents of the retirement home. In fact, despite her own mobility around her house, she was in a worse situation. She didn't have as many visitors or the option to go play checkers or Scrabble. Day in and day out, she sat alone in her house, dependent on the infrequent visitors from members of the *g'may* and the worship service held every two weeks. Any outings were at the mercy of other people who still had a horse and buggy. Was she truly any better off there than if she *did* move to such a facility?

2012

Grace set the table for two. Again. With the colder weather, visitors were less frequent, and their evenings were often spent in quiet solitude after a light supper. Tonight was no different. Outside, the snow was starting to fall. She could see the large snowflakes falling against the window in the glow from the kerosene lantern that hung above the kitchen sink.

The door opened and Menno hurried inside, a gust of wind accompanying him. He slapped his arms against his chest and shivered before removing his coat and hat.

"Sure is cold out there," he said as he hung both items on hooks from the wall. "Wouldn't want to be out there in a buggy, that's for sure and certain. Roads gonna be slick." He coughed into his fist.

"Getting a cold, Menno?"

"*Nee,*" he responded, moving to the table to pull out his chair and sit down. "Just a tickle in my throat."

She wanted to tell him that he'd been coughing a lot of late. And wheezing too. But she didn't want to ruin the good mood or create unnecessary worry. Instead, she dished boiled potatoes into a bowl and placed thin slices of ham onto a plate. She carried the two dishes over to the table and sat down next to Menno.

"Do you think they'll have the school program tomorrow night, then?" she asked, her eyes hopeful as she searched his face for an answer.

"Aw, I don't see why not, Grace." He smiled at her. "No reason the roads won't be clear by afternoon. If not, they'll just reschedule." He reached out and touched her hand, a gesture meant to comfort her. Then he bowed his head to pray.

As she had done for almost every breakfast, dinner, and supper for forty-seven years, Grace did the same, following his lead. She shut her eyes and prayed, thanking the Lord for the food that was set upon the small table in the small house that she had moved into with Menno just two years ago.

She had long ago given up any hope of a true reconciliation between Menno and Ivan. After that night, that one horrible night when Susan showed up at Ivan's house after the school program, father and son were never at ease with each other again. Within days, Menno had convinced Grace that it was time for them to retire from farm life. After all, he explained, he was sixty-seven years old and ready to relinquish the work that began with early morning chores and lingered until the late afternoon hours.

But Grace knew the truth: he was running away from Susan. Without a word, Grace packed up the few things they needed: clothing, cookware, and some canned goods to help get them through the rest of the winter. She contemplated leaving Barbara's china plates at the house, knowing it would be better to leave them for Ivan and Jane. Menno, however, insisted she pack them. While Grace knew that Barbara would want them passed down to the grandchildren, she wasn't about to argue with her husband. That was something they could sort out later.

A rented truck arrived to move their bed, dresser, sofa, recliner, rocker, grandfather clock, side tables, and kitchen table and chairs. And just like that, they left what had been their home since the beginning of their marriage.

Menno found a small ranch house on the outskirts of a community in Akron, just two towns away from Ivan, and located in a stricter, more conservative district. Among other things, the move signaled that Menno rejected the leadership of their previous bishop, who had softened the rules about shunning at Ivan's request.

The move wasn't Grace's wish or idea, but she felt that Menno's happiness was worth her sorrow. After all, these were the autumn years of their lives. She thought better of arguing with him over the location of the house or the fact that there was little backyard to garden and no paddock for the horse to graze. Instead, she merely smiled when he asked if she liked it and commented, "It'll suit just fine."

The truth was that as long as she was with Menno, it didn't matter where they lived. Her love for him was so great that she forced herself to find happiness in the *Englische* house, even though she could no longer be in daily contact with her beloved grandchildren.

During the warmer months, they often sat outside on the small porch, Menno critiquing her meadow tea. He could still recite the same recipe that he had told her years ago at the youth gathering when they were just beginning their courtship. It became a game for them: she'd make the tea and he would judge it. On most occasions, he scored it a nine out of ten, claiming that a ten was perfect and only God could make better tea.

But now that it was cold, they spent most of their time indoors. While they were close friends with their neighbors, James and Hannah Esh, the weather was too cold for social visiting in the evenings. With icy roads and slippery sidewalks, it just wasn't safe to walk the short distance between their houses in the early dark of evening.

"I hear tell," Menno began to say as he scooped potatoes onto his plate, "that the *g'may* is splitting."

Grace gasped. While it was a good sign that the community was growing, a split in the church district meant they'd have a new bishop and preachers. "Oh, Menno! Say it ain't so!"

He nodded his head. "*Ja*, I'm afraid so, Grace." Using his fork, he mashed his potatoes before reaching for the plate of butter. He cut off a large piece and dropped it onto the potatoes so that it could melt. "The farming families just east of here are too large, and the Amish folk that are moving over here are increasing. Just not economical to keep living on the farms when the young ones need the land."

That was always his excuse when asked why they had moved: it was time to turn over the land to the next generation. But everyone knew the truth. After all, Ivan's oldest son wasn't even married yet and didn't need the *grossdawdihaus*, and too many people had seen Susan around town. Still, the people of the *g'may* respected Menno's discretion about the matter, and no one challenged his decision or the reason behind it.

"The church leaders are meeting today to discuss the matter. If they decide it's time, they'll be drawing the new district lines before the weekend," Menno continued. "Then we'll be choosing new preachers after worship this weekend."

"And what of the bishop? Who will the bishop be for the new district?"

"*Ach*, Grace," he said, a disappointed look on his face. "That's up to God, not us, to decide. You know that."

He was right. The church leaders were nominated by the members in a secret ballot. Then those men with enough nominations were called to the front of the room and asked to select a Bible from the table. In one of those Bibles was a slip of paper; the man who chose that Bible would become a preacher, chosen by lot—a process guided by the hand of God. When a new bishop was needed, the preachers would be called to the front of the room, once again choosing a Bible.

The bishop set the tone for the community. He had the authority to implement transformation and change or maintain strict control over the people. Typically, younger bishops were more likely to argue for adaptation and integration with the *Englische* world, while the older ones opted for more conservative measures.

With so many elderly people living in their section of Akron, Grace suspected that they'd have a pool of conservative men in the lot. Conservative men meant fewer changes, something that Menno would like. But Grace often wondered how he would react if a new bishop offered reform, little things like air conditioning in the hot summer months or crocheting on Sundays. Clearly he had rejected the reform offered by their previous bishop, a softening of the rules for shunning.

Oh, how she missed her old church district. Ever since they had moved into this new neighborhood, with its sprinkling of *Englische* and Amish homes, Sunday had become the most dreaded day of the week. Of course, she loved the worship service and fellowship. But since they didn't know many people in the church district, their afternoons and evenings were spent sitting quietly at home instead of visiting. Thankfully, they already knew the Yoders, David and Lizzie, as well as James and Hannah Esh, since Grace had grown up in the same church district as David and Hannah. But they had family nearby, and especially on the off-Sundays when there was no worship, they would visit with their children or siblings.

On those days, Grace and Menno sat in the house. Menno would read from the Bible, sometimes discussing specific passages with her, but for the most part, it was a long and quiet day.

If only he would reach out to Ivan, she often thought. She missed seeing the children and being a part of their lives. She loved baking but had no one to bake for anymore. To make a pie at home meant that it would be enjoyed only by Menno, and usually he didn't care for the same dessert multiple days in a row. She wound up throwing most of it out.

Only once had she broached the subject with Menno. He remained silent for almost two hours before responding. It was the longest silence between them. Initially, she took his lack of response as anger. That was a typical response among the Amish. When offended or upset, they tended to shut down and remain quiet, knowing that foolish words came from angry tongues. But when he finally did speak, she realized that he had been reflecting on her request, perhaps even praying for guidance from the Lord in helping him find a proper response.

"I understand your feelings, Grace. I miss the little ones too." He gave her a look that mirrored his sentiment. "But unless she repents of her sins and is accepted into the church again, we have to honor the ban. And Ivan has disrespected his parents. That is a sin. How can I forgive him when he hasn't repented and accepted responsibility for what he has done?"

"He's our son," she pleaded. "Of our four children, we have none."

Menno shook his head. "God first, Grace. Always God first." Then he reached out and took her hand in his. It had been a long time since he had made such a gesture. When he lifted it, his fingers entwining with hers, he gave a small smile. "And we have each other. Hasn't that always been enough?"

And that was the end of the discussion.

They never talked about the future, about the big "what if" that loomed ahead. It was a thought that Grace always tucked into the back corners of her mind. When she looked at Menno, she still saw him as that young, confident twenty-two-year-old at the youth gathering, asking her if she had turned eighteen yet. In her eyes, he hadn't aged. She did, however, wonder what he saw when he looked at her.

Years of pregnancy had thickened her waist. Her hair had turned almost completely white. She wore glasses now, for she could barely see anything after years of working by the dim light of a kerosene lamp in the winter evenings. Without doubt, she knew that age had taken its toll on her and she was certainly no longer "pretty" as her sister Anna Mae had once called her, oh, so many years ago.

And while she knew she shouldn't fret about such vain ideas, she couldn't help but look in the mirror when Menno wasn't around and see the toll that time had taken on her. Even now as she sat with him at the table, listening to him talk about the possibility of new church district lines being drawn and what that would mean for the split *g'may*, she wondered how he felt about her after forty-seven years of marriage.

The following day, Menno took the horse and buggy to visit with David Yoder and James Esh. He was gone for almost three hours when Grace started to worry. What on earth could they be talking about for so long? She paced the floor, occasionally looking out the window as she waited for his return. The later it became, the more she fretted. What if something had happened to him?

When he finally returned, her relief was so great that she wanted to hold him and tell him how worried she had been. But he breezed past her, leaving his hat on the table as he began to tell her what he had heard.

"The new district lines have been drawn, Grace, and we will be in the new district," he said, sounding rather excited. "What a wise thing the bishop has done!"

She wasn't so certain. Change was not always accepted by the people. Dividing a church district often created a sense of uncertainty among them. Men would be nominated by the members of the church to fill the vacant roles, but the lot would choose who was selected. This often left the future of a *g'may* in a state of transformation and conflict. One bishop might permit change while another might deny it, creating neighbors who followed differing *Ordnungs*. But when she recognized the glow in Menno's eyes, she did not feel comfortable expressing her true feelings. Instead, she merely responded with a meek "Oh *ja*?"

"They'll have the lot on Sunday for two new preachers."

Grace gasped and clicked her tongue. "Two? Have you ever heard such a thing?"

Menno shrugged and shook his head. "Both districts need at least two preachers and a bishop. Bishop Riehl has decided to remain with our district while we choose two new preachers, and the other district will keep its preachers and choose a new bishop by lot."

Grace sighed. Each district needed preachers, experienced and well versed in the *Ordnung* as well as Scripture, before a bishop could be chosen, always by lot. Still, she was more than content that Bishop Riehl would remain with them in their newly formed district.

He was a conservative bishop, and Grace liked his sermons very much.

On Sunday after the worship service, the bishop called a members-only meeting, the children and unbaptized adults being asked to leave the room. Since it was cold outside, they went upstairs and stayed on the second floor during the meeting. The bishop told the worshippers what most of them already knew: the church district had grown too large and needed to split. She barely listened, for Menno already had told her about the new district line and which families would remain with the existing *g'may* and which families would be switched to the new one.

What she was most curious about was the nomination of the new preachers. As she looked around the room, she wondered who would be nominated. She had never experienced the formation of a new church district, so she was most curious about how the choosing would happen.

"As everyone knows, the new district will need two preachers," the bishop said. "This is a time that requires prayer, not just before and not just today, but afterward for the two men who are called by God to serve our church." He stared at the men, all seated to his right. "When you accepted the Lord and committed your life to this church, you agreed to answer if God chooses you. Serving God as a preacher is another lifelong commitment. I ask the rest of the members to pray now as the eligible men step forward and participate in the lot selection."

Grace sat up straighter at this announcement.

On the other side of the room, the men looked at each other before, slowly, a few began to stand up. Fifteen men walked to the front of the room. Among them stood Menno. That was almost all of the men in the one district, the only three exceptions being young baptized men who weren't married yet and the two young men who, while married, had no children.

One by one, the men took a step forward and selected a Bible from the table. Grace's eyes remained on Menno, her heart racing as she silently prayed. Becoming a preacher of a church district brought too much responsibility, she thought. *Please, Lord, if it is Your will, do not select my Menno.*

But when he opened the Bible, a white slip of paper fluttered to the ground. Before her eyes, she saw the color drain from his cheeks as he realized what had happened. Now, for the rest of his life, he would be known as Preacher Beiler. Grace felt tears well up in her eyes. *No, no, no,* she thought, knowing all the time that her emotions were selfish. God had selected Menno; she should be humbled and supportive. Instead, she felt angry and scared, both emotions at the same time causing her to feel physically ill.

She barely paid attention when the second piece of paper fluttered from the Bible held in the hands of David Yoder.

The selection completed, the men returned to their places on the benches and chairs. When she looked up and sought out Menno from the other side of the room, she saw tears in his eyes. As a preacher, he would visit the sick and infirm, he would minister to the spiritually weak, and he would be a role model for the rest of the community. If there ever was a chance of Grace seeing her grandchildren before, she knew that, unless Ivan repented and asked forgiveness from Menno, there was no chance of it happening now.

One Bible. One slip of paper. And Grace knew their lives would never be the same.

2015

The group of visitors stood just inside the entrance, waiting for their van to arrive. Outside, the sky was gray and overcast with a strong hint of more snow on its way. Grace stood there beside Hannah and listened to the women chatter while she stared around at the lobby. People were smiling as they walked past one another. The fresh flowers on the receptionist's desk livened up the welcome area. A young Amish woman walked with an elderly man, undoubtedly a great-granddaughter visiting a relative.

"This isn't such a bad place," Grace said, mostly to herself, but Hannah overheard her.

"Oh, come now!" Hannah said, a mixture of disbelief and discouragement in her tone. "You'd not want to come live here, Grace! You're the picture of health and have a lovely *haus*!"

Lizzie turned her attention toward them when she heard Hannah's comment. "What did Grace say?"

Hannah shook her head, clicking her tongue. "She said she likes this place and would consider living here."

Holding up her hand as if to stop Hannah, Grace tried to argue back. "That wasn't exactly what I said."

"Oh, now, Grace!" Lizzie jumped into the conversation. "You know that Menno would be sorely disappointed if you chose to move into such a place."

Grace wanted to ask how Lizzie would know such a thing. Who knew what Menno would want? He hadn't left a letter for her. Neither one of them had expected the cancer and subsequent health issues. After all, he too was once the picture of health. Her silence answered Lizzie's unspoken question.

Taking the hint, Lizzie tucked her arm around Grace's and led her a bit farther from the group. "It wouldn't be proper for you to retire here, Grace. You have family to tend to you when that time comes. It's our life-right! They must take care of us!"

"What about these people?" Grace asked, a little sass in her voice. "Where is their life-right?"

Pressing her lips together, Lizzie frowned. "It's different, Grace. You know that. You are still young, and you have time to reconnect with your two children and grandchildren."

"Oh, Lizzie! Do I really have to say it? For sure you know about *that* situation," Grace responded. "Menno always believed that God chose him because he followed his vows. God chose him because he did not bend to his daughter's choice for worldliness and his son's choice for rebellion."

Lizzie gasped. "He thought that was why?"

Grace nodded. "*Ja*, Ivan and Susan."

"I know the elders always respected him for standing so firm, but I never thought that God chose him because of that!"

"So you can see," Grace continued, "I may have no choice but to consider relocating to such a place when I can no longer care for myself."

For a moment, Lizzie seemed to contemplate her next words. But Grace already knew what she was thinking: How could a bishop's wife retire to a home?

Menno had been a preacher for just a year when Bishop Riehl died. During that time, Menno studied the Bible and met with Preacher Yoder and the bishop. The three men spent hours discussing the growth of their *g'may* and how to deal with the issue of land development because Amish farmers were selling parcels of their property. Many afternoons, the three men traveled to the farms in their church district, talking with the farmers and trying to find a solution so that younger Amish couples wouldn't be faced with a choice of leaving Pennsylvania for another more remote community in another less expensive state.

But when Bishop Riehl died, everything changed.

Another lot selection was scheduled, this time between the two preachers. Neither Grace nor Menno slept for several nights before the selection. With only two members in the selection, they both recognized the reality of the odds.

The members-only meeting was held on Sunday after worship. Grace had sat on her hands to keep them from trembling. If she had prayed that Menno not be selected for a preacher, now she begged the Lord to make him choose an empty Bible.

But he didn't.

Indeed, Menno picked the Bible with the slip of paper and became the next bishop.

In hindsight, Grace recognized that Menno had been destined for this role. His faith in God and devotion to the *Ordnung*, a devotion that had split apart her family, made him the perfect candidate. The older church members respected him for his commitment, even if it had caused Grace so much pain during her life. But he was a good bishop: stern but fair. During his short tenure, he visited each family at least once a month, encouraging Grace to come along with him.

She usually found an excuse unless it was one of the older women in the *g'may*, for she didn't want to visit the younger women, with their children clinging to their skirts or running around the kitchen. It reminded her too much of what she had sacrificed in order to obey her vow to abide by her husband's authority.

While Menno was bishop, she often wished her parents were still alive. The irony of her father thinking that Menno was a wild young man during his *rumschpringe* was not lost on her.

And then he had the stroke.

He hadn't been a bishop for more than a year. With his speech impeded and his mobility limited, the *g'may* was forced to choose a new bishop. This time, the lot fell on David Yoder.

"Grace," Lizzie said. "I understand how your Menno felt, but you cannot consider moving into a retirement home." She lowered her voice, glancing around quickly to make certain no one would overhear. "A bishop's wife does not go into a retirement home."

Grace frowned and shook her head. "Doesn't say that anywhere, Lizzie. And it's better than living alone, *ja*? I have to consider these things. What if I fell and broke a hip? You know that happened to Mary's *maem*. No one found her for a few hours! And she was living in the *grossdawdihaus*! I could fall, and it might be days before someone found me."

Lizzie dismissed her with a wave of her hand. "That's just living for the unlikely, Grace Beiler! You're making excuses now!"

But she wasn't.

Deep down, Grace knew she had some serious thinking to do. Even though Menno had died not quite six months ago, enough time had passed that she needed to begin thinking about her future. She wouldn't make any decisions. Not yet. But she couldn't continue living on her own for the rest of her life. It wasn't healthy, mentally or physically, nor was it sensible.

During the ride back to her house, for the first time in her life, Grace dreaded the thought. Without Menno, the house was just that: a house. What she longed for was a home.

CHAPTER TEN

December 18, 2015

For the fifth time that afternoon, Grace walked to the window, pushing aside the sheer curtain and gazing outside as she wondered what was keeping Hannah and James. They had promised to stop at her house on their way to the children's program. *Where are they?* Grace thought, her anxiety level rising as she turned away and began pacing.

Her bag of little gifts for the children sat on the edge of the kitchen table, which she already had set for Ivan and his family. The food was prepared too; all she would need to do was heat it when she returned. For two days, she had fretted over Ivan's visit, making list after list of what needed to be done, in which sequence and at what time. Her small trash can was filled with crumpled pieces of paper, each one representative of her indecisiveness.

The pretty china plates that she had used for this special supper had been in Menno's family for two generations. Barbara had indicated in her last letter, the one that was tucked in her hope chest with her wedding dress, that she wanted the china to be left to Menno and Grace.

Grace had found the letter when she had gone searching for that dress after Barbara passed away. Just as Grace had her own wedding dress neatly folded and stored in a white cardboard box, so did Barbara. After all, it was the way of the Plain people to have Amish women buried in their wedding dresses, which they usually stored in their hope chests. And, folded within the dress, the women often had a farewell letter that outlined any special bequeathments, such as a quilt to be given to a daughter, a vase to a grandchild, or a set of china to a son and his wife.

Staring at the china, Grace remembered that letter and how, for the first time, she realized the true meaning of faith. Life was a cycle that ended the same way for everyone: death. But for believers, those who turned their lives over to God and lived according to His Holy Word, death was only the beginning of a joyous new journey in heaven, a place where pain and sorrow did not exist.

The thought of Barbara's last letter reminded Grace of Menno. Had it been only less than six months ago that he died?

She shut her eyes, swallowing the wave of grief that began to wash over her. She remembered that particular morning, one that had started out like every other morning. She had awoken and hurried into the kitchen to start some coffee before he would need her help getting out of bed. Only he never called for her. After the coffee was ready, she wondered why he was still sleeping. She took her time, actually finding the time alone enjoyable as she began to prepare breakfast so that when Menno woke up, she'd only have to cook the scrambled eggs and heat up the morning sausage.

But he never woke up.

When she entered the bedroom, she noticed a certain stillness in the air. Outside their bedroom window, the familiar birds' chirping that normally accompanied her early morning routine was nonexistent, as if her surroundings were trying to tell her that something important and unusual had just happened. The room simply felt different from the way it had felt on other mornings. She called out his name, not once but twice, with no response.

And then she knew.

For a long while, Grace sat by his side, just staring down at his face. Death seemed to have robbed him of age because, to her, he looked younger and at peace. She fought the urge to cry, instead taking his cold hand in hers and just praying that he knew how much she had loved him throughout their long journey together.

Later, she stood up and forced herself to go through the motions of the morning, getting dressed and fetching his burial clothing, his freshly laundered Sunday suit. She knew better than to look for a letter, his stroke having deprived him of the desire and ability to write, at least clearly, and for Menno, if it couldn't be done properly, he wouldn't do it at all. And then, knowing she would never have another moment alone with her husband, she paused one last time to stare at his earthly body and prayed one last time that she would see him again in heaven with their son James and all of their family members who had gone on before them.

The walk to Hannah's house had seemed very long that morning as she forced herself to put one foot in front of the other, not eager to alert people to her husband's passing.

Now, almost six months later, she was facing a long afternoon and evening. While she was looking forward to the school program, she couldn't help but fret over Ivan's impending visit. She had seen him only twice since the funeral, and that had been back in August. As for Linda, Grace hadn't seen her at all since Menno's death.

Her oldest daughter's lack of familial interest had begun long before the rest of the family issues, something Grace had never quite understood, though she suspected that her daughter felt more comfortable with her in-laws, especially since she lived with them. And who wouldn't want to avoid the pain and guilt that had fallen upon their home after the rebellion of Susan and the tragic death of James? Just as Anna Mae, in marrying a widower with children, had fled the gloom that fell upon their home after Benny died, so had Linda busied herself with her own young family, rarely visiting Menno and Grace and studiously avoiding the issue that divided their family: the shunning of Susan.

The destruction of a family, all because of one decision made during the heat of an argument, weighed heavily on her.

When James and Hannah finally arrived at her house, the horse and buggy pausing in the driveway, Grace quickly picked up her bag of gifts and hurried to the door. She saw Hannah smile at her from inside the buggy, and immediately Grace began to feel better. She would enjoy the program, and then, with God's blessing, she would enjoy her visit with Ivan and his family.

By the time they pulled into the parking lot, it was already full of horses and buggies. In the distance, Grace saw two more buggies headed down the road toward the school.

"Oh my!" she said as she took Hannah's arm to walk toward the door. "There's a full crowd tonight, *ja*?"

Indeed, the schoolhouse was filled with people, all relatives of the students: grandparents, parents, brothers, and sisters. Lizzie Yoder motioned to Hannah and Grace that she had reserved seats for them toward the front of the classroom. With the desks moved out and benches lined across the floor, there was enough room for most of the people to have a seat.

Lizzie reached over and grasped Grace's arm. "I'm so curious as to what Catharine has these little ones doing tonight!"

Grace smiled but did not reply. There were so many memories of forty-nine previous school pageants, all with Menno nearby. Tonight, however, she felt more alone than ever and wondered if she should not have come at all.

Her eyes scanned the room. Battery-operated candles with one small pine branch sat in each of the deep windowsills. The light glow and fragrant scent created a warm and welcoming room. Around the tops of the walls was a familiar ABC border that Grace remembered well from the schoolhouse she had attended so many years ago. She smiled as she turned her head back toward the front of the classroom where the children stood at attention, their eyes on their teacher as they waited for her cue.

Catharine waited until the last guest arrived before she took a step forward toward the gathered audience. Grace saw the confidence in the young woman's eyes as she looked out at the many faces staring back at her.

"*Wilkum* to our school program," she began, her voice loud and clear so that everyone could hear. "The students have been working very hard this year as we have a special project that someone asked us to work on."

Grace felt Lizzie shift her weight, perhaps sitting up a little bit straighter as Catharine spoke.

"Tonight, we'd like to start the program with something a little different than in past years," Catharine continued. She paused and smiled again, her eyes lighting up as she stood there in front of her students' families. Then she turned toward the children and nodded her head.

In unison, the older children began to sing, the voices lifting as they used the tune of another song, "What a Friend We Have in Jesus," to sing a special greeting song:

> *As we greet you at this season*
> *With our hearts so full of cheer*
> *We would like to tell the reason*
> *Why we are gathered here*
> *This is Jesus, God's Son's, birthday*
> *Born in Bethlehem long ago*
> *Wrapped in swaddling clothes and resting*
> *In His manger bed so low.*

Then the younger children took over and continued with the second verse. Grace couldn't help but feel joy spreading throughout her as she watched their cherubic faces, so happy and pure, singing with love and faith:

> *We're so glad to have you with us*
> *As we celebrate this day*
> *May our hearts feel the true meaning*
> *Jesus came for us this way*
> *Not for presents or for candy*
> *Did he come to earth to live*
> *But God sent Him down from heaven*
> *Here for us His life to give.*

When the song finished, the students stood still for a moment. The silence let everyone take a moment to reflect on the last two stanzas of the song. And then one of the older students, a young girl whom Grace knew as Susie Eicher, stepped forward and said, "'And she shall bring forth a son, and thou shalt call his name Jesus: for he shall save his people from their sins.'"

The younger children began to sing:

> *Christmas time again is here*
> *Grandest time of all the year*
> *That is why we like to sing*
> *Honor Christ the newborn King.*

Susie Eicher stepped back and a younger boy, Timmy Hostetler, took her place. He avoided eye contact with the audience, his pale cheeks flushed with patches of pink as he recited another verse from the Bible, this time from the book of Luke: "'And she brought forth her firstborn son, and wrapped him in swaddling clothes, and laid him in a manger; because there was no room for them in the inn.'"

Once again, the younger children sang:

No room for them, no room for them
None in the inn of Bethlehem
Mary and Joseph, night is nigh
But in the stable you must lie
No room for Jesus—small and wee
But in a manger He must be
Wrapped in his swaddling clothes He lies
Jesus the King of Paradise
No room for Jesus yet today
Many to him are saying nay
Open your hearts and let Him in
Jesus will cast out every sin.

And so it continued: an older child would step forward and recite a verse from the book of Matthew or Luke that related to the birth of Jesus Christ, and the younger children would sing a short song that corresponded to it. Grace found it a clever way to tell the story of Christmas, one that was, indeed, quite different from years past. She watched with delight as the children continued telling the story of Jesus's birth. The room took on a new level of energy, one that pulsated with genuine interest from the audience.

When it was time for the verse about the wise men visiting the young child Jesus, the last of the older children standing in the back row came forward and recited his Bible verse: "'And when they were come into the house, they saw the young child with Mary his mother, and fell down, and worshipped him: and when they had opened their treasures, they presented unto him gifts; gold, and frankincense and myrrh.'"

For the last time, the younger children began to sing another song.

> *Far from the east came the wise men of old*
> *With myrrh and frankincense and treasures*
>   *of gold*
> *Led by a star they had come all the way*
> *To worship the Christ child asleep on the hay*
> *Just think! In a manger this Christ child was born*
> *And that was our first glad Christmas morn.*

The families seated before the children began to applaud, and as Grace looked around her, she saw the beaming faces of many parents. Of course, when she glanced at Lizzie, she noticed the distinct look of pride on her friend's face. Grace smiled to herself and returned her attention to the teacher at the front of the classroom.

Catharine waited until the room was silent again before she stepped in front of her students. Once again, she scanned the room before she began talking. When her eyes caught sight of Grace, Catharine paused.

"While the children worked very hard on practicing their recitation and singing, there was another project they worked on," she said, her eyes still on Grace. "A project to truly bring a little joy to the world, or, in this case, to one person in particular."

A murmur of curiosity filled the room, and Grace felt the heat flush her cheeks as the rest of the audience began to look at her. Immediately Grace suspected she knew where this was leading. While she didn't like being the center of attention, she was pleased that finally she might know the answer to the recent mystery of those secret sister gifts.

One of the smaller boys nudged the little girls next to him and they quietly slipped away. No one spoke as they returned carrying a plain brown wrapped package. Standing before Grace, they handed it to her.

"Oh my," Grace gasped. "What is *this*?"

Catharine nodded her head and indicated that Grace should remove the wrapping.

With her cheeks still flushed from too much attention and too embarrassed to speak up, Grace did as she was instructed. No one seemed to mind that she had been singled out from the rest of the church district.

Inside the paper was a plain black three-ring binder. She looked at the binder and then looked at Catharine who, once again, smiled and nodded.

Carefully, for she didn't know what was inside the notebook, she flipped the cover and saw plastic sleeves inside, each filled with two pieces of paper back-to-back. "Oh, help," she muttered as she turned one page after another. Each paper had a Bible verse written on it with a note of encouragement for Grace during her time of mourning. She could hardly believe what she had been given by these wonderful children.

"The children wanted to do something special for Grace Beiler," Catharine explained. "They created a book of scripture verses and letters to help Grace during her first holiday without Bishop Beiler."

There were nods and murmurs of approval from the parents seated on the benches. It was important for children not only to respect but also to care for the elderly in their community. Their efforts to cheer up Grace during a difficult season were truly appreciated by everyone in the room and were a wonderful gift to give to a member of their church district.

Grace glanced at Lizzie and then handed her the black notebook so that she could peek through the pages before passing it farther down the bench. Each of the mothers would certainly want to see such a special and thoughtful gift, especially since their children had taken part in this project.

"Why, I...I don't right know what to say," Grace stammered. "I thank you children. Your gift will be treasured during the holidays and throughout the year, indeed!"

The children kept smiling, pleased with Grace's reaction as well as the looks of praise from their parents. The book was making its way around the gathering as the children returned their attention to Catharine, waiting for her to guide them through the last part of the program.

"Now, before we close this program," Catharine said, "we've had a special request to sing one last song, a very specific and secret request." Again Catharine glanced in Grace's direction when she said this. "We invite all of you to sing along with us."

As the children began to sing, a chill went through Grace's body. Memories of past holiday seasons flashed through her memory, and each one contained this song. She could barely open her mouth to form the words, although she knew them by heart. It was, without doubt, her favorite holiday song.

Silent night! Holy night!
All is calm, all is bright
Round yon virgin mother and Child
Holy Infant so tender and mild
Sleep in heavenly peace
Sleep in heavenly peace.

Silent night! Holy night!
Shepherds quake at the sight
Glories stream from heaven afar
Heavenly hosts sing: Alleluia
Sleep in heavenly peace
Sleep in heavenly peace.

Silent night! Holy night!
Son of God, love's pure light
Radiant beams from Thy holy face
With the dawn of redeeming grace
Jesus, Lord, at Thy birth
Jesus, Lord, at Thy birth.

Beside her, she heard Lizzie sigh as the program came to an end. It was the sound of elation, a grandparent proud of a job well done. When Grace didn't respond, Lizzie tapped her lightly on the knee and leaned over so that her words could be heard over the din of everyone talking at once. "Takes my Catharine to do something so special and thoughtful," she said into Grace's ear, almost as touched as Grace by this beautiful gesture. "How clever to integrate the scriptures with verses from different songs, *ja*?"

Grace couldn't respond. While her eyes started to fill with tears, her mind was racing with different thoughts, so she merely acknowledged Lizzie's words by nodding her head. But she wasn't really paying attention to Lizzie; her mind was elsewhere. She searched her memory to early August when Catharine Yoder was sitting on the sofa, visiting with Menno when she had returned from shopping with Hannah Esh. The seeds of suspicion were planted, and Grace needed to see if there were any roots to them.

The black notebook made its way back to her hands, several people pausing to tell her what a special gift the children had made for her. Graciously, Grace acknowledged their words and commented that she wasn't certain why the children had singled her out for such a memorable gift. It was but her attempt at modesty so that people wouldn't think she had experienced any feelings of pride over receiving the gift.

With the notebook in one hand and her little bag of gifts in the other, Grace maneuvered through the other parents as she headed toward Catharine. It took a few minutes for Grace to have her turn to speak to the teacher. She waited patiently, knowing that the parents wanted their time to express their gratitude for a program that was different, interesting, and very well done. Grace, however, had something else on her mind that she wanted to discuss with Catharine.

Finally, her turn came.

"Grace!" Catharine exclaimed, a broad smile on her face. "I hope you will enjoy reading all of those letters from the children. They were quite excited about the project."

"Oh *ja*," Grace said, nodding her head. "It's a lovely gift."

Catharine tilted her head, still smiling as if waiting for Grace to continue speaking.

"I…I made some little gifts for the students," Grace finally said, handing over the bag containing the crocheted bookmarks. "I thought they might like them."

"Why, that was right *gut* of you to think of them!" She accepted the bag and took a quick peek inside. "Oh my! How thoughtful!" She gave a little laugh and looked back at Grace, her dark eyes staring directly into Grace's gray ones. "My *grossmammi* used to make them all the time. Not *Mammi* Lizzie but *Mammi* Anna," she added, clarifying which grandmother she referenced. "She's passed now, but I still have all her crocheted bookmarks."

"Ja, vell…" Grace started and paused, uncertain how to proceed. It wasn't usual to confront someone about being a secret sister. But there were too many signs pointing toward Catharine Yoder, especially after Grace

received such an unusual gift and the children had sung her favorite Christmas carol. And there was still one more clue that pointed toward the young teacher. "I did have a question, Catharine, that mayhaps you might be able to answer."

Something flickered in Catharine's eyes, but she continued smiling. "If I have an answer...," she responded, leaving the sentence unfinished.

"Back in August," Grace said, lowering her voice so others couldn't hear. "I came home and saw you visiting with my Menno."

"Oh *ja*!" Another soft laugh. "Such a *wunderbaar gut* man and such a strong faith! We had a lovely visit."

Uncertain how to proceed and actually formulate the question that lingered on the tip of her tongue, Grace finally took a deep breath and just blurted it out. "I'm wondering if there is a coincidence between that visit and this gift."

Catharine pursed her lips. "Why, no. Not at all."

"Then you aren't..." Her voice trailed off again. She felt foolish for even asking the question. After all, the entire point of a secret sister was to remain secret.

"Aren't what, Grace?"

The hope that she had finally found the person, the one person who had secretly been pushing her along, guiding her through the holiday season, suddenly vanished. "I'm awful sorry, Catharine," Grace apologized. "It's really not my place to ask, but I had so hoped that I had found my secret sister. I just have so many questions to ask her."

An expression of understanding and empathy covered the young woman's face. "I'm sorry, Grace," she said, giving her head a slight shake to emphasize the point. "It's not me."

Feeling disappointed, Grace forced a smile. "*Ja, vell*, I'm not supposed to know anyway, ain't so?"

"Mayhaps you'll find out," Catharine replied, her eyes sparkling once again. "You might be surprised after all." And then her attention was turned to a waiting parent who wanted to tell her what a fine job she had done in creating this year's school program.

Clutching the notebook to her chest, Grace wandered through the thinning crowd. For the first time she truly thought she knew the identity of her secret sister. While she knew that anonymity was an unspoken rule to the secret sister game, the small gifts and verses and songs had been so personal that Grace just felt she needed to know the truth.

The light pressure from a hand on her shoulder startled her out of her thoughts. She looked up to see Hannah standing beside her. "You ready, then?" Hannah asked. James had already gone outside to untie the horse and waited for them to join him so that he could bring Grace home before her company arrived.

Her company! When she remembered that Ivan and his family would be arriving soon, she hurried her way outside, Hannah practically having to jog in order to keep up with her.

The ten-minute ride back to her house seemed to take an eternity. She couldn't wait to pore over the letters from the children, to share the love and caring of her community with her son. Maybe then, she thought, their relationship might change into one that was warmer and more compassionate. If only he knew that others cared and held her in such high esteem, maybe he would finally forgive her for that night twenty years ago, when Susan had walked out, James was killed, and she had done nothing to prevent either occurrence from happening.

The guilt lay so heavy on her shoulders all of these years! What if she had not supported Menno? What if she had gone after Susan? And more recently, what if she had supported Ivan's decision to reach out to Susan? What if she had clasped her daughter in her arms, welcoming her home? What if she had refused to move away? But every time she questioned why she hadn't done those things, she reminded herself of her vow to Menno, to love and obey him as long as they both should live. But now... now that Menno was gone, could she make her own decisions about Ivan and Susan? And if she did, what should those decisions be?

Back at her house, she hurried to light a few candles and the kerosene lanterns, which she had polished and refilled earlier that day. The soft glow made the room feel warmer and cozier. She took a look around to ensure that everything was in its right place and the house looked tidy.

During the five years that she and Menno had lived here, her children had visited only a handful of times. On the few occasions when Menno arranged to visit

Linda, they hired a driver. But the cool reception at Linda's had not encouraged them to plan many more visits. While Grace longed for a relationship with her oldest daughter, she felt an invisible wall between them, and she didn't even begin to know how to breach it.

When she heard the rhythmic sound of a horse and buggy approaching, she could hardly breathe in antici-pation. Unlike other buggies that passed by her house, this one pulled into the driveway. Nervously, Grace paced a few steps and then smoothed down her apron. She had just changed it after finishing the meal prepa-ration so that she wore one that was freshly laundered and ironed.

The door opened and Grace pressed her lips together, willing herself not to become emotional as Ivan stepped through the doorway.

To her surprise, he was alone.

"Maem," he said. Just one word softly spoken, and she suddenly didn't care that he had come alone.

"Oh, Ivan," she whispered, unable to stop a tear from trickling down her cheek. "It's so *gut* to see you here."

There was an awkward moment of silence as he stood there, his eyes glancing at the table that was set for his family.

"I felt it best that I come alone, *Maem,"* he finally said. "Verna has a cold anyway and Jane's feeling poorly."

Verna. The last grandchild Grace had held in her arms. And now she was already five years old.

"How…how are the *kinner*?" she asked. The ques-tion sounded so ordinary: a grandmother asking about her grandchildren. But they felt so far away, almost strangers now after five years of living apart and only occasional visits.

"*Gut*," he answered. "They're *gut*."

She'd only seen them most recently at the funeral. During the first month after Menno's death, Ivan had stopped by twice to check on her, Linda only once. There hadn't been a lot of dialogue then, Grace still being in shock and neither of her children having much to say.

"I was glad to get your letter, Ivan. It was most unexpected and greatly appreciated."

He lifted an eyebrow and stared at her. "You know why I'm here, *ja*?"

A moment of panic coursed through her veins. There was a reason? A reason that she should know? All along, she had thought his visit was just to reconnect. Now he was telling her that there was a specific reason?

When she didn't answer, Ivan removed his hat and wiped at his forehead. Despite the cold weather, he was sweating. *Is he nervous?* she wondered.

"Mayhaps we best sit down, *Maem*."

Obediently, she walked toward the sitting room and sat down in her recliner. Her palms grew sweaty and she felt as if her heart would jump right out of her chest. What on earth was he going to tell her? She didn't think she could handle any bad news.

"I received a letter," Ivan said slowly, reaching into his coat pocket. He withdrew an envelope and held it between his two hands. The envelope was crinkled, as if it had been handled frequently, either by the sender or by Ivan, Grace couldn't tell. But when he turned it around, slowly and with his eyes watching her expression, she saw something right away that caused her to gasp. She pressed her hand against her chest with one hand and reached out for the envelope with the other.

"That's your *daed's* handwriting," she exclaimed, lifting her eyes to look at Ivan. "How long ago did you receive this?"

She expected to hear Ivan tell her that the letter was old, perhaps several years, for he certainly could not have written so clearly after his stroke. So when he responded, "Last month," she felt as if all of the air escaped from her lungs.

"Last month?" The idea was inconceivable. He had died in August!

But Ivan nodded his head. "Last month, *Maem*. Oh, he wrote it long ago. It's dated 2013. But the postmark is from November of this year."

"Oh, help." She sank back in the recliner. A letter from the grave. That's what she held in her hand. A message from her Menno, written when he was healthy and able, but sent months after his death. "And what, if I may ask, does the letter say, Ivan?"

Ivan took a deep breath and leaned forward. Hesitantly, he reached out for her hand and held it between both of his. The feeling of warm skin against hers startled her. When was the last time anyone had done such a thing? And to have her son, of all people, extend such a gesture? Her head began to swoon as if she were dreaming.

"*Maem*," Ivan said, staring her straight in the eyes. "It's time for you to come home."

Words evaded her. She merely concentrated on breathing. In, out, in, out.

"What happened twenty years ago may have been God's will," Ivan said, speaking in a deliberately slow manner as if he had practiced this speech numerous times before now. "This letter from *Daed* asked for my forgiveness, *Maem*. And he asked me to come to you. To bring you home." He looked around the small sitting room, taking in the shelf of books and the windowsill with plants. "This is your house, *Maem*, but it will never be your home. You need to be with family. It was *Daed's* last wish, and I choose to forgive him."

She still could not speak, but merely sat there in stunned silence.

"I've even prayed for forgiveness for my role in the matter." Ivan released her hand and sank back into the sofa. He ran his hand through his hair and sighed. "I reckon I was just angry about James. And then when Susan came back, she needed help, and I couldn't imagine a father turning his back on his own *dochder*." He went on. "Verna! Look at Verna. She needs our help on a daily basis. Could I deny *her* that?"

"Oh, Ivan…"

He cut her off, wanting to finish what he clearly had practiced before coming over that evening. "You never knew this, I'm sure, but Susan left shortly after that day, *Maem*. I hear from her once or twice a year," he said, lowering his eyes. Grace could tell from his expression that Ivan was hesitant to continue. She waited, both anxious and fearful of what he would say. "Her life isn't easy, *Maem*. Her marriage didn't last. He left her a few years after they married, and she's had to fend for herself." Ivan lifted his eyes and met her worried gaze. "But she's a survivor and refuses handouts. I've offered her money in the past and she always refuses."

Grace took a deep breath. Finally! Precious details of her daughter's life. How many years had she longed to know? How many nights had she prayed to God to protect her daughter, the lost sheep? "Do you think…" She hesitated. *After so many years and so much hurt, would it be possible?* she thought. "Mayhaps you might contact her and arrange that I could see her?"

Ivan studied her face. Grace wondered what he saw there. Certainly she could not hide the inner conflict that she felt, a mixture of both grief and guilt. How long had she battled to remain loyal to both her husband and her daughter?

"I can do that," he replied, his words drawn out and thoughtful. "Might be good for you both to reconnect, I reckon. But I want you to realize that *Daed* was right in his way, you know. A vow taken and broken is not something to be overlooked lightly. She became a part of the world, and not one that was kind to her. She abandoned her heritage and faith after committing to honor it and to honor God. I understand now why *Daed* did what he did. And I understand how I too contributed to our rift. So I'm also here to ask you for your forgiveness."

Forgiveness? The earnestness in his voice reminded her so much of Menno from that night fifty years earlier when Menno had begged for her parents' blessing on the night prior to their wedding. The memory made Grace smile. "My dear son," she said, a feeling of joy filling her whole body. She couldn't remember a time when she had felt such elation. "There has never been anything to forgive!"

There was so much catching up to do that neither one of them knew where to start. For five years, Grace had not been a mother to her son. But she found that she slipped back into the role with ease. After all, it was one of two roles that she treasured: that of mother as well as wife.

Suggesting that they move into the kitchen so that she could fix him some supper, Grace could hardly keep herself from doting over him. She asked about each of the children and if he had heard from Linda. He told her about the farm and how the crops had been abundant last year, a fortunate blessing after the previous year when too much rain had flooded the fields.

By the time she served him homemade pumpkin pie with coffee, her mind wandered back to the letter. She had hoped that Ivan had something to do with her secret sister; now she knew otherwise.

"Don't you wonder who sent you the letter, Ivan?" she asked before taking a sip of her coffee.

"There was another note in the envelope with his letter, an unsigned note that said *Daed* wanted me to come here to you on this very day."

She raised her eyebrows, surprised by this news. Could it be, she wondered, that her secret sister had orchestrated this reunion? And why? "That's rather curious," she managed to reply. "And why today, then?"

With a shrug of his shoulders, he started to cut the piece of pie with his fork and then paused. "You never asked to see the letter. Aren't you curious to read his words?"

She shook her head. How could she explain the emotions that she felt at that moment? Elation at returning to the farm? Joy at being reconnected with at least part of her family? Pride that Menno had corrected a wrong done so many years ago, but in a way that did not compromise his faith? But there was something else, lingering under the surface of her emotions: disappointment. Disappointment that he had thought to leave a letter for Ivan and even prepared to have it sent after his death, but there had been no letter for her. After giving so much of her life to Menno, she couldn't possibly understand why he had the foresight to communicate with Ivan, writing a letter two years before he died, but he had not taken the time to write one to her.

"I think you might want to," Ivan said. "There's something in the letter, *Maem*, for you."

"For me?" she asked incredulously. "*Ach*, Ivan! You should have told me so!"

He reached back into his pocket for the letter. Reaching inside, he withdrew a small slip of paper. It had her name on it. As he handed it to her, Grace immediately knew two things: the handwriting was a woman's, and the note was not from Menno.

But she took it from Ivan anyway and unfolded it.

"What on earth?" She squinted through her glasses and leaned closer to the light. Her eyes read the words, but they didn't make sense. "It's a riddle!"

"I saw that," Ivan admitted. "Do you know what it means?"

She read it once again, this time out loud. "'A Christmas program. A Christmas book. Between the pages, take a good look.'" Grace clicked her tongue and shook her head. "I never heard of such a thing! This secret sister is such a mystery," she said.

But as she read the words again a third time, something dawned on her. Hadn't she attended the students' program that very afternoon and received a notebook filled with letters and scriptures from the children?

"Why, I just wonder..."

Without saying a word, she stood up and hurried into her bedroom where she had left the binder. She hadn't had time to read through it when she returned, for she had focused on the preparations for Ivan's visit. Carrying it back to the table, she showed it to Ivan and explained what had happened at the school program.

Together, they flipped through the pages, reading each letter and Bible verse. She smiled at some of the drawings from the smaller children; the little people they drew were simple circles with stick legs and arms. She remembered when her own children drew the same way. Toward the end of the book, their handwriting and drawings became a bit more intricate and sophisticated.

And then she turned a page and her eyes fell upon a drawing that made her catch her breath.

"What is it, *Maem*?"

She lifted her hand and pressed the back of it to her lips. For the second time that evening, she was speechless. It was a purple iris drawn in the lower corner. Around the edge of the paper was a crisscross drawing in the same colors as the handkerchief she had been given. She turned the next page and there was a poem, funny and clever, about pumpkin bread. In anticipation, she looked beside it to the right page, and sure enough, someone had written out the words to Song 51. And so it continued, each page representing one of the gifts from her secret sister: the blue diary, the scripture from Thanksgiving, a recipe for sugar cookies, and a drawing of the retirement home. On the last page, the words to "Silent Night" were written. But unlike the other pages, this one did not lie flat. There was something tucked behind it.

As she slipped her hand into the plastic sleeve and in between the two pieces of paper, she felt it: another envelope.

"I don't believe this," she whispered.

Her hands shook and she had to take a few deep breaths before she could turn it over. But she already knew without having to look. The envelope was addressed to her and the handwriting was Menno's. Only this handwriting was not from 2013. It was harder to read and was most certainly written after he had the stroke.

The color drained from her face, and despite her best efforts not to cry, her vision blurred and she quickly wiped the tears away with her free hand.

> To my Grace,
>
> We have spent nearly fifty years together, enjoying the good times and holding up each other during the bad ones.
>
> We have truly honored our vows.
>
> I know my time to leave this world is coming. And if I know you, my Grace, you will continue to honor me after my death.
>
> But I want you to know that I release you from respecting my wishes. Too much time has passed and you need to be with your family.
>
> Now that you are holding this letter, you should have received my gifts, reminders of the important events in your life. And it is high time that you return to the farm and live out the rest of your life where you belong—right alongside Ivan, Jane, and their kinner. That is my final gift to you, my faithful fraa.
>
> Blessings and love,
> Your husband,
> Menno

Stunned, she sat there at the table, the letter clutched between her two hands and pressed against her heart. *How is this possible?* she asked herself. How could it be that her secret sister was not a sister at all but her husband? Her *deceased* husband?

"I just don't believe this," she whispered, tears returning to her eyes. "It's just not possible."

Ivan reached out and touched her arm. "You all right, *Maem*?"

She looked up, still in a daze from the letter's revelation. "What?" she asked.

"Are you all right?"

Steadying her nerves, she folded the letter and slipped it back into the envelope. She laid it flat upon the table and ran a finger across the shaky lettering on the front. From the horse auction where they had met until this very moment when she received this treasure, this glorious letter that Menno had crafted along with a clever trail of gifts that coincided with such important and life-changing events, she had been blessed. Even during the times of hardship, the tough decisions and tears, she had been blessed because Menno had been by her side. Even now, during the very time when she had been contemplating her future, Menno had been beside her all along, supporting her.

She smiled, no more tears in her eyes.

"Oh *ja*, Ivan," she said, placing a hand over his that still rested on her arm. "I'm more than all right. After all, I'm going home at last."

EPILOGUE

December 24, 2015

THE SOUND OF the children, the younger ones running about the room, made Grace smile. She sat in a padded rocking chair, her feet gently pushing against the floor. In the kitchen, Jane and her oldest daughter, Lydia, were busy preparing for the Christmas feast. The room smelled like fresh pecan and pumpkin pies mixed with the scent of smoky ham. Levi and Ivan walked into the room, carrying a long folding table from the basement. It needed to be set up in order to accommodate all of the family members who would arrive the following day.

Both Barbie and Samuel followed behind them, each carefully carrying a large box. When Grace saw them, she set down her crocheting and hurried to her feet. "Let me help you with that," she said, reaching out to take the heavy box from Samuel's hands.

But he shook his head vigorously. "I got it, *Mammi* Grace," he said, and made certain that he gently set down the box on the other table. At ten, Samuel clearly wanted to show his grandmother that he was almost a man, if not as strong as one. She held back a smile and merely went about unpacking the boxes.

They contained Barbara Beiler's china. Grace had insisted that they use the china for the Christmas meal. With Jane's two sisters and one brother bringing their families to the meal, the extra place settings were welcomed. By Grace's calculations, over forty people would share fellowship together, celebrating the birth of Jesus Christ.

Ivan rubbed the base of his back and assessed the two long tables. "Best go fetch the other one, *ja*?" He didn't wait for a response, adding, "These two might not quite do it, I reckon." He proceeded to return toward the basement, twenty-two-year-old Levi quietly following him.

"Do you think we'll have enough benches and chairs?" Grace asked, stepping back for a moment while Barbie spread a white tablecloth over the one table.

"For sure," Jane replied, looking over her shoulder. "Levi has two benches and I'm almost certain we've got another two down in the cellar. With the folding chairs, we should be right as rain!"

"Snow, *Maem*," seven-year-old Benjamin corrected. "It's winter!"

Jane made a show of thinking about that for a second before she quipped, "Right as snow? That don't sound right, now, does it?"

The children laughed at their mother's joke and Grace felt the warmth of the household fill her from the inside out. *What a glorious present*, she thought as she looked around the room. It was a gift from Menno to be reunited with the family.

Beside her, she felt a hand tug at her skirt and she turned around to see five-year-old Verna. "Oh, my, Verna," Grace said. "Would you mind helping your *grossmammi*? I need to set these plates out on the table. That sure would be a big help."

Verna grinned, still shy around Grace. But she happily began moving the plates from the box onto the cloth-covered table.

"Someone's come visiting," Jane called out, standing on her toes as she looked out the window over the kitchen sink. "Wasn't expecting anyone." She glanced at Lydia. "Were you?"

"*Nee, Maem.*"

Wiping her hands on a dish towel, Jane turned around and quickly looked about the room. Grace followed her gaze and saw the toys on the floor, left from the two youngest ones, Benjamin and Verna. The floor also needed a good sweeping. With so many people walking in and out, from outside and downstairs, the dirt had collected.

"Now don't go fretting about that," Grace said, her voice soothing as she tried to calm down her daughter-in-law. "It's Christmas Eve and no one can expect a perfect *haus* before such a day."

"I reckon," Jane admitted, but without sounding overly convinced. Since Verna's birth, she had become a fastidious house cleaner, always concerned that things be put away orderly. "Best go see who's come."

Verna and Grace had just finished setting one half of the table, Barbie busy covering the other half so that they could continue setting out the plates, when Jane walked back into the kitchen, a young woman following her.

"Grace, you have company," she said with a quizzical smile.

The young woman stepped out of the shadows and removed her dark bonnet. Grace recognized her at once and caught her breath from the surprise. "Why, Catharine Yoder," she exclaimed, unable to conceal her astonishment. "Whatever brings you here on this night?"

Catharine stepped forward, the same spring in her step as Grace remembered from the school program, less than a week ago. Her eyes sparkled and she reached out to grasp Grace's hand. "I can stay for only a few minutes," she said. "But when I heard that you had moved back with your family, I knew that I needed to stop by to wish you the most blessed Christmas ever."

Grace wasn't certain how to respond. If someone had asked her to take twenty guesses who might surprise her with a Christmas Eve visit from her former *g'may*, she never would have guessed Catharine Yoder. "I must confess that I'm quite taken by surprise."

The young woman laughed, a sweet sound that made Jane and Lydia smile as they looked over their shoulders, equally curious as to the purpose of this visit.

"I wanted to let you know how honored we were," Catharine said. "It was a true blessing to help Bishop Beiler with his special project. The students and I had such a *wunderbaar* time trying to figure out how to get his gifts to you."

Reaching down, Grace put her hand onto the tabletop to keep herself steady. "You?"

Another soft laugh was accompanied by an enthusiastic nod of her head. "*Ja*, and the students!" She sighed. "When Lizzie told me that Bishop Beiler wanted to speak with me, I was surprised. But then he explained his plan and how he wanted the school to be involved. He had everything organized and with specific instructions all written out when he discovered he had cancer. After his stroke, he knew his time was near, and that's why he asked to see me. When he passed away shortly after and I realized the purpose of the secret-sister gifts, I was truly humbled to be a part of his plan."

Grace's mouth dropped open and she tried to find the words to speak. Hadn't she specifically asked Catharine if she was the secret sister?

"Oh, I know what you're thinking," Catharine said. "That's why I wanted to come see you before Christmas. That night after the school program when you asked if I was the secret sister, I answered honestly: I wasn't. Your husband merely asked us to be the *messengers*."

"I...I don't know what to say."

Catharine smiled. "Don't say anything. It was so romantic, what your Menno did. A true gift of love."

Standing behind Grace, twelve-year-old Barbie giggled, and Grace suppressed a smile at the young woman's openly expressed sentiment.

"*Vell*, anyway," Catharine added. "I wanted to share that with you. I felt it was important, being that you were so curious and it was such a special Christmas present, don't you think?"

Despite Jane's offer to stay for a cup of coffee, Catharine begged off, explaining that she had planned this visit to coincide with another one nearby. But before she left, she gave Grace an embrace and held her for just a moment, whispering into her ear, "Merry Christmas, Grace." And, like a whirlwind that had blown in through the door, she bid her good-byes and quickly left.

The room remained quiet for a few long moments, Grace standing there at the table as she realized what she had just learned. The question of the *who* and the *why* had been answered. Now the missing piece fell into place: the *how*. The thought of all those children working so hard in unison to help her husband fulfill his final wish—to bring together the family and correct the wrong from so many years ago—left her bereft of speech. And he had orchestrated it all to come to fruition at Christmas, the time for rejoicing and celebrating with loved ones.

Menno had known that his death was imminent, and his final wish had been to ensure that she'd be cared for, that she would enjoy her life-right. Yet he knew her well enough that a simple letter outlining his final wishes would not be sufficient. She would remain faithful to his memory after his passing just as she had been faithful to his words during his life. So instead, he had guided her along the path leading to the golden years of her life, including the visit to the retirement center just two days before Ivan's visit. He had known what she would be thinking and that she would not want to live alone for the rest of her life. Only when her emotions were so raw would she be ready for the visit from Ivan. And while Menno didn't know whether Ivan would accept the request from his deceased and estranged father, Menno did know that Grace understood her choices. While guiding her under the pretense of a secret sister, he had left her the chance to decide on her own whether to live out her days in the retirement home or to accept a home with Ivan's family.

Such was the man she had married fifty years earlier—loving, caring husband and the most righteous man she ever knew. He had been her source of comfort throughout their life together, in good times and in bad times, guiding her thoughts and prayers toward God the Almighty when his own earthly presence was not enough to help her face adversity. And now, even after his death, he had found a way to ensure that her later years would be filled with the love and care she deserved.

Standing by the table, she shut her eyes and envisioned Menno standing before her. In her mind, she felt his arms around her, embracing her as he would sometimes do when they were alone. Only this time, instead of a simple hug, she heard the distinct sound of his voice in her ear as he whispered the same words as the young woman who had just left: *Merry Christmas, Grace.*

GLOSSARY

ach—oh

aendi—aunt

Ausbund—Amish hymnal

boppli—baby

bruder—brother

daed—father

danke—thank you

dochder—daughter

Englische—non-Amish people

Englischer—a non-Amish person

ferhoodled—confused, mixed up

fraa—wife

g'may—church district

grossdawdi—grandfather

grossdawdihaus—small house attached to the main dwelling

grossmammi—grandmother

gut mariye—good morning

haus—house

ja—yes

kapp—prayer cap worn by Amish girls and women

kinner—children

kum—come

life-right—the right of the elderly to continue living under the care of their children and/or on their property without payment or rent

maem—mother

Mammi—used with the first name by children as a title for grandmothers

mayhaps—maybe

nee—no

Ordnung—unwritten rules that govern the *g'may*

rumschpringe—period of "running-around" time for youths

schwester—sister

vell—well

vorsinger—song leader

wie gehts—What's going on?

wilkum—welcome

wunderbaar—wonderful

OTHER BOOKS BY SARAH PRICE

THE AMISH CLASSICS SERIES
First Impressions
The Matchmaker
Second Chances

THE AMISH OF LANCASTER SERIES
Fields of Corn
Hills of Wheat
Pastures of Faith
Valley of Hope

THE PLAIN FAME SERIES (WATERFALL PRESS)
Plain Fame
Plain Change
Plain Again
Plain Return

Priscilla's Story (contains four novellas:
*The Tomato Patch,The Quilting Bee, The
Hope Chest, The Clothes Line*)

An Amish Buggy Ride (Waterfall Press)

An Empty Cup (Waterfall Press)

Amish Circle Letters

Amish Circle Letters II

A Gift of Faith: An Amish Christmas Story

An Amish Christmas Carol
(Amish Christian Classic Series)

A Christmas Gift for Rebecca:
An Amish Christian Romance

A complete listing of Sarah Price's books can be found on her Amazon author page at http://www.amazon.com /Sarah-Price/e/B00734HBQM.

ABOUT SARAH PRICE

*T*HE PREISS FAMILY emigrated from Europe in 1705, settling in Pennsylvania as the area's first wave of Mennonite families. Sarah Price has always respected and honored her ancestors through exploration and research into her family's history and their religion. At nineteen, she befriended an Amish family and lived on their farm for several years.

Contact the author at sarah@sarahpriceauthor.com. Visit her weblog at http://sarahpriceauthor.com or on Facebook at *www.facebook.com/fansofsarahprice*.

MORE FROM
SARAH PRICE

BEST-SELLING AUTHOR OF AMISH FICTION

These Amish retellings of popular Jane Austen classics are beautiful takes on the power of love to overcome all obstacles.

AVAILABLE IN BOOKSTORES AND IN E-BOOK
www.CharismaDirect.com

13619

REALMS

WHEN CULTURES COLLIDE, CAN LOVE SURVIVE?

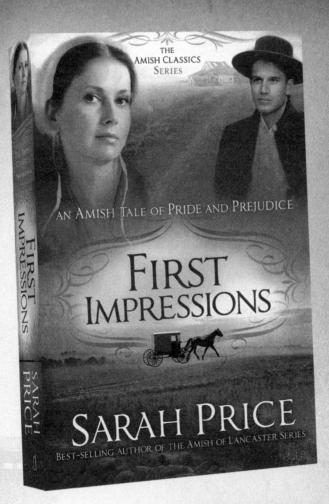

THE AMISH CLASSICS SERIES

AN AMISH TALE OF PRIDE AND PREJUDICE

FIRST IMPRESSIONS

SARAH PRICE

BEST-SELLING AUTHOR OF THE AMISH OF LANCASTER SERIES

This Amish retelling of a popular Jane Austen classic is a beautiful take on the power of love to overcome class boundaries and prejudices.

12932

AVAILABLE AT BOOKSTORES AND IN E-BOOK

REALMS

Be Empowered

Be Encouraged

Be Inspired

Be Spirit Led

FREE NEWSLETTERS

Empowering Women for Life in the Spirit

SPIRITLED WOMAN
Amazing stories, testimonies, and articles on marriage, family, prayer, and more.

POWER UP! FOR WOMEN
Receive encouraging teachings that will empower you for a Spirit-filled life.

CHARISMA MAGAZINE
Get top-trending articles, Christian teachings, entertainment reviews, videos, and more.

CHARISMA NEWS DAILY
Get the latest breaking news from an evangelical perspective. Sent Monday-Friday.

SIGN UP AT: nl.charismamag.com

CHARISMA MEDIA

P0780